STATE STREET PRESS

Copyright © 2007 First Novel LLC.

This edition is published by State Street Press
by special arrangement with
Ann Arbor Media Group LLC
2500 S. State Street
Ann Arbor, MI 48104

Printed and bound in the United States of America
by Edwards Brothers, Inc.

Library of Congress Cataloging-in-Publication Data

Santora, Nick, 1970-
Slip & Fall / Nick Santora.
p. cm.
ISBN-13: 978-0-68112-749-4
ISBN-10: 0-681-12749-X

1. Lawyers--Fiction. 2. Brooklyn (New York, N.Y.)--Fiction.
I. Title. II. Title: Slip and fall.
PS3619.A587S56 2007
813'.6--dc22
2007012265

For
JANINE

PROLOGUE

THICK MORNING FOG rolled in off New York Harbor as the old immigrant was led to a secluded spot in the back of the lot. The hanging mist and a sun that was still a few minutes from rising made him and the younger man who guided him invisible even to those who were filtering through the chain-link gate for a day's work, just fifty or so yards away.

They stopped behind a green dumpster. The old man was told to get down on his knees, and even though at seventy he was twice the age of the younger man, he did what he was told. The young man stuffed a white sweat sock into the immigrant's mouth.

"You make a sound, I'll smash your fuckin' head in, understand?" the young man threatened.

The immigrant nodded.

"Gimme your hand."

The old man complied. At first he tried to get away with offering up his left hand, but it didn't fly.

"Not that one," the young man ordered. "The one you write with."

The immigrant pulled his left hand back and slowly pushed his right hand forward, along the ground, making grooves in the earth with his fingers.

The young man removed a hammer from inside his coat pocket.

"Remember, not a sound," he warned.

The immigrant pressed his eyes closed tight.

The hammer swung down with full force. Blood shot out from all sides of the old man's hand as if someone had stepped on a sponge soaked in dark red paint. The grooves in the dirt filled in black. Despite the sock and the warnings, the immigrant let out a wail that couldn't be heard over the sound of workers unloading flatbeds by the gate.

"Mother-fucker," the young man barked, and he quickly drove the hammer down into the hand two more times as punishment for the old man's disobedience.

The immigrant collapsed onto his side, grasping his mangled paw. He wept silently, the pain too great for any more screams. The young man grabbed the dumpster by its side and pushed it over. The immigrant didn't even see it coming; he just felt it land on his hand, crushing already broken bone into smaller pieces. The pain was so bad, the old man passed out.

When the other workers found him about twenty minutes later, he was unconscious, bloody, and alone.

The immigrant wasn't the first guy in Brooklyn to catch a beating—and he won't be the last. Everyone in Bensonhurst pays their dues eventually. Some pay what's fair; some pay tenfold. A lot of people feel I didn't pay nearly enough; they think I got away with murder—figuratively and literally.

And if that is how people want to look at me, I won't try to convince them otherwise. The blood on my hands and the hands of others—I caused it all. It's that knowledge that gives me the nightmares that keep me awake every night. But I deserve them; I deserve everything I got. It's my never-ending penance for what I did. Because what I did was horrible.

ONE

MY FATHER HIRED a limousine to take my entire family from Brooklyn to Manhattan to see me graduate from law school. I watched them pour out of the vehicle in front of my apartment building on 113th Street—my stocky father, my portly mother, fat Uncle Vincent and husky Aunt Edith, and finally my chubby sister Ginny. It looked like some kind of Fat Italian Clown Car. I had tried to dissuade my father from getting the limo. He and my mother didn't have much money and a limousine definitely was not within their budget. He wouldn't listen.

"This is the proudest day in Principe family history," he told me. "We're going to celebrate it properly."

My grandfather served under Patton and stormed the beach at Normandy but me becoming a lawyer was considered the family's finest hour. Makes you think.

To my family, and especially my father, my graduation was

validation that everything my family had gone through was not in vain—from my mother's father leaving Italy as a stowaway in the bowels of a cargo ship to my dad's dad, and my old man as well, destroying their bodies, one day at a time, as overworked, underpaid, journeyman carpenters. I was the big payoff, the jackpot, the scratch-off ticket that when rubbed with a quarter revealed three perfect cherries. I was the one who would transition the Principe family from blue collar to white, from tool belt to leather belt, from work boot to dress shoe. I was the Golden Boy.

Despite my parents' aspirations for my career, I never wanted to stray far from my roots. Even though I was recruited by all of the top Manhattan corporate law firms, I turned them all down. Instead, I opened my own practice immediately after law school. I was so goddamn naïve—I thought I had outsmarted everyone. While my classmates from Columbia were working hundred-hour workweeks for behemoth firms such as Sullivan & Rose and Warren, Kugler & Curtis, I'd have my own personal injury practice.

My father provided a built-in client base. He had worked with every lather, carpenter, and laborer from Coney Island to the Bronx. These guys knew him and respected him, so why wouldn't they hire his son if they ever got hurt on the job? Construction sites are dangerous places and guys get hurt all the time, and their lawsuits are very lucrative. Why the hell would I want to work at some stuffy firm representing banks and hedge funds when I could represent *real people*, people I knew and grew up with; people who truly needed my help—people who wouldn't be able to feed their families if they broke their leg or fractured an arm? I was going to get rich doing God's work. I truly started out with the best of intentions.

I realize now that a big reason I went out on my own was

because of my dad. I think subconsciously I knew I could never pay him back for all he'd done for me, putting me through college and all—working his ass off so I could get an education. The least I could do was help his Union brothers when they needed help the most. That kind of thinking was my first mistake. A son can never pay back his father. It's impossible. You can give him everything in the world and still come up short.

So after graduation I opened an office above Morelli's Deli in Bensonhurst, at the corner of 18th and 71st, just a few blocks from where I grew up. The space was big, but reasonably priced, mostly because on hot days the smell of headcheese and pimento loaf would seep through the cracks of the old wooden floorboards. There was a reception area with a secretarial station, a large office, a small bathroom, and a smaller office that was so jammed with old furniture, boxes, and other junk from the prior tenants that you couldn't walk more than a few feet inside. The space needed some work—a coat of paint, some rewiring, and a few holes in the walls had to be patched—but it was nothing my father couldn't fix over the course of a weekend, which he did of course. It wasn't much, but it was more than adequate for a sole practitioner just starting out.

The large office had a great view of the neighborhood. Sometimes, when I was at work, I'd look down on 71st and see guys I grew up with riding the sanitation trucks or humping Sheetrock for Fortunato Construction for a three-story that was going up across from Morelli's. I'm ashamed to say it, but there were times when I looked down on them in more ways than one. Even though I was raised by and grew up idolizing men who worked with their hands for a living, once I knew I'd never meet the same fate, I sometimes felt I was a little bit more important than my former peers who dug ditches for a living.

Don't get me wrong—I wasn't an elitist, and most of the time I didn't feel that way. It's just that every once in a while, right after I had first opened shop, I'd strain my shoulder patting myself on the back.

My father was so excited when I first hung my shingle. Actually, it wasn't a shingle at all. I had a glass door at street level that opened to a staircase that led up to my office. I put those gold, stick-on letters with black trim on the inside of the door—ROBERT R. PRINCIPE, ESQ.—ATTORNEY AT LAW. My dad kept telling everyone in the neighborhood that I "was a partner in my own law firm."

The old man had a tendency to exaggerate the accomplishments of his children. Once, in junior high, Ginny brought home one of those paper certificates you got in gym class for the President's Physical Fitness Challenge. She did more sit-ups than anyone else in her class or something like that but my father told anyone who would listen that his daughter got a personally signed "Commendation" from President Carter. A couple dozen Americans were holed-up in some basement in Tehran, gas prices were skyrocketing, and the United States had just boycotted the Moscow Olympics, but somehow my dad had convinced himself that Carter could sleep at night because my sister clocked a good time in the shuttle run. But you gotta cut the guy some slack. There are a lot worse things you can say about a man than he thinks the sun rises and sets on his children.

Besides, he wasn't the only one who was excited about my new firm. I couldn't wait for my first case to come in. I'd be helping the injured in their time of need. And if I got rich in the process, what was the harm of that? I figured I'd settle a few big injury cases after I graduated from law school, save carefully, and be retired within five years. That was eight years ago.

TWO

THE MOST INTERESTING THING I learned in law school was the theory of "causation"—the idea that no event is an island unto itself; that everything that happens is just part of a long cosmic chain; and each link in the chain is the result of a prior link having already occurred. I'm convinced that when the world comes to an end you'll be able to backtrack and find a single occurrence, even if it occurred a million years in the past, that set off a reaction that eventually led to the event that caused the downfall of mankind. In other words, I believe everything has a clearly defined genesis. You need not go back a million years to find the genesis of my personal downfall. It was when I learned that Mrs. Catalano was dead. I had just gotten the news when I heard the phone ring.

"I'm not here, take a message," I called out to Joey from my office. I didn't feel like speaking to anyone. I was still sort of in shock. The phone kept ringing. Joey must have been on the other line but I wasn't about to answer the call. Besides, Joey knew how to use the damn hold button.

I had hired Joey two weeks after I opened my firm and she had been with me ever since. She was a secretary, receptionist, legal assistant, paralegal, and unlicensed lawyer all rolled into one petite, curvy, twenty-five-year-old Puerto Rican frame. Frankly, she was more important to the everyday happenings at the firm than I was and she knew it. But she got three weeks' vacation, a small cash bonus at Christmastime, and was allowed to leave early whenever she needed if she had to do something with, or for, one of her three kids. In exchange, I paid her a pittance and during rough patches she let me miss a paycheck or two and then make it up with interest when some money came in.

She was like a younger sister to me—so much so that when other lawyers commented on the "hot Puerto Rican piece of ass" I had working for me, it took all of my professionalism to refrain from knocking them out. Eventually, word got around the courthouses that you shouldn't comment on my secretary, no matter how tight her blouse was or how short her skirt, because I would be pissed off. Some mistook my protective nature of Joey as the by-product of romantic feelings, but nothing could have been further from the truth. Those rumors would have bothered me except that Joey and my wife, Janine, knew they were bullshit and that was all that mattered to me.

Joey entered my office holding a pink phone message slip. I didn't notice her at first because my face was buried in my hands.

"What's wrong?" she asked, concerned.

I looked up at her. My eyes were red and swollen.

"I just got a phone call," I explained. "Mrs. Catalano is dead."

"Oh my God. I didn't realize you were so close to her. I'm so sorry, Bobby."

"Fuck Mrs. Catalano!" I shouted. "She was one of the best cases in the office." This business could turn you into a bastard sometimes.

Joey's face registered concern. "Was she the pedestrian on the sidewalk case?"

"Yes."

"The one who was hit by the Mercedes?"

"Yes."

"The one with the million dollar insurance policy?"

"That's the one."

"How did she die?" Joey wanted to know, as if it made a difference.

"Malignant brain tumor," I said as I stood and stared out the window.

"I didn't know she had cancer."

"Apparently neither did she."

"Can you settle the case?"

I kicked my trash can over. The prior day's *New York Law Journal* spilled out and a brown, half-eaten apple rolled across the floor.

"Sure I can, for about ten grand! This case was worth half a million if it was worth a penny. Perfect liability, surgery with hardware to the leg, huge insurance policy. The whole goddamn case was based on future pain and suffering but you can't have future pain and suffering when you're fuckin' dead, now can you, Joey?"

Like I said, the business could turn you into a bastard—a callous, unfeeling bastard.

"Shut your mouth right now. You sound like a horse's ass," Joey shot right back. "Mrs. Catalano's family is in mourning and all you can think about is your stupid fee? You know better than that, Robert. And I know you better than that."

"Maybe you don't know me as well as you think because *all* I'm thinking about right now is my stupid fee. Money that you and I are never gonna see now."

"You think I work here for the great pay and the benefits? Or maybe the luxurious surroundings?" Joey said sarcastically. "I've stuck it out because you're the only lawyer I know who actually cares about his clients. So don't go and turn into an asshole now 'cause I don't have the energy to start lookin' for another job."

Joey stared at me, unblinking. Man, she could be a tough son of bitch at times. She won.

"You're right," I yielded. "I'm sorry. But damn it, when are we gonna catch a break? We're almost completely tapped out." I slumped back into my chair. I grabbed the classifieds from my desk and gently tossed them to Joey. "You better start checking the want ads."

Joey caught the paper and threw it back at me, *hard*, hitting me in the chest. "Check 'em yourself, 'cause I'm not going anywhere. We're just going through a bad stretch is all."

"It's more than a bad stretch. After expenses, I took home no pay last year. If it weren't for Janine's salary, we'd be out on the street. Joey, I don't know how much longer I can pay you. You need to understand that. You're a single mother."

"You never need to remind me of that, trust me," Joey joked.

She walked behind me and rubbed my shoulders. It didn't help. I was as tense as a high wire.

"We'll worry about payroll problems if and when the time comes," she said, trying to calm me down. "Besides, we still have the Smyth case. When that settles you'll be a millionaire and you can give me a big, fat bonus. In the meantime, why don't you go home early, spend some time with Janine, and get your mind off things for a while?"

I stared through the door at the practically empty shelves in the reception area.

"Why not?" I said. "I've hardly got any cases to work on anyway."

I instinctively grabbed my briefcase, although there was no work to be done inside of it, and left my desk. During the months leading up to the day Mrs. Catalano died, there was so little business coming in that I hadn't had any work to do in the evenings when I went home. But, like a trained seal, I reached for my briefcase every day before leaving the office and took it home with me. And every morning, I'd walk back to work carrying the same empty briefcase. It was almost as if I would have been admitting defeat if I stopped bringing it home each night.

As I headed out the door, Joey called after me. She waved the pink phone message slip above her head. "That phone call before was from Mrs. Guzman. She wants to talk to you."

"Tell her I'll get back to her," I said without turning around. I was in no mood to speak with Mrs. Guzman.

THREE

MY OFFICE WAS TWELVE BLOCKS from my house so my "commute" to work was a fifteen-minute walk. I loved that I didn't have to sit in traffic like the schmucks coming into the city every morning from Jersey, Westchester, and Long Island. Instead, I was able to stroll through my hometown, one of the few perks of my job. Childhood memories from the neighborhood would wash over me. Every day I'd pass Saint Joseph's Church, where I used to play CYO basketball; Town Circle Barbershop, where my dad and I both went to get our hair cut on the days before we each got married; and Junior's Diner, where in seventh grade Angela Valario let me feel her up in the back booth when no one was looking.

The past would cloak me and protect me in a way that only someone's hometown can. I felt safer in Bensonhurst, Brooklyn, than I did anywhere else on earth.

But the day Mrs. Catalano died, my walk home didn't

make me feel better. I had "stomach issues"—the euphemism I gave my severe intestinal problems that started soon after I began practicing law and which got progressively worse over the years. A specialist told me my problems were the result of stress and anxiety, which I found funny because no one who ever saw me in court would have ever guessed that I suffered from stress. Whether on trial or arguing a motion, I never showed any signs of anxiety despite the fact that, very often, beneath my calm façade, my heart often raced, my organs drowned in adrenaline, my blood pressure soared, my synapses burned, and my stomach percolated. All of my episodes ended the same—with me sitting on the toilet, doubled over, pissing out of my ass. After Janine, diarrhea had become my closest companion.

No one besides Janine knew I had a problem, not even Joey. There had been times when I argued entire motions before the court while in the midst of a full-blown anxiety attack. No one could tell a thing was wrong. I made sure that neither the judge nor opposing counsel became aware of my condition. I'd check my breathing, wipe my sweaty palms on the inside of my pants pockets, sometimes I'd even have to clench my sphincter—whatever I had to do to keep my competitive edge and get out of court alive. But trying to keep the attacks hidden just made them worse, and a vicious cycle ensued. The more anxious I felt, the more I made sure to hide it, and the more I tried to hide it, the more anxious I became because I was scared I wasn't hiding it well enough.

The impetus of my attack that particular day was clear—I had been counting on the Catalano case to bring some very substantial, and very *needed*, money into the firm. Now I realized I would be lucky to get five percent of what I had hoped to settle the case for. The pony I had bet on came in dead last. Hell, the pony died in the starting gate. All I wanted to do was get home without shitting my pants, hit the bathroom, and then crawl into bed.

Just when I thought no one in the world had it worse than me, I crossed the street toward Crown Car Wash and spotted my cousin Jackie Masella. He was behind the car wash entrance, pushing some bald, sixty-year-old Chinese guy into the back seat of Jackie's Cadillac. One look at the fear in the Chinaman's eyes and I knew that the self-pity party I was throwing for myself was totally inappropriate. The Chinaman had it worse than I could ever imagine. Or so I thought at the time.

If you asked Jackie what he did for a living, he'd tell you that he was a *labor negotiator* and *consultant* for the United Brotherhood of Carpenters and Joiners of America. If you asked anyone in the neighborhood, they would tell you the same thing. And everyone would be lying. Everyone in Kings County knew my cousin Jackie had been a thief, crook, gangster, and junior wiseguy for most of his three and a half decades on this earth. But no one ever talked about it.

His father was my grandfather's sister's son, which made Jackie my second cousin. But if you know anything about Italians and how we view family, you'd know that such labels are meaningless. If he's your nephew, you treat him like a brother. If he's your cousin, you treat him like a brother. If he's your aunt's niece's son's second cousin on your mother's side, you treat him like a brother. So long as he is blood. And Jackie was more than blood. He grew up around the corner from me, and since he was only a few years older than I was, we were basically inseparable when we were kids. And we stayed like that until I went off to college. After that we drifted apart a bit, which people tend to do when they grow in different directions. I had studying and internships, and Jackie had the unions and collecting for his boss, Big Louie Turro, or *BLT* as he was known in the neighborhood. I had made a point of telling Jackie about all the classes I was taking and the incredible people I had met in college, hoping that maybe he'd turn his life around, go to night school or something. I would even lie to my cousin about all the girls I was scoring at school, anything to get him interested in leaving the neighborhood and doing something with his life other than running around for Big Louie.

But every Christmas break, every summer vacation, whenever I came home from wherever I had been, there were two things that never changed. First, Ferro's Bakery would give away free zeppoli every Fourth of July and Christmas. You could go as many times as you wanted, eat as many zeppoli as your stomach could handle, so long as you said, "Happy Birthday, Jesus" or "Happy Birthday, America," depending on which holiday it was. No "Happy Birthday," no zeppoli—Tom Ferro's rule. He said they were the two most important birthdays in the history of the world and they had to be respected.

The other constant was that Jackie would be hanging out at Patsy's between 6 p.m. and 9 p.m., because those were the hours that guys who "owed" BLT would come by to settle up with my cousin. If they didn't, Jackie would go looking for them. And everyone in Bensonhurst knew that if Jackie Masella came looking for you, well, you better hope you couldn't be found.

But Jackie had found the Chinaman. As I watched, Jackie slipped a C-note to the owner of the car wash, who then conveniently "alibied" himself by walking across the street to a coffee shop. I wondered if the poor old guy in the Caddy had any idea of what was in store for him, because I sure as hell did.

Jackie got into the back seat, next to the Chinaman, and closed the door. A metal track pulled the Cadillac into the bowels of the building, where the sounds of gears churning, water spraying, and buffers buffing would drown out any cries coming from the Eldorado. The car disappeared from view. I checked my watch. I felt sicker than before, knowing what was happening inside the car wash, amongst the hot wax and spinning brushes.

Exactly one minute later, Jackie's car emerged glistening. The back door opened, Jackie got out and walked away from the car. The Chinaman stumbled out after him, his face badly beaten and blood all over his shirt. He looked around, unsure of what to do until Jackie motioned to him to get lost. A swarm of Puerto Rican workers descended on the car, scrubbing the blood off the tan leather interior, just as their boss, I am sure, had instructed them to do.

What had the old guy done to deserve Jackie's wrath or, more accurately, BLT's wrath? Had he borrowed money he couldn't pay back? Did he play the numbers and actually think he'd collect after he won? Or maybe he refused to sell hijacked cigarettes in his bodega? Didn't really matter. Once you'd gotten a "waxing at the Crown," as it was called in the neighborhood, the reason you got it was irrelevant. You just knew you didn't want it to happen again. I had heard about guys getting "waxed," but I never knew if it was real or just Brooklyn legend. Now I knew. What I didn't know was that soon enough I'd be getting an up close and personal look at how Jackie did business and that it would make a waxing at the Crown look like a walk in the park.

Jackie grabbed a towel from one of the Puerto Ricans and wiped blood from his hands. I was only about fifty yards from him, so I put my head down and walked quickly so that he wouldn't spot me. I didn't want him to know I had seen him "work"—it just would have been awkward. I passed by the car wash without looking up and covered the last few blocks to my home in record time.

I walked the stone path leading from the sidewalk to my brick row house. I remember how proud we were the day we closed on it. Janine and I were barely able to scrape together enough for the down payment, but the house was in good shape and in a safe neighborhood so we made it work. Well, at least we did for a while. Janine was unaware of it at the time, but I had skipped a few mortgage payments in order to pay some law firm bills. And I was finding it hard to catch up.

I remember our first night in the house—Janine and I watched the movie *The Flamingo Kid*. We kept thinking of excuses to get up from the couch.

You want a glass of water, honey? Let me get it for you.

Are you cold, sweetheart? Let me go upstairs and get a blanket.

Why don't I run into the kitchen and make us some popcorn?

We really just wanted to strut around our great big house. Truth be told, the house isn't big at all. But the apartment we had been living in was only two rooms and so small that you couldn't stretch your legs without kicking over a lamp. All Janine and I had done was buy a tiny two-bedroom, one-and-a-half-bath row house in a middle-class neighborhood, but we thought we had bought the Taj Mahal.

As I turned the key in the lock to my front door, my stomach started to settle down. Going home always made my anxiety attacks subside. That's because Janine was there. No matter how stressed I ever felt, all I'd have to do was ask her to wrap her arms around me and tell me she loved me and I'd almost immediately start to feel better. That's why I always told Janine

I didn't want her coming to my office. I didn't want those two worlds to mix—the one that caused all of my worries and the one that was a panacea for the very same.

My wife called out as soon as I entered. My stomach did not remain settled for long.

"Hi, sweetheart!" she shouted as she ran over to me and threw her arms around my neck. She kissed me repeatedly on the cheek and lips.

"Hey! What did I do to deserve this welcome?" I asked.

Janine was all smiles. "Sit down," she said. "I've got news for you."

"What kind of news? I don't like news that I have to sit down for before I can hear it." I was wary and my instincts would prove to be correct.

"Just sit down and I'll tell you," Janine said as she led me into the kitchen. She was absolutely giddy. That alone spelled trouble for me. I don't claim to know a lot about women. In fact, I know less than nothing. But there is one thing of which I am certain—there is a direct correlation between the excitement a woman feels in response to an event and the dismay a man will experience over the exact same thing. For example, a woman will jump for joy when she finds out her mother is coming in from Tucson to spend a month at her house while a man, upon hearing the same news, will jump out the window. It was my knowledge of this phenomenon that caused my stomach to gurgle much faster when I saw how my wife was behaving.

"Is it good news or bad news?" I asked tentatively, already knowing the answer.

"The best kind of news! I'm pregnant!"

I collapsed into the kitchen chair. My stomach played "Babalu."

"How did this happen? I thought we were being careful?" With over a million different responses from which to choose, I had managed to pick the absolutely worst one. I'm gifted that way.

Janine became defensive, and rightfully so. "It just happened. Why? Aren't you happy?"

"I just thought we were going to wait until we were a little more set financially is all." Once again, this was not the response my wife was looking for.

"Hey," she argued, "I'm not exactly the Virgin Mary over here. You played a part in this, too, you know."

I said nothing. I was numb, except for my stomach, which, like clockwork, began to really hurt like hell.

"Oh, forget it. You can be such an asshole sometimes," Janine said as she turned to walk out of the kitchen. It was obvious I had hurt her, and she was, and still is, the last person in the world I would ever want to hurt. Unfortunately, I have the tendency to do exactly the opposite of what I intend.

I reached out and grabbed Janine gently by the wrist.

"Sweetheart …" I said softly.

She pulled away. "Don't touch me."

I wrapped my arms around her waist and pulled her onto my lap and hugged her tightly. It was damage-control time.

"Of course I'm happy. I'm thrilled. I'm just … I'm just a little surprised is all. Believe me, I couldn't be happier." Like most lawyers, I can shovel bullshit with the best of them but shortly into this particular apology I realized that I wasn't spin-doctoring at all. I truly meant what I was saying. I was thrilled and excited to be having a baby with this incredible woman. It literally almost scared the crap out of me. But I was excited nonetheless.

Janine leaned in and kissed me sweetly on the lips. Like

always, when she kissed me, I forgot all about lawsuits and bills and mortgages.

We were mid-kiss when the front door swung open wildly, smashing against the table that sat behind it, causing our wedding photo to fall over, face down. My sister Ginny ran into the house, shrieking like only she can. Her live-in boyfriend, Ian, followed behind her. Ian was a spoiled rich kid from Long Island who was in his mid-thirties and still trying to make it as a musician. Ginny was attracted to his alleged "passion to his art" and his refusal to accept any kind of support from his father. But he had no problem letting my sister support his no-talent ass. I had heard his band, Gator Spoonful, play only once, and that was more than enough— imagine a bad 80's hair band except the members don't fit into the tight spandex and they don't have that much hair anymore. He had been living with Ginny for a few years. She was four months pregnant with his child and was beginning to show. I disliked Ian immensely and I didn't hide it.

"Oh, my God! Oh, my God!" Ginny yelled as she embraced Janine and kissed her. "My mother called and told me the news! I had to come right over!"

"You told my mother before you told me?" I asked, a little hurt.

"You were in court this morning and I had to tell somebody," Janine explained. "Besides, I wanted to tell you in person."

"Congratulations," Ian said insincerely, extending his hand toward me. I shook it, for Ginny's sake. Ian patted my wife's stomach and winked at me. "Glad to see you guys are finally catching up to us."

"Bullshit," I corrected. "When there's a ring on my sister's finger, then *you'll* be caught up to *us*. Until then, you're way behind."

Ginny placed her arm around Ian and kissed him on the cheek. "That'll be coming soon enough, won't it honey?" Ginny asked.

"As soon as the baby is born," Ian reminded her.

"That's a little ass backwards, isn't it?" I said under my breath.

"Are you gonna start in again?" Ginny snapped. "This is my life, Bobby, not yours."

"And you're doing a fine job fucking it up, aren't you? You hit Mom and Dad up for any more money this month?"

"Enough!" Janine put an end to the argument. "There will be no fighting. Not tonight."

Everyone was silent. Janine rarely, if ever, raised her voice. So when she did, you knew she had a good reason. For a petite, quiet woman, Janine commanded more respect than anyone I knew. In a family of boisterous, insane Italians, Janine stood out as our own one-hundred-twenty-pound E.F. Hutton—when she talked, people listened.

"You're right. I'm sorry," I apologized to Janine before turning to Ginny. "I'm sorry, Ginny. I just had a bad day at work and I'm taking it out on you."

"That's okay. I've had a few days like that myself," my sister said as she gave me a tight hug. "I still can't believe my baby brother is going to be a father!"

Neither could I.

FOUR

THAT NIGHT I lay in bed and watched my wife get changed into flannel pajama bottoms and a T-shirt. My God, Janine was stunning. She looked at herself in the full-length mirror that hung on our closet door and ran her hands over her stomach. My stomach hadn't been as flat as hers since I was twelve.

"Will you still love me when my belly's big and fat?" she asked.

"My belly's big and fat and you still love me," I answered.

Janine climbed into bed next to me and kissed me on the nose.

"Your belly's not fat. You're very handsome." She was being kind. I had ceased being handsome in my mid-twenties, and it was a shame, too, because in my day I was a damn good-looking guy. But during my first year of law school my hair started to fall out in clumps—partly genetics, partly stress. Studying replaced working out and I soon gained twenty pounds. I carried the extra weight fairly well, but I hardly looked thin. Janine called me "stocky" but what that really meant was I had grown love handles. By the time I turned thirty a few lines had become fixtures on my face and "handsome" was a distant memory. A few more years and I had become invisible to all women except desperate, single secretaries who didn't care that I was married because all they wanted was to land a lawyer. But Janine would always tell me I was handsome. I don't know if she was lying, blind, or retarded but I wasn't about to complain. She was beautiful and mine and if she was happy with me, then so be it.

I placed my hand on Janine's stomach. I was worried.

"I don't know how we're going to afford this, honey," I said. "I'm not exactly setting the legal profession on fire, if you know what I mean."

Once again, Janine defended me from myself. "You're a great lawyer," she argued. "You just need a break is all."

"No shit."

"We'll be fine. The school said I could work part-time as a teacher's aid once the baby is born. I'll be making a lot less, but we'll make it work. Besides, after the Smyth case is settled we'll be on easy street."

"I hope you're right. The case is on for a defendant's motion in a few days. I'll beat it. But I still have to win the trial."

"I know I'm right," Janine said confidently as she turned off her bedside light. "Now spoon me so I can get some rest. I'm really tired."

Janine rolled over onto her side and got into the fetal position. I did the same and pressed my front against her back and wrapped my arms around her from behind. As we lay there in the spoon position, I drifted into a nervous sleep, dreaming of dead clients and new babies and a wife I did not deserve.

F I V E

"DEFENDANT'S MOTION for summary judgment is granted. Case dismissed."

I watched in disbelief as Judge Hall raised his gavel. Its ascent seemed to take place in slow motion. It reached its apex and then began its free fall toward the bench, Hall's liver-spotted fingers wrapped tightly about the handle, grasping my fate. The head of the small wooden hammer crashed with a loud thud, three times, as was Judge Hall's trademark disposition of a case. Each bang caused a sharp pain in my chest as if the judge was using his gavel to drive a nail into my heart. He was throwing out the Smyth case, the case that was supposed to save me, Janine, our impending child, and my law firm in one fell windfall of cash. And I was powerless to stop him.

"Your Honor, I strongly object!" I shouted so that I could be heard above the din of the *ham-and-eggers* packing the courtroom. *Ham-and-eggers* is supposed to be a derogatory term. Its intention is to separate the working-stiff schmucks who hump it into the courthouses every day, five days a week, to litigate cases from the Ivy League, thousand-dollar-suit-wearing, Midtown-office corporate lawyers who wouldn't know which end of a gavel was up because they never had, and never planned to, degrade themselves by stepping into a courtroom. The ham-and-eggers were considered the lower end of the legal profession and the joke was they would bring their lunch, such as a ham-and-egg sandwich, to work in a lunch-box while the corporate lawyers would eat out at places like Le Cirque and Gotham. To be honest, I sort of liked being called a ham-and-egger. In fact, I took pride in the term. My old man brought a lunch-box to work every day of his life and had eaten his share of ham-and-egg sandwiches. I figured if it was good enough for him, it was good enough for me.

On the day I argued the Smyth case, Kings County Supreme Court in Brooklyn was a madhouse as usual, overflowing with ham-and-eggers. The thing that surprised me most about the legal profession when I first started practicing was the informality and disorganization of the courtrooms. On any given day a judge would have anywhere from twenty to one hundred cases on his or her docket. Courtrooms that were designed to hold thirty people were forced to accommodate one hundred fifty. Lawyers would fill the gallery, the jury box, the aisles, and, more often than not, they would overflow into the hallway. All the while, the attorneys would shout out the names of their opposing counsel's client, in the hopes that opposing counsel would hear them above all of the noise. If the name was heard, opposing counsel would call out the name of the first lawyer's client in response, and then, upon spotting each other, the two adversaries would fight their way through the sea of suits so they could meet and discuss the motion or conference that was scheduled for that day. It's like some kind of pathetic mating call ritual that only lawyers understand and it creates probably the most inefficient system possible for the administration of justice. That is why I kept shouting out my objection to Judge Hall's ruling—I had to make sure he heard me above the din of the courtroom before his bailiff called the next case.

"I heard you the first time, Counselor," Judge Hall admonished. "And you can object as often and as loudly as you like, but I'm not changing my ruling."

"But Judge, there are several issues of fact here that, with all due respect, should be decided by a jury and not by you!"

"And that's where you and I disagree and that's what makes the world go 'round."

"But Judge …"

"Look, your client slipped on applesauce in a Food World. You have no witnesses and Mr. Smyth has no idea how long the applesauce was in the aisle. You can't establish notice so I have to toss the case. Summary judgment is warranted."

Judge Hall was right, and I knew he was right, but I wasn't about to let him know it. I had to keep fighting.

"Your Honor, may I approach the bench?" Whenever I was about to kiss a judge's ass, I would switch from calling him "Judge" to "Your Honor."

"Make it quick," Hall snapped.

I had argued in front of Hall more times than I cared to remember. He was a decent enough guy, but he had been on the bench about ten years too long and had seen all the tricks in the book. He was "surfing"—lawyer lingo for riding out his last few years before hanging up the robe and collecting a sweet government pension. He knew I had no chance of changing his mind but he figured to give me a shot at it, maybe out of professional courtesy, maybe out of morbid fascination—like watching a spider try to struggle his way out of the toilet bowl right before you flush him.

I hurried up to the bench but my adversary, John McDonough, had beaten me there by a few seconds and was already making his case to Judge Hall.

"Your Honor," McDonough pleaded, "I don't understand why you're entertaining this conversation. You've already made your ruling. If Mr. Principe has a problem with it, he can always appeal."

"Shut up, John," the Judge snapped back.

Once you were at the bench and no one else could hear your conversation, formalities were over—at least for the judge, anyway. The lawyers still had to grovel, which put me at a distinct disadvantage as McDonough's obsequiousness was finely honed. In fact, he was famous for it. He was a toady's toady, a real bench-bitch, the type of lawyer who worshipped judges and dreamt of being one, even though he knew there wasn't a chance in hell of that ever happening. If you looked up *sycophant* in *Webster's* you wouldn't find a picture of McDonough's face—you'd find a picture of McDonough with his head firmly shoved up some judge's ass. And if you had X-ray vision, you'd be able to see McDonough, stuck up in there, smiling from ear to ear, more than content to be snugly nestled in the warmth of the judge's colon. God, I hated the son of a bitch.

Judge Hall turned to me. "You've got thirty seconds to change my mind."

"Your Honor," I started, "Mr. Smyth testified repeatedly at his deposition that the Food World in question was where he shopped *every* week, and that whenever he was there the aisle where he fell was *always* covered with garbage and debris. That is more than enough to establish that the store had notice of the dangerous condition." My argument was weak at best, and McDonough pounced on it.

"Plaintiff counsel is well aware, *or at least he should be*," McDonough said smugly, "that a persistent, but *general*, dirty condition does not create notice. To make a case, Mr. Principe would have to demonstrate that my client had notice that the *specific* applesauce that allegedly caused Mr. Smyth to fall had been in the aisle for a *specific* period of time. He can't do that." McDonough stared at me, proud of himself, waiting for my response. He had no idea how close he came to my response being a crack to his smirking mouth. But McDonough was saved from that fate by Judge Hall, who leaned forward so that we could hear him whisper.

"Look, Rob," he said, in an almost fatherly tone, "I don't want to throw your case out, especially with the type of injuries your client suffered. I mean, a skull fracture is pretty serious. But unless you can show notice, I have to toss you. Give me something to hang my hat on and you stay in the game."

"But Your Honor …," McDonough blurted.

"Quiet, Counselor," Hall raised his hand, palm out, in McDonough's direction.

"Your Honor," I began, "*Warren v. Flanders School District* holds that a general, consistent dangerous condition is enough to establish constructive notice if the defendant is responsible for allowing that condition to persist. In that case, garbage cans in the school cafeteria were always overflowing with garbage, and …"

Hall cut me off.

"I'm familiar with *Warren*. It's a Third Department case. You have case law relevant to Kings County?"

He knew I didn't. He was a bastard for even asking. I was down to desperate measures.

"Your Honor," I pleaded, with eyebrows raised, trying to make my face appear as sincere and earnest as possible. "This is the biggest case in my office. I'm begging you, please don't throw it out."

"I'm not about to ignore Second Department law simply because you feel this is your 'biggest case,'" the judge shot back, annoyed that I had tried to play on his sympathies. "Now do you have anything else for me to consider or not? You're wasting the court's time."

"No, my argument stands," I shot back defiantly as if suddenly trying to appear like I had balls would make a difference.

"Then my decision stands as well. Case dismissed." The judge turned to the bailiff. "Call the next case."

"Number fifty-seven on the Calendar, *Tonelli v. Merrick*," the bailiff shouted so his voice could be heard throughout the courtroom.

The attorneys for the next case took their places at counselors' tables, but I wouldn't step down from the bench. I had a choice—suck it up and appeal with only a one percent chance of having the decision overturned or lose my shit and act like an insane person in front of my colleagues. I chose.

"Judge," I shouted. "Do you want to clear a case from your docket so badly that you're willing to ignore the fact that my client suffered a fractured skull because the defendant can't keep his store clean?" I had just suggested that a judge dismissed a case in order to lessen his workload. Truth is, judges do that all the time, but it's a dirty little secret that no one ever acknowledges. That's a line you don't cross, but I crossed it anyway. I not only crossed it but then I turned around, whipped out my dick, and pissed on it—all in open court.

Judge Hall turned crimson. "Sanctions!!" he screamed. "Five hundred dollars!!"

"Who cares? I don't have the money to pay it anyway!!"

"Get him out of my courtroom!"

The bailiff grabbed me by the arm and attempted to lead me out into the hall. I pulled my arm free and walked out on my own.

The eyes of every lawyer in the room watched me as I exited. I was aware that, by noon, every attorney in Brooklyn would have heard about how Rob Principe had a total breakdown in court. By three o'clock the story would be that I slugged the bailiff. By the next morning, the rumor mill would have me getting dragged out in cuffs, crazy eyed, screaming "Free Manson."

As a lawyer, all you have is your reputation, and mine was a well-deserved one for being honest, almost to a fault, and for being levelheaded. In a single morning, I had done much damage to that reputation. And it was all the result of choosing to lash out at the judge instead of just walking away from the bench. As bad choices went, I was just getting warmed up.

SIX

ROLAND HAD BEEN CALLING my name for about half a block but I didn't turn around because I wasn't in the mood for talking. The noise of the traffic was loud enough for me to pretend I couldn't hear him but he eventually caught up to me when I was waiting for the light to turn at the corner of Church Street and Montague. Don't get me wrong, I love Roland. He's been my best friend since we were kids. We went to grade school, high school, and even college together—everything but law school; Roland got his JD at Brooklyn Law. But like I said, I just wasn't in the mood to talk, even to a pal.

"Hey, Prince," Roland said as he finally caught up to me. "Slow the hell down, man. I've been calling your name since the courthouse. Ya didn't hear me?"

"No," I lied. "Sorry, my mind is sort of elsewhere."

"I'd be loopy, too, if I had my ass handed to me the way you just did."

"Did you see that bullshit?" I asked.

"Yeah, I was in the back. Tough loss," Roland sympathized.

"Yeah, well, Hall's an old mummy."

"He was right, ya know."

"Shut up."

But he didn't shut up.

"How the hell did you let your client testify that he didn't know how long the applesauce was on the ground? That's borderline malpractice."

"Malpractice? Why? Because I didn't tell Smyth to lie at his deposition?" I asked sarcastically.

"No," Roland responded, "because you didn't tell him the consequences of *not lying*. There's a big difference."

I was about to lecture Roland on legal morals and ethical responsibility when we were interrupted by Jimmy Fargas, a man for whom these topics would have been completely foreign. Jimmy was a fat personal injury attorney from Staten Island who had gotten rich on pediatric medical malpractice suits. He was famous for landing huge cases and he did whatever he had to do in order to keep the clients coming through his door. He set up "chasers" in hospitals, he bribed nurses and physician assistants for referrals, and he paid off parents who had already hired lawyers so they would fire their counsel and retain him. He was a millionaire ten times over and was two years younger than me. I hated him. He greeted us looking like a fat cat with a mouthful of canary.

"Roland, Rob," he said, bubbling over with excitement. "Anything new with you guys?"

I could tell he wanted nothing more than for us to ask him the same question.

"Fargas. What's with the shit-eatin' grin?" Roland asked, falling right into the fat bastard's trap.

"I just signed up a brain-damaged baby case!" he burst out with glee, like a woman telling her best friends that she just got engaged. Roland immediately peppered Jimmy with questions.

"Liability?"

"Solid. Misuse of forceps at delivery. Crushed skull injury."

"Coverage?"

"Doc's got a two million policy. Hospital's got five."

"Parents?"

"They 'no-speka-the-english,' man. They'll do whatever I say. I tell them to hold out for more money, they'll hold out. I tell them to settle, they'll settle."

"Solid score." Roland high-fived Jimmy as if they had just combined on a perfect give-and-go in a pick-up basketball game.

What struck me was that Roland never thought to ask the child's name, and Jimmy never thought to offer it.

Roland, with great admiration, watched Jimmy walk away. "Now that guy is on the ball, you know what I'm sayin'? You gotta be more like him, Prince."

"You mean a scumbag?"

Roland smiled. "C'mon, let's grab some lunch."

SEVEN

GOING TO ROLAND'S LAW FIRM always made me feel bad about myself. His space was huge, with ten individual offices, a large secretarial pool, two conference rooms, a copy room, and a kitchen with an espresso machine that cost more than my car. Everything was mahogany and leather, real top-shelf stuff. The work of hip young SoHo artists decorated the walls. Not that I wasn't happy for Roland's success. It's just that after spending a few hours at his place, I always felt depressed when I went back to my deli-meat stinking office on 71st and 18th.

As usual, Roland had gone a little overboard with lunch. The conference table was covered with food—tomatoes with mozzarella, rice balls, eggplant parmesan, and potato-and-egg sandwiches that were so good they'd make you cry.

"You want anything else, Prince?"

"No, thanks. I'm stuffed."

"How about some wine?" Roland offered, reaching for a bottle of red from a vineyard out on Long Island's North Fork.

"No, I'm good, thanks anyway."

"Some dessert then? Johnny V on the corner makes the best cannoli in town," Roland pressed, as if I hadn't been eating Johnny V's pastries since I was five. In fact, my first solid food was one of his half-moon cookies that my mother gave me to suck on when I was teething. "Since I settled his wife's car accident case, he gives me whatever I want for free," Roland continued.

"I've had Johnny V's cannolis, Roland," I said, maybe sounding a little annoyed, or possibly even defensive, but Roland didn't pick up on it. "I just can't eat anymore."

"I'll just get a few then." Roland never took no for an answer. That's what made him such a good lawyer. Roland spoke into his intercom. "Nancy, sweetheart, call Johnny V and have him send over some cannoli, biscotti, and some spumoni. Thanks."

Despite my earlier refusal, Roland poured me some more wine.

"Prince, you're my best friend and you know I would never, *ever*, try to steer you wrong, right?"

"Right."

"So I want you to listen carefully to me, okay?"

"Sure."

"No one's telling you to tell your clients to lie. I don't tell my clients to lie. But you can't make it in this business unless you explain to your client the effect his words will have on his case. For example, in this Smyth case you just had thrown out, do you want to know how I would've prepped the guy?"

"Thanks, but I've prepped clients for depositions hundreds of times," I said annoyed.

"I'm sure you have," Roland responded. "Now let me show you how to do it right. I'd have said: 'Mr. Smyth, I understand that you fell on some applesauce in a store. Under New York law you have *no case whatsoever* unless you can show that store workers knew that the applesauce was there, which they'll never admit. Or, you can show that the apple- sauce had been there for a long enough period of time so that the store *should have known* it was there.'"

"That's great. Why don't I just get sworn in and testify for him myself?" I asked sarcastically.

"You want an office like this one day or do you wanna stay in that dump above Morelli's, no offense, for the rest of your career, which, by the way, is almost over if things don't turn around?"

"You're telling the client what to say!" I argued.

"No, I'm not," Roland defended. "I'm telling him the *consequences* of what he *might say*. There's a big difference. And it's totally legal."

"It may be legal," I countered, "but it's not ethical."

Roland smiled at my ignorance. "Ethics are like clouds, Bobby. They change shape depending on how the wind is blowin' at the time. All that matters is whether or not you're breaking the law and I don't break the law. The law is my ethics, not some bullshit code of morality that differs from person to person. I pay the best doctors to be my experts, I cross examine little old ladies to tears if I have to, and I prepare the shit out of my clients before they testify. And I do it all *within the law*."

Roland took a sip of his wine and looked me over.

"You know what your problem is?" he asked.

"Enlighten me."

"You went to Columbia Law School to become a personal

injury attorney. That's like buying a fuckin' Ferrari to be a goddamn cab driver. You think you're above the rest of us, that you can make your money without getting your hands dirty. But Princey, sooner or later, we all gotta roll around in the mud."

"Yeah, well you *wallow* in it."

"Perhaps. But I clean up nice, don't I?" Roland retorted. "I mean, look at me. Bottom of my law school class. But I've got a brownstone in Brooklyn Heights, a summer home in East Hampton, and I get more tang than Neil Armstrong. All because I play the game aggressively, *all* within the boundaries of the law."

I couldn't take it anymore. "I have to get back to my office," I said as I stood and headed for the door.

"What about the pastries?"

"I've got a stomachache."

EIGHT

THE LAST FEW RAYS of a setting sun slipped through the blinds of my office window as I was getting ready to go home to Janine for an evening of television and singing to my wife's stomach.

I had taken to singing to our unborn child. I sang songs like "You Are My Sunshine" and "Bushel and a Peck." I didn't really know all of the words, so I sort of fudged it at places and made up my own lyrics. I found it really fun for some reason.

Janine kept telling me that I was nuts—the baby was way too young to hear anything at this point; she hadn't even developed ears yet. Janine was convinced we were having a girl. But I liked the singing anyway. It calmed me. And it made me feel close to my kid. So, despite the fact that I would most likely soon become an unemployed thirty-three-year-old lawyer with no prospects for a decent job, I started to feel good for the first time in a long time. I had a beautiful wife, a belly full of food that Roland had paid for, and I was going home to sing to my child.

And then the phone rang. I usually screened calls after 6 p.m. but for some reason I answered this one.

"Hello?"

As soon as I heard the voice on the other end, I wished I hadn't picked up the phone.

"Mr. Principe?"

"Yeah?"

"Mr. Principe, this is Paul Stevens from American Home Savings."

I said nothing. I was hoping that if I stayed quiet and held my breath, Mr. Stevens would just hang up and leave me alone. No such luck.

"Mr. Principe, are you still there?"

"Uh. Yeah. I'm still here. Sorry, I've been having some problems with my phone."

"Oh. That might explain why I've been having so much trouble getting in touch with you. I've been leaving you messages for weeks, Mr. Principe ..."

"Well, like I said, I've been having trouble with my phone system. Phone, voice mail, everything ..."

"Mr. Principe, I've left several messages with your secretary as well ..."

"Oh, well, I apologize. That's inexcusable. I will certainly have a talk with her first thing tomorrow morning. You know it's impossible to find anyone in this town who can take a good message. I mean, how hard is it? You answer the phone. You write down the message. You hand the message to your boss. You know what I'm talking about?"

I was stalling. It didn't work.

"We need to discuss your mortgage situation. You're three months in default, Mr. Principe."

The son of a bitch kept saying my name, as if he had read in some book on how to be an effective manager that you should keep repeating the name of the person you're talking to again and again. It really pissed me off, so I did it back to him.

"Sure thing, *Mr. Stevens*. Now that I think about it, I did get a message that you called, *Mr. Stevens*, but I've been so busy, I haven't had time to get back to you. I'm in the middle of settling a big case. Should be done in a few days though. Then I'll be able to make all my back payments. How does that sound, *Mr. Stevens*?"

"You told me that last month, Mr. Principe. You said something about a case of yours. Smyth was the name."

"That's right, *Mr. Stevens*. Smyth. You've got a good memory. Case is still going strong. Insurance carrier just made a solid offer, but it's too low. I'm gonna squeeze 'em for a few more bucks. Should be wrapped up any day now."

"Mr. Principe, the bank can only be so patient. If you don't pay soon, we'll have to take action."

"I understand your position. Don't worry. I'll have the money to you soon."

"Okay. Why don't you send one month's payment now, as a sign of good faith?"

"Okay," I said. "I'll send that out first thing tomorrow."

"I should have it by the end of the week then?"

"Scout's honor. Keep an eye on your mailbox."

"Good. Have a nice evening, Mr. Principe."

"You too, *Mr. Stevens*, you pretentious, smug, son of a bitch."

I said that last part after I had hung up the phone.

I grabbed my briefcase and headed for the outer door.

Once I got there I stopped and turned around. I walked back into my office and I put my empty briefcase back on my desk and left it there. Then I walked home. Scared. Tired. And defeated.

NINE

I WAS ABOUT HALFWAY when I heard Jackie's voice.

"Hey!" he shouted. "Johnnie Cochran! Over here."

Whenever Jackie would see me, the first thing he'd do is call me Johnnie Cochran, probably because other than me and his own criminal attorney, Johnnie Cochran was the only lawyer he had ever heard of.

Across the street, Jackie was sitting on a wooden folding chair next to a metal patio table in front of Patsy's—the social club of choice for local mobsters since the Mafia first stepped foot in Brooklyn. My father, a long time ago, had done the drywall for the building that Patsy's called home. He always said that if he knew what the place was going to become, he would've burned it down as soon as the last nail went in.

My father was embarrassed by Jackie and Jackie's late father, Joseph. He loved them both—they're family. But he was ashamed of how they made their living and enraged at what they did to the names of honest, hardworking Italian-Americans. Sometimes growing up, I'd get razzed at school a bit by kids, especially the Irish, about how my uncle was a mobster.

"Remember," my father used to tell me. "This country is named after Americus Vespucci. It was discovered by Christopher Columbus. Thanks to two Italians, we can live in this land and call ourselves Americans. Other than a pub, what's ever been *named after* an Irishman? Other than the bottom of a whiskey bottle, what's ever been *discovered* by an Irishman? Tell those Irish donkeys *that* the next time they give you any grief."

One day, in eighth grade, I got serenaded with "guinea" and "wop" on the way home from school. So I took my old man's advice and set forth a clear and lucid comparison of the respective contributions made by the Italian and Irish cultures, just like my father had told me to do. It was a presentation worthy of any future lawyer. When I was done, Conor Slattery and Brian McMahon proceeded to kick the shit out of me. When I got home and my dad saw what had happened, he wasn't angry I'd been fighting.

"Don't ever let anyone make you feel ashamed of who you are," he said.

When I was growing up, my old man was very big on giving advice, usually in the form of a saying. "*A coward dies many deaths, a valiant dies but once.*" That was one of his favorites. He was also fond of "*Money only makes a man wealthy, but family makes a man rich.*" But I was a child and I didn't always listen to my father's advice. Now I wish I had "*because the insolence of the boy is often paid for by the man.*" Damn, was he right about that last one.

I crossed the street toward Patsy's. Jackie stretched his arms wide apart—almost as wide as the big grin on his face.

"Sorry, Jackie, I didn't even see you there," I said.

Jackie turned to Choo Choo and Tony, two more of Big Louie Turro's boys.

"Would you look at this guy?" he asked Choo Choo. "Big time lawyer."

Choo Choo laughed, causing his entire three-hundred-fifty-pound frame to shake and his D-cup man-breasts to jiggle like two bags filled with Jello. Tony didn't laugh. In all the years I had seen that guy sitting outside of Patsy's, I'd never seen Tony crack a smile or heard him say so much as "Hello."

"He's probably deep in thought about his next big case," Jackie continued. "But you're never too busy to give your cousin a hug, now are ya?"

Jackie wrapped his arms around me tight. I kissed him on his cheek, hugged back, and gave him a weak smile. It was the best I could do considering I still had Paul Stevens' phone call on my mind.

"What's wrong? You look like shit," Jackie asked, genuinely concerned.

"Nothin's wrong. I'm just a little tired is all."

"My ass. Something's wrong. Come on. Let's go in, have a drink. We'll talk about it."

"Jackie, I swear, nothing's wrong. I've just been working some long hours and I really need to get home and go to bed early. I'll give you a ring next week. We'll get together."

I took a step to leave but Jackie grabbed me by the arm. Wiseguys aren't used to anyone ever saying no to them and, when it happens, they don't know how to react.

"What? You're too busy to have a drink with me?"

"No, I'm just beat …"

"Come on. One drink. Fifteen minutes and you're on your way."

I looked down at Jackie's hand on my forearm. He hadn't let go and he wasn't going to let go unless I started to walk into Patsy's with him. He would've stayed there all night, into the next morning even, staring at me, waiting for my answer to his invitation. He was that persistent. And crazy. Jackie was used to getting what he wanted. So I went inside.

What harm could one drink do? I thought.

Turned out, it could do a hell of a lot of harm.

TEN

PATSY'S WAS ALMOST pitch-black inside. It was always like that, on account of Lou Turro's demand that the curtains be pulled shut at all times. He allowed the door to remain open but no one was allowed to stand where you could be seen from the outside. All of the tables, and even the bar, were pushed far off to the side walls so that anyone sitting at them couldn't be spotted by cops or feds staked out in vans across the street. Big Lou was paranoid about that kind of thing.

The rumor mongers of 71st Street have it on good authority that in the early eighties Turro found out that the FBI was staking out Patsy's from the rooftops across the street. Obviously, he couldn't have that, so he bought the three buildings directly across from the club and tore them down. No rooftops, no rooftop surveillance. Problem solved.

Then, to really piss off the feds, he turned the lot into the Louis J. Turro Memorial Playground for the neighborhood

kids. It had a big plaque at the base of a flagpole and everything. The fact that he was still alive didn't stop Big Louie from
making it a "memorial" playground. Jackie once told me that
he was pretty sure BLT didn't know what "memorial" meant,
but Lou had it placed on the plaque because he had seen the
word used in the names of other parks and thought he had to
use it. To this day I don't think anyone ever had the guts to tell
Big Lou about his mistake.

I sat at a table way in the back while Jackie got us each a
drink. I didn't even bother to tell Jackie what I wanted, because
no matter what I said, he would have said it was a "pussy
drink." If I had ordered a Jack Daniels and Coke, he would've
said I was a pussy for not drinking the Jack Daniels straight. If
I had ordered a boilermaker, he would've given me shit for
needing the beer chaser. So years ago I learned to just let Jackie
get me one of whatever he was having.

Jackie sat down and dropped a scotch in front of me. He
raised his glass.

"Salute."

I lifted my glass and tapped it against his.

"Salute."

Jackie slammed the scotch. His glass was empty in seconds.
I took a sip and put the glass down.

"What are you, a pussy? Drink the drink."

Jesus, I can't win, I thought to myself.

"Nah. Gonna take it easy tonight. Gotta go back to the
missus sober, ya know?"

"Yeah, yeah. I know. Always a Boy Scout, you were."

Jackie looked me up and down.

"So, who shit in your potato salad?"

"What? Nobody."

"Well, something's bothering you. Problems with the squaw?"

"Problems with Janine? No. Actually, things are pretty good, I guess. We're having a baby. We just found out."

Jackie shot out of his seat like his ass was spring-loaded.

"You gotta be shittin' me! You and Janine are having a baby! That's amazing! That's fuckin' amazing!"

Jackie grabbed me from my chair and pulled me into a tight embrace. He patted me hard on the back. So hard in fact that some of the guys turned their attention toward us. Jackie turned to everyone in the bar.

"Hey, everybody! My cousin's gonna be a father! I'm gonna be an uncle!"

Everyone raised their glasses and toasted. Not because they gave a shit about me, Janine, or our baby, but out of respect to Jackie, his father, and partially to my dad, whom everyone in the neighborhood knew as an honest man and a talented carpenter.

Jackie sat back down, but he was turbocharged now. His feet were touching the floor, but his legs were shaking up and down like maracas and he was talking a mile a minute. He was truly excited and happy for me. For a moment, he looked like he used to when he was a kid, on his birthday, right before he got to smash open his piñata with an antique, hand-carved bat his dad would let him use. One year, when Jackie was ten, he got so excited waiting for his dad to lower the piñata, he pissed his pants right in front of all the other kids. A kid in our class, Victor Artusa, made the mistake of laughing, so Jackie swung and buried the bat into the side of Victor's head. The guy has a visible dent in his skull to this day and he no longer has a sense of smell.

"You know what this is, Bobby?" Jackie asked, rhetorically. "This is a blessing from God. A mother-fucking blessing from God, that's what this is."

"I know it is," I said in a way that didn't seem to satisfy my cousin.

"Then what the hell's wrong with you? I'm more excited than you are."

"I am excited. I am. I swear. I may not show it on the outside, but I am. It's just that the timing isn't so good. It might've been better if we had waited a while longer."

"Bobby, you're thirty-four. How much longer you gonna wait?"

"I'm thirty-three."

"Whatever. You got a beautiful wife, you got a nice house, you're a lawyer. Have a kid. Shit, have a litter for Christ's sake. You got nothing to worry about."

I took another sip of my scotch.

"Actually, that's not exactly true. My firm isn't doing well. At all. I've got debt up to my eyeballs. Creditors are up my ass. No money is coming into my practice. I'm in some kind of trouble, Jackie. I'm treading water, man. Have been for almost five years now, and it's getting harder and harder to keep my head above sea level, ya know what I'm saying?"

"You kiddin' me?" Jackie seemed truly shocked. Not in a surprised way, though. But more in a disappointed way, as if he had just learned that Joe DiMaggio had corked his bat or that Martin Scorsese was half Irish.

"I thought you were doing great. Uncle Bobby's always braggin' …," he said.

"My father brags when I take a shit."

"I'm sorry, man. I didn't know."

"Yeah, well, now you know. And now that we have a baby coming. And we might lose our home. I'm telling you, Jackie, I'm desperate, man. I feel like I'm at the end of my rope."

Jackie smiled and took my hand.

"You need some money?" he asked. "Say the word, I'll get you whatever you need."

I didn't mean to, but I laughed.

"No, thanks," I said. "I know what happens to guys who can't pay you back."

Jackie's smile vanished. Instantly. I had offended him.

"Did I say anything about a loan?" he asked, pissed off.

"No, Jackie, I didn't mean to insinuate …"

"Did I say anything about you having to pay me back?"

"No, I just assumed …"

"That's the problem with you goddamn lawyers. You're always assumin' things. You know that?"

"You're right. I'm sorry. I shouldn't have assumed that. I didn't mean to hurt your feelings."

Jackie wouldn't let it die.

"You know what happens when you assume, Bobby?" Jackie pressed. "You make an ass out of yourself. That's what happens. I mean, come on, Bobby, did I say anything about paying me back or not?"

I didn't have a chance to answer. Jackie's attention had quickly shifted away from me and toward the door, where a man who had entered the club was standing nervously in the entrance. He made eye contact with Jackie and nodded slightly.

"Speaking of payback," Jackie said as he stood up. I watched him cross the floor toward the man. The contrast between the dark club and the outside sunlight made it difficult to clearly make out the features of the man's face but I didn't need to see them to know that he was terrified. He stiffened as Jackie approached him—his shoulders hunched up and pushed forward, his jaw tightened, and his fingers curled into tight little balls. He looked like a cat that you startle in an alley—all tense and ready to run, but too scared to move a muscle.

From where I sat I couldn't hear what Jackie and the man were saying to each other, but I didn't have to hear their conversation to know what was going on. The man reached into his jacket pocket and handed Jackie an envelope. Jackie opened it, pulled out some cash, and quickly flipped through it. I could tell from the man's body language that he had come up short. Jackie put the cash in his pocket, balled the envelope up in his fist, and threw it against the man's chest. I watched my cousin grab the man by the jacket collar and slap him twice, very hard, with his free hand. No one else at Patsy's seemed to notice, even though you could hear the slap throughout the club. To everyone there, this was business as usual. Jackie might as well have been validating the guy's parking.

Normally I would have been taken aback by this violence because I've never been a violent man. Even as a child, I detested it. When I had to, I'd scrap it up a bit—to defend my heritage or my sister's honor if some playground punk commented on her chest (Ginny had a full C cup in ninth grade). When that happened, I was more than able to hold my own. I'd won more fights than I had lost. But the very notion of violence as a means to an end always seemed to me to be the most inefficient form of problem solving. If you kicked someone's ass, chances are they'd hold a grudge and then come back for more. Except the next time, they'd bring a friend or a weapon, and you'd have the same problem you had before, only worse. I always felt that if you were smarter than someone, you could diffuse almost any situation through rational, and sometimes manipulative, communication that would make your antagonist feel like he had come out ahead even if he really hadn't. That way, you not only took care of the problem, you made an ally who might help you with your next adversary. Since I knew at an early age that I was smarter than most of the mutts I grew up with, I rarely found myself resorting to fighting unless it was absolutely necessary. It was my inclination to communicate and negotiate that made me want to be a lawyer.

That's why I was surprised that day, when I watched Jackie by the door, that I wasn't instantly repulsed by his actions. Instead, I was intrigued. I was engrossed. But more than anything, I was envious. Envious of Jackie. Envious of his strength. His decisiveness. His ability to solve a problem immediately. *Either you have my money or you don't* was Jackie's position. And if you don't, you get a smack. If you don't have it the next time, you get a piano wire necktie. Problem solved. Nice and easy.

It was then, watching Jackie, that I made the decision that changed the rest of my life, a decision I never in a million years thought I'd make. It was a decision made by a man who was too proud to admit he had failed at something that he had worked at so hard, for so long. It was a decision made by a man who was incredibly desperate and scared—a man who didn't want to disappoint his family or let down his father.

It was a decision that I wish I had never made.

But we all have to live with our decisions. Some people learn this the easy way. Some learn it the hard way.

I learned it the impossible way.

Maybe if I hadn't run into Jackie on the same day I lost the Smyth case and got that call from Paul Stevens, things would've turned out differently. No one would've gotten hurt. Maybe. Who the hell knows?

But like I said, I was desperate and scared. I felt like I was all alone, in the middle of the ocean drowning. And at the time, I thought maybe Jackie was my way back to shore.

ELEVEN

JACKIE SAT BACK DOWN at the table. He was agitated. I didn't notice it at first but he had grabbed my scotch and downed it. He was talking but I wasn't paying attention. I was sort of numb at the realization of what I was about to say to Jackie.

"Hey," Jackie barked. "Are you even listening to me?"

"Yeah. No. I'm sorry. I lost my train of thought for a minute. What were you saying?"

"I was sayin' that if you think you have problems, you should have my job. I gotta chase deadbeats like that around every day. Everyone's tryin' to screw you out of a buck, you know what I'm sayin'? No one's honest nowadays. No one's a man of their word. Everyone's lookin' to get over on you."

I leaned in close to Jackie, careful that only he could hear me.

"It's funny you should mention that, because that's what I

was just thinking about," I said.

"Thinking about what?"

"Your problem. You know, collecting from people who aren't able to pay you. And my problem. Not being able to pay the people I owe. Like the bank and my bills at the firm."

"What does one thing gotta do with the other?" Jackie asked, confused.

"Well, nothing really," I answered. "But I think I have an idea that might solve both of our problems."

"Oh, yeah?" Jackie said skeptically. "What?"

I looked around. "Not here."

"What's wrong with here?"

"I want to talk somewhere more private."

I stood from the table and headed for the door. As I walked out of the darkness of Patsy's and into the daylight I took a quick glance over my shoulder and saw that Jackie was right on my heels.

TWELVE

JACKIE AND I SAT on a bench in a playground next to Franklin Elementary. A group of young black kids was playing basketball; they couldn't have been more than twelve years old. We watched for a few minutes. Neither of us spoke. Jackie was smoking a Chesterfield and I was too scared to open my mouth. I knew that once I said what I wanted to say, I was going to ring a bell that could never be unrung. But once I started talking, I was surprised at how easily the words came out.

"That old guy who just came into Patsy's? He owed you money, right?"

"No," Jackie smart-mouthed. "He was selling Girl Scout cookies but he was outta the Thin Mints so I smacked him around."

"What do you do," I asked, "with these guys who owe you money? You know, when they can't pay you? What do you do?"

"Hey, fuck you, Bobby."

I had asked a question that no one in my family had ever asked Jackie. Partly because we were scared of what his reaction would be, but mostly because we already knew the answer. But I wouldn't drop the issue.

"Alright, fine," I said. "I'll assume I know what happens to them and I'll also assume that once that happens, you and Louie Turro have pretty much resigned yourself to taking the loss and never getting your money back."

"Cost of doing business," Jackie said matter-of-factly. He took a long drag from his cigarette and exhaled through his nose. He looked like a stocky, hairy dragon. "You better have a goddamn point."

"I do," I said as I looked around to be absolutely certain no one else was within earshot. "What would you say if I could fix it so when someone couldn't pay you, not only would you get your money back, but ten times what was owed you?"

"I'd say you were fucked in the head." Jackie flicked his cigarette butt onto the blacktop and immediately lit another.

"Jackie, listen to me for a minute. There are so many laws protecting workers on construction sites that you can't cut a fart without violating something."

"So?"

"So, if a guy gets hurt on a job site, there's always someone to blame. Someone to sue. And the beauty part is that the contractors are required by law to carry at least a million dollars in insurance. And they all carry more. Just to be safe."

Jackie turned his attention from his cigarette to me. I could see his interest increase when I mentioned the money.

"There are even laws on the books that say if a construction worker falls from a scaffold on a job site, the owner of the property and the general contractor are *strictly liable* for that worker's injuries. Do you know what *strictly liable* means?"

"No. I must've been sick that day of law school."

"It means that no matter what the worker did before he fell, it can't come in to evidence at the time of trial. A guy can be carrying a piece of sheetrock on each shoulder while climbing a scaffold, not paying attention to where he's going, and if he slips and falls, the owner and the general contractor are liable. Period. Story over. The only thing to do after that is to negotiate how much money the guy gets."

Jackie put his second cigarette out. I could almost see the wheels turning in his head. He so desperately wanted to put it all together, so badly wanted to figure out where I was going with all of this. But God bless his heart, he was dumber than dog shit. He finally gave up and asked me to spell it out for him.

"And this all helps me how?" he asked.

"Let's say a guy owes you fifty large. He flakes. Repeated warnings, you rough him up a bit, but he can't pay. Now you've got a situation on your hands. You can't let the guy off the hook, because then everyone will know that you can stiff BLT and get away with it. So you gotta bump him off ..."

"Hey, watch it Bobby ..."

Jackie was not happy with me. Everyone knew what happened to the guys who tried to get over on Big Louie. Tommy Palmese, Johnny Tiso, Jeffrey "the Jew" Tannebaum—they all disappeared. No one ever talked about them or what happened to them, but we all knew. One day they were at Ferro's buying bread for their families; the next day, they were ghosts. But it was understood that you don't talk about it. And I had just come right out and said it. Right to Jackie.

"Look, Jackie. Forget I said the last part. Let's just say that you can do whatever you normally do when someone stiffs you, and you'll be out the fifty grand forever. Or you can use your connections with the unions and get the guy a job on a construction site. He fakes a flop, I represent him, and then settle his case. I take my one-third legal fee and you and Big Louie take the rest, which will be a lot more than what the guy originally owed you anyway."

"Wait a minute. If the guy ain't getting any of the money, why the hell would he do this?"

"Because BLT will wipe his slate clean. If the guy takes a dive, retains me as his attorney, and keeps his mouth shut, he owes you nothing. No matter how the case turns out."

"But if you lose the case, I'm out fifty grand."

"If the guy can't pay you, you're out the fifty grand anyway! Besides, we're never going to go to trial on these cases. I'll settle them for half their value. Insurance companies will be thrilled to throw a hundred grand at me for a case that's really worth a quarter million."

"Why would the insurance pay if the guy isn't really hurt?" Jackie asked.

"Because we'd have medical records saying he is hurt."

"How?"

"Leave that to me."

THIRTEEN

IT'S STRANGE, but I think every chiropractor I've ever met is over six feet tall. In my entire life, I've never seen a short one. My theory is that they're a bunch of dumb former jocks who became interested in physical therapy and stuff while nursing high school sports injuries. Since they weren't smart enough for medical school they went to chiropractic college. I mean, it doesn't take a genius to be a chiropractor. It's not like there's a lot of diagnostic ability required in the job. If you tell a chiropractor you have a headache, he'll crack your back. If you tell him you've got a sore knee, he'll crack your back. You could go into a chiropractor's office and tell him you have AIDS, and the only thing he'll suggest is a nice adjustment to your lower lumbar region. It's a racket. There's a saying—if you have two years to kill and nothing else to do, become a chiropractor. But then again, I guess if you have three years, you could become a lawyer.

Tim Bass was at least six-foot-six. He was thin, young, maybe thirty or so, and he had cropped black hair that was spiky in the front and sunken cheekbones that made his face look like a skeleton. He was a handsome guy, though, and I think most of his female clientele saw him for reasons other than neck pain. When he entered his back office to speak to Roland and me, he was wearing khaki pants and an untucked Hawaiian shirt. His office walls were decorated with pictures of him surfing in Montauk at the very tip of the eastern end of Long Island.

"Aloha," he said as he extended his hand. "Roland, good to see you again. Is this the guy you told me about?"

"Rob Principe," I said as I shook his hand.

"Dr. Bass," he responded as he took a seat behind his desk. *Who the hell is this guy kidding?* I thought to myself. He's no doctor. He's not an MD. Hell, I had a *juris doctor* from Columbia University for Christ's sake, but you didn't hear me asking to be called *Doctor Principe*. I was there to do business, so I was forced to humor the only guy in Brooklyn dumb enough to wear a Hawaiian shirt and say *Aloha*.

"What can I do for you fellas?" *Doctor* Bass asked.

"Well," Roland answered. "Like I told you over the phone, my pal Rob here has finally wised up and decided to listen to me. He's going to start advertising aggressively in the blue-collar areas of Brooklyn."

"Trying to bring in the construction crowd," Bass surmised.

"Exactly," Roland continued. "So I told him that if he was going to do it, he had to do it right. And that means using the best doctors. So here we are."

Bass turned his attention to me.

"The guys you hope to represent, they'll all be working on the books? No migrant workers? Puerto Ricans? Illegals?

Shit like that?" he wanted to know.

"In Bensonhurst?" I asked rhetorically. "No. All my guys will be union men."

"Good. So Worker's Comp will pay for everything." Bass leaned back in his chair and kicked his feet up onto his desk. "Now, let me tell you how I work. As soon as you send me a client, I'll get them in for physical therapy three times a week. I'll run every test you can think of—MRIs, CAT scans, EMG, the works. It's all covered by Compensation so your client won't have to go out-of-pocket for anything. If there's anything wrong with these guys, I'll find it."

Bass flashed a game show host smile and gave me a quick wink.

"And I always find something," he finished.

The pure, unadulterated sleaze of the moment caused a wave of anxiety to wash over me. Acid splashed in my stomach like breakers pounding the jetties in Far Rockaway, Queens. *Was I actually going through with this insane scheme?* I thought. Of course I was. I had had that conversation with Jackie at the playground a few days earlier and now I was meeting with an obviously crooked chiropractor who Roland had said was the best in the city. Every day I was getting closer and closer to committing countless crimes. But my plan was to just do it once, just so I could get out from under my debt. Just so I could stop treading water. *Just once*, I promised myself, *and then never again*. But my stomach didn't believe me.

"Can I use your bathroom?" I asked.

"Second left down the hall," Bass responded.

I barely made it in time.

FOURTEEN

"DIDN'T I TELL YOU he was impressive?" Roland asked,
quite pleased with himself, as we walked through the parking
lot behind Bass's office.

"You sure this guy is legit?"

Roland stopped at his car and fumbled for his keys.
Actually, to call it a car would be inaccurate. Roland drove a
rocket ship—a Mercedes CLS 500 AMG, silver with leather
interior, heated seats, five hundred seven horsepower, zero to
sixty in 4.3 seconds, with an eight-speaker, twelve CD changer
Bose system that could blast the paint off the doors—not that
I was jealous.

"Don't worry about a thing, man. Bass is the best there is.
I've been using him for years. He's *aggressive*, but he's on the
up and up." Roland looked me over and laughed. "Man, you're
just hiring an expert, not marrying the guy. You need to relax."

I couldn't relax, for several reasons. First, considering what

I was planning on doing with Jackie, I wanted to make certain that I wasn't using a crooked whore of a doctor who might bring attention to me or my phony lawsuit. Second, the last thing I wanted was to somehow get Roland into trouble simply for introducing me to the guy. Roland didn't know about my scam and I didn't want him to get involved. If he got in any kind of mess because of me, I never would have been able to forgive myself. And I also couldn't relax because my stomach was acting up again and I felt another rush of diarrhea approaching. I was quickly learning that I couldn't stomach a life of crime.

"Roland, listen, I just want to make sure ..."

"Look, an MRI is like one of those ink blot tests," Roland rationalized. "One person sees a butterfly, another sees his mother with an ice pick in her neck."

"But how can that be?" I protested.

"Because it just is, okay? One doctor might look at an MRI and only see a mild back sprain. Dr. Bass looks at the same MRI and sees a severely herniated disc that will prevent my client from ever returning to work. Is Bass merely telling me what I want to hear because I pay him, *legally mind you*, a fifteen hundred–dollar fee for his expert opinion? Frankly, I don't give a shit because he's a medical professional and I'm not about to question his judgment."

"Come on, Roland, you and I both know that he *is* only telling you what you wanna hear. And if you and I know that, chances are someone else knows that, too."

Roland got inside his car and closed the door. A few seconds later he lowered his tinted windows. He had put on sunglasses that cost more than my suit.

"Bobby, if I thought Bass was only telling me my client had bad injuries because I was paying him for an expert's report, then, under the law, I'd have to stop using him. But I don't know that for a fact. And you don't know that either. The only way I will ever know that is if I ask him."

Roland turned the key in the ignition. The motor purred like a thousand content kittens. He smiled.

"And I don't ever plan on asking him that question. You'll see. You're scared now, but investing some capital in advertising is the best move you could make. Like I said, if you want to win in this game, play aggressively and stay within the law, and you'll never get hurt. Now I gotta run. I'm getting a new pool put in and I want to see how it's coming along. Ciao."

And with that foreign good-bye, Roland peeled out in a matter of seconds, leaving me alone except for a spray of parking lot pebbles and my own 1992 Ford Taurus with one hundred twenty-seven thousand miles on it.

During the drive home, I didn't mind the usual bumper-to-bumper traffic on Flatbush Avenue because it gave me an opportunity to sit and think without any distractions, other than the homeless woman urinating on the sidewalk three feet from my open window.

Roland's words played over and over again in my mind, like a skipping record: *If you want to win in this game, play aggressively and stay within the law, and you'll never get hurt.* I knew I was playing the game way too aggressively and I was far from staying within the law. I wasn't even in the same zip code as the law. If I looked in my rearview mirror, the law wasn't even a speck on the horizon, and that made me real uncomfortable. Too uncomfortable. I decided, right then and there on Flatbush Avenue, that it was time to turn around and head back to the law.

I laughed out loud at the absurdity of what I had almost done. I must have been crazy to think I could have ever brought myself to commit such an egregious fraud on the legal system. I resolved that I would tell Jackie that I had changed my mind, that I realized that I had made a mistake, and, as an Officer of the Court, I could never go through with such a dishonest plan. Just imagining the conversation made my stomach feel better.

FIFTEEN

FROM MY DESK I saw Jackie enter my reception area, a spring in his step and a slice of *Ray's Famous* in his hand. He was followed by an older gentleman, who I later learned was Salvatore Tangelino. Mr. Tangelino wore a faded red-flannel shirt tucked into gray, cotton work pants. His worn, tan leather belt matched his beat-up work boots. He looked like every man in my family had ever looked when he came home from a job site—neat and presentable but wearing the honorable scuffs of a hard day's work. Jackie pointed to a seat and Mr. Tangelino dutifully sat, his hands resting on his knees.

"Is Bobby in?" Jackie asked Joey.

"He's in his office. I can buzz him for you …"

"Don't bother. He'll be glad to see me," Jackie said as he blew past Joey's desk, leaving her with Mr. Tangelino.

He entered my office and closed the door behind him, his smile as wide as the Midtown Tunnel. I was smiling, too, because I was going to tell him I had changed my mind and finally get a good night's sleep.

"Hey, Jackie. I'm glad you're here," I said.

"I bet you are. Have I got a surprise for you."

"What kind of surprise?" I asked warily.

"I spoke with Big Louie about our little talk the other day and he's very interested. He gave me the green light to go ahead with this thing. On a limited basis. You know. To see how things work out. But if he's happy … Oh, Bobby boy, we'll all clean up big time."

I could have sworn I felt my stomach get sucked directly into my colon. It was a miracle I didn't have an accident. Honestly. I was a grown man. Thirty-three years old. An Ivy League law school graduate. And I almost made in my pants.

"You spoke to BLT! Are you insane? How the hell could you do that?" I shouted.

"The man *is* my boss," Jackie reasoned. "What did you think? I was gonna go into a deal with you without letting Big Louie know first? Now *that* would be insane. That's how guys end up waterlogged, if you follow me."

I stood and began pacing.

"Jesus Friggin' Christ," I shouted.

"What's the problem?" Jackie asked.

"God Dammit!" I continued. I guess at the time I thought all my problems could be solved by breaking the Third Commandment.

"What are you so worried about?" Jackie said nonchalantly as he took the last bite of his pizza slice and threw the crust in my garbage. He grabbed some tissues from my desk and wiped the cheese grease from his fingers. "This is gonna work out great! You know, I could really move up in the ranks if this thing pans out."

"What am I worried about? I was about to tell you that I didn't want to do this thing anymore! I must have been crazy to have even *considered* it!"

"But it was your idea," Jackie very accurately pointed out to me.

"I wasn't thinking straight. Because I have no money. And this lousy firm's going under. And I've got a baby on the way. I just wasn't thinking straight!"

My pacing became faster. I was dizzy and my stomach was killing me. I stopped, faced Jackie, and whispered to him.

"I can't go through with this, Jackie," I said softly. "It's *illegal*."

Jackie stared back at me. He shook his head, clearly amused by my reaction.

"*Illegal Schmeegal*," he practically shouted. "What are we doin' here? Screwin' a few insurance companies who got billions to spare, and who are always fuckin' the little guy anyway. All we're doin' is returnin' the favor."

Jackie sat in a chair and crossed his legs. He lit a cigarette and exhaled a perfect smoke ring.

"Would you just relax already, man?" he said coolly. "I told you, we're gonna take it slow at first. Nothing too big. Nothing that will get us in any trouble. Besides, you can't back out now. I brought a client with me."

"You did what?"

"I brought a client with me," Jackie repeated.

I hurried to my door and peeked out.

"The guy you came in with? The guy who is sitting in my reception area right now?"

"Yeah. What did you expect me to do? Sit on my ass? You told me to set some guy up on a site to take a fall, so I set a guy up on a site to take a fall. One thing you gotta know about me,

Bobby—I'm a hard worker. Something needs to get done, I get it done. That's why you're gonna love workin' with me."

I looked out my door again. Mr. Tangelino was sitting where Jackie had left him. He hadn't moved an inch. His hands were still on his knees.

"His name is Salvatore Tangelino," Jackie explained. "Degenerate fuckin' gambler. In to Louie for *thirty*. Can you believe that? Guy don't have a pot to piss in, but he runs a thirty grand tab up on Big Louie Turro. Talk about your bad business decisions. Anyway, I got him to lay under a four-foot scaffold yesterday and say he fell from it. Fall from a height— that's strict liability, right? See, I was really payin' attention the other day! I'm gonna be good at this!"

I fell back down into my chair and buried my face into my hands.

"Jesus Christ, Jackie! Why didn't you talk to me first? I thought we agreed that we'd talk about this again before we did anything."

"We're talkin' about it right now," Jackie reasoned as only he could. "Look, don't worry about a thing. Tangelino really wants to do this. He's no dummy. He knows what woulda happened to him if he hadn't paid up. He gets outta payin' back thirty grand just for tellin' a few lies. And I told him exactly what to say. I'm tellin' you, we're gonna make a killing. I'll go get him."

Jackie headed for the door. I could have argued with him some more. I could have told him that I wasn't going to go through with it no matter how excited he was about the scheme and no matter how disappointed Big Louie would be once he heard I had backed out. I probably could have told Jackie a million things that would have changed how everything eventually turned out. I could have. But I didn't. I didn't because I was scared how Jackie would react and was *terrified* how BLT would react. But most of all, I didn't because I kept hearing a voice. It was soft at first, but it grew louder and louder. The voice kept saying: *Just do it this one time. Just do it this one time*—over and over again. The voice was my own. Unfortunately, as a litigator, I had learned to be pretty damn persuasive. So I convinced myself that I would just do it once, and then never again.

"Wait a minute," I called out to Jackie before he left the room. "If I'm going to do this, we have to have an understanding. This is *my* client and this is *my* firm. I don't want you coming to this office anymore. Not to bring a client. Not to have lunch. Not even to just say hi. If we're going to do this, it needs to be done discreetly. I don't want the client to know that I'm involved in this in any way. He has to think that I just happen to be the lawyer you're making him use. Understood?"

"Yeah. Absolutely. What do you think? I'm a moron or something? Sal doesn't know a thing. He thinks I told him to use you because you're my cousin. He thinks you're a legitimate lawyer."

"I *am* a legitimate lawyer," I bristled. I actually had the nerve to sound indignant.

"Yeah. Sure. Whatever," Jackie replied. "I'll go get him."

And with that, Jackie left my office. For a few moments I was alone. Just me, a legitimate lawyer, with a rationalizing voice in my head that I wished would shut the hell up.

SIXTEEN

SALVATORE TANGELINO SHEEPISHLY entered my office and sat across the desk from me. I stood and extended my hand to him. He extended his in return. His hands were familiar. They were dry and bruised. His fingertips were cracked; the skin was split apart and had healed that way. His pinky had no fingernail. The fleshy part of his hand, just below the thumb, had been rubbed raw from years of swinging hammers and vibrating skill saws. He had worker's hands—the same kind of hands that had held me as a child. He had the hands of my father and my grandfather. We shook. The hand of an honest day's work wrapped around mine. Our hands looked nothing alike.

"So, Mr. Tangelino" I said, pretending as if I didn't know why he was really in my office, "Jackie told me that you might need some legal help."

"Yes. That's-a-right," he responded. He had a thick Italian

accent and sounded just like my mother's grandfather, my Pop-Pop who died when I was only seven, but I remembered him very well. He was a gentle man from Benevento, just north of Naples, who gave me uneven haircuts and miniature chocolate bars that he always seemed to carry in his pocket. I was surprised at how much the similarity to my great-grand-father unnerved me. Mr. Tangelino said nothing else. He was obviously terrified that he would say something wrong, somehow mess up. He looked to Jackie for guidance.

"What the hell are you looking at me for? Look at him, he's your lawyer," Jackie scolded, rolling his eyes.

Mr. Tangelino looked back at me. He still didn't say anything.

"Tell him about your accident," Jackie demanded, running out of patience.

Mr. Tangelino finally spoke. His lies came forth in an unsteady, nervous stream of broken English.

"I was-a-working by-a myself. On a four foot-a high scaffold. The scaffold, she begins to a-shake. She wasn't a-steady. So I lost-a my footing, and I fall. Boom. Onto the ground."

Mr. Tangelino had been coached better than an Olympic athlete.

"Were you injured from the fall?" I prompted.

"Oh, yeah," he said. "I hurt-a myself here, in-a my neck, and back down-a here, on-a my back. Now, I have a lot of-a pain."

Mr. Tangelino was able to contort and point to his back pretty easily for someone in "a lot of-a pain." I'd have to tell Jackie to get him to stop doing that, I thought to myself.

"Where else?" Jackie glared at Mr. Tangelino, scolding him like an impatient parent whose child couldn't remember their multiplication tables.

"Excuse-a me?"

"Where else did you get hurt? You told me that you got hurt in three places."

"Oh, yeah. My-a head. I have-a the pain in-a my head, too."

Mr. Tangelino looked back to Jackie, seeking approval. Jackie gave him nothing but a dead-eye stare. So Mr. Tangelino continued.

"After I fall, I call out. And one-a the workers, he runs over and calls the ambulance. They take-a me to Kings County Hospital. They take-a the X-rays and the next day they let me go home. I went to the job site today to tell-a the foreman I'm-a hurt and can't work-a no more. He gave me this."

Mr. Tangelino took a neatly folded piece of paper from the front pocket of his flannel shirt. He reached across my desk and the paper passed from one liar to another. I unfolded the paper carefully, so as not to tear it. It was an accident report, noting the time, location, and description of the incident. It also contained Worker's Compensation and insurance information. It was signed at the bottom by the job site foreman. Such reports were standard in construction accidents. I had seen scores of them. I was struck by how this one, which set forth the details of a bogus, staged accident, looked as real and legitimate as any other.

"Well," I said, "the good news is I think I can help you. The first thing we need to do is find out the extent of your injuries. You could be very seriously injured and not even know it. The human body can mask pain, even when you are very hurt; it's part of our natural defense mechanisms. So I'm going to send you to see Dr. Bass. He's an excellent doctor. He'll take an MRI of your neck, back, and head and tell me exactly what's wrong with you."

"Okay," Mr. Tangelino replied.

"He'll also set you up on a physical therapy schedule. I can't stress how important it is that you don't miss any appointments. Not just for your health, but for your lawsuit. If you don't take your rehabilitation seriously, then the insurance carrier won't take your claim seriously. So you have to go. Every week. Three times a week."

"I'll drive him there myself," Jackie chimed in.

I gave Jackie a disapproving look. I wasn't crazy about the fact that he was in my office, and I sure as hell didn't want him talking. I opened one of my desk drawers and flipped through several files of preprinted forms. I stopped at one file and pulled out a Retainer Agreement.

I could have put an end to the whole thing right then. The truth is I had already had several opportunities to do so. At Patsy's I could have disregarded my plan as the desperate musing of a desperate man. Or I could have told Jackie to leave Mr. Tangelino in the reception area as I wasn't going to go through with this. Or I simply could have left the Retainer Agreement in my desk and regretfully informed Mr. Tangelino that I didn't feel my firm had the resources to handle a complex construction case at this particular time. I could have done a lot of things. The only thing I actually did do was slide the Retainer Agreement across my desk and hand Mr. Tangelino a pen.

"Before I can take any action on your behalf, I'll need you to sign this retainer. By doing so, you agree to allow me to represent you in this lawsuit in exchange for one-third of the money I get for you." I stared at Mr. Tangelino, secretly hoping he wouldn't sign. I prayed that he would have the fortitude I lacked, the guts to say: *I don't want any part of this.*

As trapped as I felt, Mr. Tangelino only could have felt a

million times worse. He owed thirty thousand dollars to Lou Turro. And he couldn't pay. In Brooklyn, that was the equivalent of jumping onto the subway tracks and letting the Five Train plant a big kiss in the middle of your forehead. Mr. Tangelino was as good as dead, and he knew it. He knew he had no choice but to take Jackie's offer to fake an injury and bring a lawsuit.

He picked up the Mont Blanc pen my father had given me when I graduated from law school. My dad got it second-hand but he had bought an ink refill for it and had my initials engraved on it. When he gave it to me he said: "Always remember that a man with no education and a hundred tools can only build a house, but a man with an education and a single pen can do anything." I watched as Mr. Tangelino put the tip of the pen to the Retainer Agreement.

"Wait. Don't," I said, stopping him before he could sign his name. Jackie stared daggers at me.

"What's the problem?" he wanted to know.

"Uh, nothing," I explained as I took the pen from Mr. Tangelino's hand. "It's just that this pen doesn't write so well."

I reached into a drawer, took out a Bic ballpoint, and gave it to Mr. Tangelino. I placed the Mont Blanc in the drawer, way in the back.

Mr. Tangelino used the ballpoint and scribbled his name on the Retainer Agreement in the chicken-scratch that was characteristic of many of the people from the old country. His signature made it official—Mr. Tangelino was my client. He was not hurt. He was not injured. He was not unable to earn a living. But he was my client nonetheless.

My door opened partway and Joey stuck her head inside.

"Mrs. Guzman is here to see you," she announced.

"Damn it. I forgot to call her back." I stood and shook the man's hand. "Okay, Mr. Tangelino. I'll get working on your case and I'll be in touch."

Mr. Tangelino said nothing. He merely nodded his head and moved toward the door.

"One more thing," I called out to my first new client in four months.

Mr. Tangelino stopped and turned toward me.

"You didn't lose your footing and fall from the scaffold. You were *caused to lose your footing* and fall from the scaffold. A plaintiff *never* falls. A plaintiff is only *caused to fall.* Understand?"

"I understand."

"Good."

Joey showed Mr. Tangelino out. Jackie grinned at me like an idiot. I couldn't believe it, but I was grinning a little, too. I was uneasy doing so but, somehow, I was grinning nonetheless. I picked up the accident report and held it up for Jackie to see.

"This may be easier than I thought," I said.

"See, I told you there was nothing to worry about."

"I'm still not totally comfortable with this though. We have to be very careful. We can't do anything stupid," I cautioned.

"Relax, you'll live longer. Meet with your client. We'll talk later," Jackie said as he walked out of my office, happy as a pig in shit.

SEVENTEEN

AS JACKIE LEFT, he held the door open for Mrs. Guzman.

"Thank you," she said, smiling at my cousin, flashing her ridiculously straight, white dentures.

"My pleasure," Jackie responded, returning the smile as he let the door close behind him, leaving me alone with Mrs. Guzman.

"Please, let me help you," I said as I rushed from behind my desk. I took her by the arm and guided the kind octogenarian across my office and into a chair.

"Mrs. Guzman," I apologized. "I am so sorry that I never returned your phone call. It's just that things have been so crazy around the office the past few days and I've sort of been chasing my tail a bit … "

"That's quite alright, Mr. Principe. I'm sure a young man like yourself is very busy and can't possibly return every phone call he gets."

Mrs. Guzman spoke very softly, as if the very subject matter of our conversation was sacrosanct, and to her I guess it was. Her flawless English was flavored with a slight Puerto Rican accent. I could tell that although she was never formally schooled, someone in her life had made certain that Mrs. Guzman received an education. She came across as a very proud woman, and, despite the fact that we were virtual strangers, I liked her very much.

"Well, I try to return calls as soon as I can."

"I'm sure you do," Mrs. Guzman assured me.

She reached into her pocketbook and took out one of those mini-tissue packs, the kind where the tissues are kept in a plastic pouch with a small slit. She pulled out a couple of tissues and left them on her lap.

"I don't mean to be a bother. I know I've been calling you a lot," she continued, "but I was wondering if you've had an opportunity to review my husband's papers."

"Yes, I have. I was going to call you today to discuss them. That's why I'm so glad you came by."

Three sentences. Three lies. First, I had hardly *reviewed* her husband's medical records. I mean, I *looked* at them. *Briefly. Very* briefly. I knew a loser case when I saw one and I honestly didn't have the time or money to waste on a case that had no chance of paying off at the end. Second, I wasn't going to call Mrs. Guzman that day. I had totally forgotten about her phone calls. If she hadn't walked into my firm that afternoon, I probably never would have called her back. Not because I'm a heartless jerk who doesn't want to help an old lady, but because I truly had a lot of things on my mind and the late Mr. Guzman just wasn't one of them. And third, I *was* not glad that she had come by. Truth is, when it comes to delivering bad news, I'm a bit of a coward. I had nothing but bad news for

Mrs. Guzman and would have preferred giving it to her over the phone, if at all.

"So, do you think I have a case?" Mrs. Guzman asked, wide-eyed and hopeful.

"Well," I stalled. "Let me find the medical records you gave me and we can go over them."

As I spoke, I pretended to search throughout my desk and file cabinets for the records, all the while knowing exactly where the file was. I was just buying time. Buying time from having to break this sweet old lady's heart, but I could only stall for so long.

"Ah, here it is."

I faked discovering the records under a stack of papers next to my laptop and then sat back down at my desk. I took a deep breath, exhaled, and broke the news.

"Unfortunately, Mrs. Guzman, I don't think you have a very strong case. You see, New York is one of only a few states that doesn't allow surviving family members to recover money for the emotional distress they suffer as the result of the wrongful death of a loved one."

"I can't make them pay?" Mrs. Guzman asked, confused, as her hand lifted one of the tissues from her lap to her eyes.

Oh crap, she's gonna cry, I thought.

"Technically, under the law all you can get is the value of the economic contributions made by your husband at the time of his death. Since Mr. Guzman hadn't worked in over thirty years and since he was on public assistance, we really don't have a valid claim for lost income."

Mrs. Guzman's back stiffened. "My husband was a sick man. He *couldn't* work."

I remember thinking I hoped Janine would stand up for me, stand *by* me like that, even after I was dead.

"Please understand that I'm not saying your husband was able to work. But the courts don't care about that. All they want to see is whether you have been hurt economically by your husband's death."

"I've been hurt every way imaginable."

"I realize that. And I sympathize. But the law is the law, and there isn't a court in this state that will allow you to recover for your emotional pain."

"What about the overdose?" Mrs. Guzman questioned.

"That's what makes this so difficult. It's pretty clear from the hospital records that your husband was given the wrong level of blood thinner and that's what killed him. But Mr. Guzman was also eighty-five-years old and a very sick man. The records note repeatedly that his doctors didn't expect him to live more than another week or so. His vitals were through the floor even before they gave him the blood thinner."

"Can't you do anything at all for me?"

Her tears were flowing now—one after another, sliding down her face. She was much too dignified to bawl or make any noise. She just sat there very quietly while tears raced each other toward her petite jawline. She didn't even bother with the tissues anymore. I tried to be as sensitive as possible.

"Mrs. Guzman, you have to understand. I'm looking at a case where a very sick, very elderly man with no income passed away about a week sooner than he probably would have died anyway. I know it sounds horrible to say, and please don't take this the wrong way, but this is a case that has little to no value from a legal perspective."

"I don't care about the money, Mr. Principe. It's just the way they tried to cover up their mistake after Pedro died. I knew he didn't have much longer. I just wanted them to tell me the truth about why he died. I wanted them to say they made a mistake. But they didn't. All I want now is for them to apologize."

I walked around to the front of my desk and sat in a chair next to Mrs. Guzman. I took her hand in mine.

"I understand your frustration. And I would really like to help you. But I'm a solo practitioner, and I only have so much time in a day. I can only take on a certain number of cases and I have to pick and choose very carefully the cases that I decide to handle."

"But I just want them to apologize."

"I know. I want them to apologize, too. But a case like this would take a lot of time and a lot of money—money that I would have to lay out with little chance of ever getting back. And I can't put one-third of an apology on the table to feed my family. I'm so sorry that I can't help you. I really wish I could."

I held out her dead husband's medical records. "I thought maybe you'd want these back."

Mrs. Guzman looked me in the eyes and patted me on the hand. "I understand. You have a business to run. I appreciate your time."

My eyes followed Mrs. Guzman as she rose slowly from the chair and shuffled toward my office door, her gait methodical but unsteady. I remember thinking about my own mother, how she was only twenty years away from being Mrs. Guzman's age and how lost she would be when my father passed away, God forbid. Mrs. Guzman's arthritic hand was barely able to turn the doorknob. The door swung open and she stepped out into the reception area.

"Wait," I called out reluctantly. I approached Mrs. Guzman and took the medical records from her. "I don't think we have a chance in hell with this case. That being said, I'll draw up the Surrogate Court papers, so we can bring a claim. I'm not promising anything, but I'll see what I can do."

Mrs. Guzman then did the most unexpected thing. She leaned forward and kissed me on the cheek.

"God bless you," she whispered in my ear, before she turned and walked out of my office.

"You're welcome" was all I could think of to say in response.

If I had known what the next few months had in store for me, I wouldn't have said "You're welcome." I would have said "Thank you for the blessing" ... and then I would have asked her for a few more.

EIGHTEEN

OVER THE NEXT several weeks, things got progressively worse. I did not bring in a single new case. Not one. And it wasn't for lack of trying. I had even contacted my former classmates from Columbia, who were all now making mid-six figures at the top corporate firms in the city.

These guys did half-billion-dollar bond offerings and nine-figure mergers that made the front page of the *Wall Street Journal* every other day. But they wouldn't know what to do with a slip and fall, a car accident, or a medical malpractice case if one crawled up their pant legs and bit them on the nuts. Sometimes they were asked to find a personal injury attorney for some corporate client's daughter who broke her arm in gym class or for some banker's mother-in-law who tripped over a case of shaving cream that was left in the aisle of a drug store. I was hoping to convince them to refer these cases to me, since I was probably the only ham-and-egger they knew.

In return for the referral, I would give them a third of my legal fee. This practice, known as "fee-sharing," is strictly prohibited by the Rules of Ethics that govern the legal profession but it takes place hundreds of times a day, every day. The rules state that a lawyer cannot share a fee with another attorney simply for referring business. Since the biggest difference between a successful lawyer and one like me is the ability to bring in clients, lawyers quickly found a way around the Ethics Rules. In short, the lawyer who received the referral would simply make sure that the referring attorney got copies of all correspondence, pleadings, and deposition transcripts associated with the case. The referring attorney would keep a dummy file in his office. If the New York State Bar ever questioned the fee paid to referring counsel, all he'd have to do is point to his dummy file and say he remained actively involved throughout the litigation by reviewing all of the relevant documents and giving advice and suggestions to the attorney actually handling the matter. Therefore, he would argue, the one-third fee that he received was not for merely *referring* the case but for providing invaluable insight and expertise throughout the litigation.

Everyone knew this was total bullshit—especially when some bankruptcy lawyer who had never tried a personal injury case in his life claimed he was helping a veteran litigator. But the veteran litigator would back the bankruptcy lawyer's story because, as the saying went, "If someone's good for *one* referral, then they're good for *two*." So if a lawyer referred a case and that case settled for sixty grand, the legal fee would be about twenty thousand and the referring attorney would get around sixty-seven hundred dollars for making one lousy phone call and then sitting on his ass, waiting for the check to come in.

Giving out referral fees was a goddamn racket, and for years everyone did it but me. I was tired of being the only one who lost because I actually played by the rules. Considering what I had just done with Jackie and Mr. Tangelino, offering up referral fees was hardly of concern any more.

But the guys I knew from Columbia gave me the cold shoulder. They were all scared of anything that sounded remotely shady. I don't really blame them. They had hundreds of thousands of dollars coming in every year, condos on the Upper East Side, and lucrative partnerships waiting for them a year or two down the road. They had something to lose.

Then again, so did I. Paul Stevens from the bank kept calling me about my house. He was probably looking for the check I had promised to send him but never did. I hadn't spoken to him since the day I first pitched the plan to Jackie. I had Joey screening all my calls. I told her Stevens was a pain-in-the-ass defense lawyer I didn't want to talk to. She didn't know any better.

The problem was that after a few weeks Stevens stopped calling altogether and that meant only one thing—he had turned over the matter to the bank's counsel and they would soon begin foreclosure proceedings against me. Eventually, we'd get a foreclosure notice. My only hope was that Janine wasn't home when the envelope came and I could somehow intercept it. She was having a tough go of it and a pending eviction was the last thing she needed.

Janine had been suffering from some bad morning sickness, which, by the way, is a complete misnomer. She was nauseous in the morning, the afternoon, and most evenings. One night, we had Ginny and Ian over for dinner and in the middle of the meal Janine vomited right into her lemon chicken. I rushed her to the bathroom but by then it was all over her shirt. I tried to help her get cleaned up but she just sat on the toilet and cried, a combination of being mortified and being flush with hormones that her body was not used to. She's the only woman I know who can still look absolutely beautiful while bawling with puke on her chin.

My point is, the pregnancy wasn't going as smoothly as she thought it would. I wasn't about to make things worse by telling her that we were on the verge of losing the law practice and our home.

Hope arrived one day in the most unlikely of forms—an MRI report. While sorting through another day's stack of useless and unwanted mail, I noticed the return address of Dr. Timothy Bass. The address was in raised print, royal blue, and the stationery was of heavyweight paper—the expensive kind. I knew this because when I first opened my firm I had bought the same kind of stationery. I had even spent a few days going over the design of the firm letterhead so that all of my correspondence would look perfect. It was not the best use of my time. Within a year I was sending letters out on copier paper and I was buying irregular envelopes in bulk at an office surplus store. At least Dr. Bass was doing well.

I opened the envelope and skimmed the cover letter. It read:

Dear Mr. Principe:
Enclosed please find a copy of the MRI report for
Salvatore Tangelino. Please remit payment of $1500.00
for same. I remain available to testify at trial, if necessary,
at the rate of $5,000.00 per day. Please advise if my
services are necessary.
Sincerely,
Dr. Timothy Bass.

I had to laugh. Bass had just bilked the Worker's Compensation insurance carrier for thousands of dollars in unnecessary medical care and now he wanted fifteen hundred bucks for a report that was nothing but bullshit. Granted, Bass was unaware that Tangelino hadn't really been in an accident, but he was still somehow able to find something wrong with a completely healthy man.

The MRI report was utter perfection. It set forth that Mr. Tangelino suffered from multiple herniations in his lower lumbar region at L2-3, L3-4, and L4-5. *Poor Mr. Tangelino*, I thought. He'd be in a lot of pain if any of this was true.

I sat down and stared at the report for a while. I thought about what I held in my hand. A report printed on some really expensive stationery? Yes. Evidence of a crime? For certain. But more than anything else, I had money in my hand. I had a report from a licensed medical care provider that established Mr. Tangelino was suffering from a severe back injury. In the world of personal injury law, that was as good as cash.

All I had to do was serve a complaint on the general contractor and owner of the job site, set a discovery schedule, get the defense attorney to see things my way, and the case was as good as settled. I'd get a few bucks, get out from under the thumbs of my creditors, and Janine and I would be home free. And I'd be done with this whole scam forever. I couldn't wait for Mr. Tangelino's deposition.

NINETEEN

THE DEPOSITION was a fucking disaster.

Before I explain why, I want to make it perfectly clear that I love my heritage. I am incredibly proud to be an Italian-American. But with God as my witness, the Italians who are right off the boat are, without exception, the dumbest, densest, most thick-headed, brain-dead clients who ever cursed a plaintiff's practice. Hands down.

Give me an Irishman any day of the week over an old-country Italian. Give me a black. Give me a Latino. Shit, give me a ninety-year-old Cantonese woman who doesn't speak English. I promise you, any one of them will make a better deposition witness than a first-generation Italian.

The reason for this is simple. Italians come from a culture where titles and positions are respected and revered. Many of the immigrant laborers I represented never completed elementary school. Blind deference and lack of education are a deadly combination that, more often than not, results in some middle-aged insurance defense attorney in an eighty-dollar suit intimidating these people to such an extent that they answer simple questions with ten-minute ramblings that destroy their cases. Sometimes you get the exact opposite effect—the witness will answer "I don't know" to every question, no matter how basic.

"What was the date of your accident?"

"I don't know."

"What is your address?"

"I don't know."

"What is your full name?"

"I don't know."

They think that they are helping their case by stonewalling opposing counsel, but what they are really doing is establishing a record that they have no recollection of how their particular accident happened. This results in no recovery because, without certain details, you can't prove an accident was the defendant's fault. It was all incredibly frustrating and it often had me wishing I had gone to medical school.

Mr. Tangelino was no different than most of his countrymen. He rambled on and on when answering questions, even though I had prepped him extensively. The deposition was held at Kolbrenner & Sklar, the firm hired by the insurance carrier for the general contractor and the owner of the job site. It lasted about four hours. It should have taken half as long but Mr. Tangelino couldn't keep his answers short and to the point. I let him know this as I walked him from the conference room to the elevators after the deposition had ended.

"I didn't do so good, did I?" he asked me.

"To be perfectly honest, no. Do you remember when I prepped you for this?"

"Yes."

"Do you remember what I told you?"

"Yes."

"What did I tell you?"

"I don't remember."

I was torn between wanting to bang my head against the wall in frustration and banging Mr. Tangelino's against the wall in anger.

"I told you," I explained for the millionth time that day, "that you need to keep your answers short. *Very* short. If a question can be answered by just saying *yes* or *no*, then you should just say *yes* or *no*. If you don't know the answer, then you say, *I don't know* or *I don't remember*."

Mr. Tangelino stared back at me with a blank expression on his face.

"Why didn't you follow my instructions?" I prodded.

"I'm-a sorry," he said. "I was just-a so nervous. The questions, they-a confuse-a me so much. I just-a wanted to tell my story and a-go home. What-a happens now? Do we lose-a the case?"

"No, but you're not a good witness, Mr. Tangelino. I can't put you on the stand. You think you were nervous today, wait until the trial. You'll get picked apart like a Thanksgiving turkey."

"So we lose?" he asked again.

"No," I said, exasperated. "My job is just a little harder, and the case is a lot less valuable."

The elevator doors opened and Mr. Tangelino stepped inside.

"Take care," I said. "I'll keep you updated."

The doors began to close but Mr. Tangelino stopped them with his hand.

"You-a gonna tell Jackie? That I no-a do good today?" he asked, wide-eyed.

A blind man could see that he was scared. My stomach erupted and sharp pains pierced my abdomen. My mind raced. *Did he know about my arrangement with Jackie? Did Jackie tell him despite his promise to me that he wouldn't? Why else would he ask? Was he assuming I was involved because Jackie was my cousin? Did he think I was crooked, too? Or did he just think I'd tell Jackie about the deposition because Jackie had referred him to my office?* If anyone other than Jackie and Louie Turro knew about the scam, I could go to jail.

My heart rate skyrocketed and my palms began to sweat. But on the outside, like always, I looked as cool as the other side of the pillow.

"Why would I tell Jackie anything?" I asked nonchalantly.

"I don't know. I just-a thought ..."

"Attorney-client privilege, Mr. Tangelino. Your case is your business and my business. No one else's. Okay?"

A small, uneasy smile appeared on the old man's face.

"Okay," he said.

He removed his hand and the elevator doors closed. I stood there for a few seconds as the elevator swallowed Mr. Tangelino into the bowels of the building. I thought that maybe I had assuaged his fears a bit. *If only I could do that for myself*, I thought. With a hand pressed against my lower stomach, I headed back toward the conference room where Kent Reilly was waiting for me.

Kent was a typical insurance defense attorney—not too bright, not much of a personality, and unmotivated bordering on lazy. Why anyone would want to do insurance defense has always been beyond me. The pay sucks because, truth be told, anyone can do it. Honestly, *anyone*. You don't even need to be a lawyer. Well, technically you need a law license but there is no special knowledge or skill that is required by the job. These guys just push paper around all day long. They have certain pleadings they use for auto cases, certain pleadings they use for construction cases, and certain pleadings they use for medical malpractice cases. All they do from case to case is change the names on the documents.

Also, they don't care about their clients, because their client on paper isn't who they really work for. On paper it will look like they represent the defendant—J & P Contracting or Dr. Jones or whoever is on the bottom of the "vs." on the summons. In reality, insurance counsel only gives a shit about the insurance carrier who insured J & P Contracting or Dr. Jones. They could care less if Dr. Jones' practice falls apart as a result of the trial or if the contractor lost bids because the suit brings bad publicity. All the defense attorneys care about is getting rid of the case for an amount less than the insurer has reserved for it. That way, the insurance carrier is happy and they will send more litigation business to the defense attorney. So, if a carrier sets up a reserve of seventy-five thousand dollars on a car accident case, defense counsel only cares about getting the case settled for $74,999.99 or less. That way, he can say he always comes in under the reserve the next time he hits up the carrier for more business.

As far as defense attorneys go, Kent Reilly was a pretty decent guy. He was about my age. I had gone up against him a few times over the years and had always gotten a vibe from him that he was an honest man. If he had money to settle a case, he didn't drag the matter out forever just so he could run up his hours and submit a higher bill to the carrier.

If he felt a matter could be resolved, he'd plead your case to the carrier and get you a fair number. He'd always say to me, "Shit, it ain't my money." Kent cursed like a teamster with Tourette's, but somehow he did it in a way that didn't come across as offensive. He was as close as you got to a straight shooter in the personal injury game. He was chuckling when I re-entered the conference room.

"How the hell do you expect to put that guy on the stand?" he laughed. "He's the worst fuckin' witness I've ever seen. And I've been doing this shit for eight years."

"Come on. He wasn't that bad," I protested.

"Bobby, he can't even answer a simple question."

"That's because you can't ask a simple question," I retorted as I packed my files and legal pads into my briefcase.

"Fuck you. I am an excellent deposer," Kent feigned indignation.

I continued to defend Mr. Tangelino. "He was nervous. This was his first deposition. Besides, if I were you, I'd be worried about how I was going to defend this case."

"How the hell do you figure?"

"Fall from a height. Strict liability, my friend. Plus, I've got an accident report and a sweet old man a jury will love."

"A jury will fuckin' *hate* him," Kent countered. "No one wants to be on jury duty as it is, and Tangelino will keep them there for two fuckin' weeks the way he testifies. You ask the guy for his date of birth and he gives you his goddamn life story."

"I told you, he was nervous."

"I've seen nervous witnesses before. Your guy was a train wreck. I'll rip him a new asshole on the stand if you're crazy enough to put him up there."

I locked up my briefcase and shook hands with Kent.

"Well, maybe we can work something out," I offered, trying my best to sound indifferent as to whether Kent responded to me or not. But I was far from indifferent.

Despite what people might believe about the practice of law from what they've seen in movies or on television, that moment when I said those six words—*Maybe we can work something out*—is the most important moment in any lawsuit. Not the deposition. Not jury selection. Hell, not even the trial itself. Because if Kent told me I was crazy and that there was no way in hell he would offer money on such a dog of a case, I'd know that I'd be in the case for the long haul and, more likely than not, it would have to be tried. But if Kent hinted, even in the most subtle way, that he had some money on the file, then I'd know the case would settle.

The one rule I learned early on in this business was that a defense attorney will not even entertain the possibility of settlement unless he has the money to back it up. So I waited— for what seemed like an eternity—for Kent's response, my lure dangling just below the surface, dancing with the current, praying for a bite.

"If you want me to throw a few bucks at you just to make this thing go away, we can probably wrap it up. You got a demand on this?"

A nibble! Now all I had to do was set the hook and reel him in.

"Five hundred," I responded, trying to make my incredibly inflated demand sound wholly reasonable.

"Dollars? You got it," Kent cracked.

"Very funny. Five hundred *thousand*. And consider yourself lucky that I'm being so nice. I could hit for seven figures on a case like this."

"No offense, Rob, but if I'm not mistaken, it's been a while since you've hit on anything."

I didn't have a comeback because Kent was right.

"I tell you what. I can probably get my carrier to swing mid-fives for this case. Forty, maybe fifty grand, tops," Kent continued.

"I get fifty grand for a broken arm, *without surgery*, where my client goes back to work within two weeks. Tangelino has multiple herniations and he'll *never* go back to work." I had the gall to sound insulted by the offer.

"Your client has questionable herniations at best. My expert reviewed the film. He said he couldn't find a fuckin' thing wrong with this guy."

"What a surprise. And how much did he get paid to say that? Look, three fifty and that's as low as I can go. This is a solid case."

"If you're lowering your number to three fifty, I can offer seventy-five to close this thing up."

"Seventy-five gets you about halfway there, Kent. Just open your purse a little more and we're done."

"You're a funny guy. Are you saying we can get this done for a buck fifty?"

"Depends. Are you offering a buck fifty?"

"Only if you're accepting it."

"Get me one fifty and we can mark it settled."

"Let me talk to my carrier and I'll call you later. You'll be in your office?"

"Yup. Give me a ring and we'll see if we can put this thing to bed."

I grabbed my briefcase, walked out of the conference room, and rode the elevator down to street level. I couldn't believe that I had just negotiated a phony case for a hundred fifty thousand dollars. I was disgusted with myself. Truly disgusted.

At the same time, I had this feeling, deep inside me somewhere, that kept trying to fight its way to the surface, but I wouldn't let it. At first I wasn't sure what the feeling was, but it soon became clear to me. It was pride of all things. Amazingly, I was somehow proud of myself. It's hard enough to get a decent settlement when you have a really strong case. I had obtained a good settlement for my client with *no real case at all*. For the first time in a really, really long time, I had done a good job. Fraudulent or not, illegal or not, it couldn't be denied I had just done some damn good lawyering.

I exited the building and walked across the street to the subway station. I descended the stairs to catch the Number Four train back to the office, my briefcase swinging back and forth in my right hand. It felt good to have something inside of it for a change.

TWENTY

THE OFFICE WAS DEAD as usual when I got back. Joey was on the phone speaking to her mother in Spanglish.

"How'd the deposition go?" she asked me.

She always asked me how my court appearances or depositions turned out, partly because she had as much riding on these cases as I did. Also, Joey had been with me from the beginning, and I know that she sort of felt like we were partners, that it was her firm as well, and considering how hard she worked for me, she had every right to feel like that.

"Okay," I said as I grabbed the day's mail from her desk and walked to my office. "It might settle."

"Mom, I'll call you back."

Joey hung up the phone and hurried back to my office.

"What do you mean, it might settle?" she asked excitedly.

"I mean Kent Reilly made a tentative offer. He just has to get authority from his carrier to settle. I'm waiting for his call."

I tried to make it sound as if it was all no big deal—*Mr. Nonchalance*—but Joey knew me too well.

"Look at you, trying to act all *'This is business as usual.'* I can't remember the last time we settled a case. This is so fantastic."

"I'm just not going to count my chickens until they're hatched, cooked, and on my plate, okay? He may not even call me today and ..."

The phone rang. Neither of us moved. We just stared at the phone, scared to approach it—like it was made of kryptonite or something. It rang again. I was too nervous to answer. It rang again, and I swear it was louder this time as if shouting at me, daring me to pick up the receiver. Finally, Joey grabbed the phone from my desk.

"Law Office of Robert Principe. Yes. Please hold a second, Mr. Reilly." Joey pushed the hold button.

"It's him!" she screamed.

"Shhh. Keep it down," I said as I grabbed the receiver from her.

"He's on hold; he can't hear you."

"Shush, anyway. We have to play this cool."

Joey sat down and leaned forward, eyes wide, waiting. She looked like a little girl right then, waiting for her favorite cartoon show to start or for her parents to give her the okay to start tearing through the wrapping paper on a present that had been placed before her. She was all innocence and joy at that moment. She had no idea what she was really watching.

I placed the receiver to my ear, pressed the hold button, and put on my best "just another day at the office" voice.

"Rob Principe," I said.

"Rob, Kent Reilly."

"Hey Kent, how ya doin'?" I asked, as if I gave a shit.

"Good. What're you up to?"

I surveyed my completely empty desk.

"Oh, I'm just trying to sort through the piles of work in front of me. Putting out brush fires. If it's not one thing, it's another. You know how it is."

"Yeah, unfortunately I do," Kent replied. "Well, good news is I can lessen your load by one case. I got you your one fifty."

I fell back into my chair. Joey stared at me, trying to read my expression.

"That's great. I'll get the paperwork together and get it out to you in a few days."

Joey popped out of her chair and jumped up and down, silently waving her arms around like a mad woman.

"Alright, Kent. You, too. Take care."

I hung up the phone and blew a windy gust of relief out of my mouth. Joey ran around my desk and hugged me tight around the neck. She planted about a half-dozen rapid-fire kisses on my cheek.

"You did it! You did it!"

"Yeah, I guess I did," I said. I grabbed my stomach and tried to stand up, which was difficult with Joey hanging on me.

"I'm so proud of you!" she shrieked.

"Yeah, it's a good thing," I said without much enthusiasm, as I tried to disentangle myself from Joey's embrace. I had a beautiful Latino woman kissing me, hugging me tight, pressing her more than ample chest against me, but all I could think about was getting to the bathroom. I freed myself and headed for my office door.

"I have to go to the restroom for a minute," I explained.

"Wait," Joey stopped me before I could escape. "How much? A scaffold case with herniations—I'm guessing three hundred?"

"No."

"Three fifty?"

"No."

"Oh, my God!" Visions of pay raises danced in Joey's head. "How much then?"

"One fifty," I said.

From Joey's reaction, I might as well have said I settled the case for a bag of magic beans.

"One fifty?" she asked, unable to hide her disappointment.

"Yeah. One fifty. You have a problem with that?"

"No. I uh, I just figured a case like this would go for a lot more."

Defensive, scared that Joey might smell something fishy and worried about the intestinal pressure building inside of me, I reached for the one thing I knew could get me out of the conversation the fastest—sarcasm.

"Oh, I'm sorry, Joey. Would you have liked to have negotiated the case?"

"I wasn't saying that."

"Did you sit in on the deposition? Do you know all the facts surrounding the accident?"

"Rob, all I was saying ..."

"Remind me again. Where exactly did you go to law school, Joey?"

Joey went silent. I knew right away that I had really hurt her, which made me feel like shit. The excited little girl I had seen just a moment earlier vanished and was replaced by a grown woman who appeared, well, stunned. Stunned because Joey had been treated like crap by all the men in her life except for me. Her father was a drunk who beat her and her mother and her brother until he drove his Valiant into a divider on the Brooklyn-Queens Expressway. The father of her first two kids cheated on her and the father of her youngest went to Aqueduct one night to play the ponies and for all Joey knows, he's still there. I was the one man who had never hurt her, the one guy who had always treated her like a person of value—a person who deserved respect. And now I had verbally slapped her down in order to protect myself. To hide my lies.

Joey looked as if she wanted to say a million different things to me. Since time wouldn't permit that, she picked the one thing that was the most accurate and effective.

"You're an asshole," she said softly as she walked past me to her desk.

How could I argue when someone was so right?

She sat down and kept her head turned so that I couldn't see her profile, but I was pretty sure that she was crying. I felt like the biggest son of a bitch in the world. I walked up behind her and put a hand on her shoulder.

"Joey," I said softly.

"Leave me alone."

"I'm sorry. I shouldn't have said that."

"No shit."

"Could you please look at me?"

Joey tried to surreptitiously wipe the tears from her face as she spun around on her swivel chair and stared at me with hurt, angry eyes. There were one or two streaks on her light brown cheeks where the tears had been.

"What?" she barked.

"You're right. I'm an asshole. But I'm a little defensive right now and a little insecure about my abilities as a lawyer, about my abilities to run this firm. And what you said hit home a little. You know, that maybe I could've gotten some more money on the case. But the case had problems, Joey. Mr. Tangelino was a disaster at his deposition. And it was a blind accident without a single witness. I felt this settlement was what was best for our client."

I waited for a response from my secretary, from my friend.

"Then you should have told me that," she said matter-of-factly. "You didn't have to be a dick."

"You're right. I should have. I was a dick, and I'm sorry."

No response, so I continued.

"Look, the problem is that when you're friends with someone, when you're close with someone, you sometimes treat them worse than you would a stranger. Because you know you can get away with it. Because you know your friend knows you for who you really are. Not how you sometimes act. And you know they'll forgive you. And I hope you do because your friendship is more important to me than any stupid lawsuit."

Joey softened.

"This is your last chance, Robert. You've been acting really weird ever since Mrs. Catalano died. You haven't been yourself and I don't like it. Cut the crap or I'm gone. Okay?"

She meant it. I raised my right hand in the peace-sign position.

"Scout's honor. Cross my heart, hope to die, stick a pitch-fork in my eye."

"It's stick a needle in my eye," Joey corrected.

"I deserve a pitchfork."

Joey smiled. "Why don't you call Janine and tell her the news," she said.

"That's a good idea." I leaned over and gave Joey a kiss on the forehead. "Thanks for the forgiveness. It's appreciated."

"You're welcome."

With my stomach pain dissipating, I headed back to my office to call my wife with the news of our sudden cash windfall. When I got to my desk I reached for the phone but, just like when Kent called, I couldn't lift the receiver because that's when it hit me.

I was about to lie to Janine. I had kept things from her in the past to protect her from the ugly truth of our financial situation. And I didn't want to upset her when she was pregnant. But I had never deliberately lied to her. Now I was going to call her and tell her that I had settled a case, and then she would ask me *What kind of case?* I would have to tell her that it was a scaffold fall with herniations. And that would be a lie. She'd ask me how I got the case, and I'd say it was a referral from a former client. That would be untrue. She'd ask me a string of questions, not because she was particularly interested in the law, but because she'd be proud of me and she'd want to know all the details. When it came to my career, Janine was my biggest fan, my greatest supporter. She'd ask me about the most boring minutia of my trials—my motions, my appeals—just to show me that even though she wasn't in the courtroom with me, she and I were in this thing together.

I could never tell her the truth about this case. Not unless I was prepared for her to never be proud of me again. Not unless I was prepared to lose my biggest fan. And I couldn't have that. I couldn't survive losing Janine.

I first met her when I was still in law school. She was finishing up her Masters in teaching at Hunter College, and she was in a class with a girl with whom I had gone to high school. I hadn't spoken to the girl in probably two years, but for some reason she told Janine that she knew a guy who would be perfect for her and she set us up on a blind date.

All I remember from that first date is the terror I felt about fifteen minutes after I had picked up Janine at her apartment. I knew by then that I was in love with her. And I knew that

I always would be. After fifteen minutes, just nine hundred seconds, I was positive that there was no one else in the world who I wanted to spend my life with except for the unnaturally beautiful, incredibly funny, down-to-earth woman sitting in the cab next to me as we rode down Second Avenue to grab dinner in the Village.

The terror I felt that night came from the fact that I knew I'd never be happy unless I could get this woman to fall in love with me, too. Since I hadn't had the best of luck with relationships, I decided to do something I had never done before with any girl I had dated.

I was going to be totally honest from the start. I would never lie to her about anything. That way, if she did fall in love with me, I would know it was real and right and meant to be because she would have fallen for the real me, not the fake, pseudo, manufactured me that I had created so often with other women I had dated. It was a secret promise of total honesty that I made with myself. And I had kept that promise since our very first date. I had never lied to Janine, for any reason, right up until that moment in the office when I stood motionless staring at the phone.

I picked up the receiver and dialed. The phone rang on the other end of the line. I prayed she wouldn't answer.

"Hello?"

"Sweetheart, it's me," I said.

"Hey, Honey. What's up?"

"I have some news," I started.

I then proceeded to lie to the only woman I have ever loved.

TWENTY-ONE

UMBERTO'S WAS the unofficial restaurant of the Principe family. We ate there to celebrate anniversaries. We ate there to celebrate birthdays. And, at Janine's insistence, we were going to eat there to celebrate my fraudulent settlement. I fought her tooth and nail about it. I told her I was tired, that my stomach hurt, and that I just didn't feel like eating out. She insisted that we go. We weren't in the restaurant very long before I figured out why Janine had been so insistent.

The maitre d' brought us through the main dining area of the restaurant to a private back room. When I entered, I stopped dead in my tracks, which was odd because my first instinct was to turn around and run. Sitting around a long table were my father, my mother, my Aunt Edith and Uncle Vincent, Roland, Ginny, and Ian. A bouquet of balloons was tied to a vase in the center of the table—the balloons read "Congratulations!" "Good Job!" and other laudatory expressions short enough to fit. Everyone broke into applause as soon as I entered. Ian even did that annoying high-pitched whistle thing where you put your pinky and index finger in your mouth and blow out really hard. I wanted to shove his hand down his throat.

"What the hell is this?" I asked Janine, stunned.

"Just a little something I threw together. You know, spur of the moment, after you called today with the good news." She kissed me on the cheek just as my dad approached us.

"Congratulations on your big win, son." My old man wrapped his bearlike arms around me and hugged tightly, patting me on the back a few times. He kissed me on the cheek, too, and then hugged me again.

"It was no big deal," I tried to explain. In reality, though, it was a big deal. In reality, it was a federal offense.

"No big deal?" my father objected. "You won a big trial today."

"No, Dad, I didn't …"

My father wasn't about to let me confuse him with the facts. He grabbed a young busboy by the arm, despite the fact that the poor kid was trying to fill water glasses for our table, and pulled him toward us.

"My son won a trial today," my dad boasted, as if this six-teen-year-old illegal alien making $4.50 an hour gave a rat's ass. The kid looked at my dad as if he was out of his mind and, at the time, he was. He was delirious with joy.

"Bueno" was all the busboy could think to say, and then he hurried away from the private room, most likely to switch tables with some unsuspecting colleague.

"Dad, I didn't win a trial. I just settled a case. There's a big difference."

"Who cares about the semantics? You got them to pay you

money, right? So you won. It doesn't matter if it's a knockout or a TKO. You still get the championship belt, right?"

I didn't say anything. I so badly didn't want to be there. I looked at my father, his eyes soaking me in. He was so proud, so happy. As far as he was concerned, I had cured cancer and split the atom. God, I hated myself.

"You'll see, Bobby. Things are going to change at that firm of yours now. Things are going to change. I guarantee it."

My father smiled at me—his big grin pushing his walrus-like moustache up against the bottom of his nose, his eyes scanning mine for a hint of confirmation of his prediction.

That was the first time I realized that my dad had been frightened—that during all those years when I had been struggling to keep the firm afloat, he was more scared than I was. I saw love in his eyes that night at Umberto's. That's for certain. But I also saw *relief*. Relief that the firm was going to survive, at least for a little while longer. Relief that his son wasn't a failure. More significantly, relief that *he* wasn't a failure. He hadn't worked all that overtime, slung all that drywall, and pounded all those nails for no good reason. He did it so his son could be a success, so that his son would never have to raise a hammer or go to work in the winter, knowing he wouldn't be warm again until he returned home that night.

For a while, my dad had been thinking that maybe I wasn't going to turn out to be the prize pig at the fair. For the past few years, it looked as if I was going to wind up just another hog for the slaughter. I think it would have been too much for the old man to take. Maybe. I'm not sure. He'd probably deny he ever felt that way if I ever asked him, but I suspect he isn't even aware of his own feelings on the subject. I swear to God, as happy as he was that night, as proud as he was, he was also just as relieved. If I were him, I'd feel the same way. I mean, considering all that the guy had sacrificed for me, I don't blame him for wanting a little return on his investment.

My dad reached into the inside pocket of his sports coat and pulled out a small plastic jewelry box.

"Here," he said. "I got something for you."

He handed me the box. I didn't want to take it.

"What is it?"

"Open it up and find out."

I reluctantly took the box from my dad and flipped open the top. Inside was a Columbia Law School class ring—gold with a blue stone. My initials were engraved on one side and on the other side there was a Scales of Justice.

"I know you always wanted one, but I knew you'd never spend the money on yourself," my father beamed.

I thought I was going to be sick.

"How did you …"

"As soon as Janine called and told us the news, I ran down by Matty K's, you know, the place over by the old brewery."

"Yeah, I know it."

"Matty's got a whole bunch of these kinda rings. He just had to, ya know, personalize it. With your initials and Columbia and all. You like it?"

"Dad, you can't afford this."

"So what? Try it on."

I tried to slide it onto my right ring finger, but I couldn't get it over my knuckle, almost as if my hand was rejecting it, as if it knew I didn't deserve it.

"You can get it resized if it's too small," my dad said.

"No, no. It fits fine," I assured him as I shoved the ring down toward my palm, securely in place. It took a bit of skin off the side of my finger, and I bled a little but I hid the blood from my dad.

"It looks great," he said, as he hugged me again. "I'm real proud of you."

"Thanks."

I had to get away. I felt as nauseous as Janine must have been feeling those past weeks. I didn't deserve a dinner. I didn't deserve a ring. I sure as hell didn't deserve the kind of family that would give me a dinner and a ring. I tried to slip out to the bathroom but Ginny grabbed me before I could make my escape.

"Hey, where are you running off to?" she asked playfully.

"Me? Nowhere. I was just going to go wash up."

"Can I talk to you alone for a minute?"

Ginny stepped out of the private room and walked toward an empty bar in the back of the restaurant. I reluctantly followed.

"You okay?" she asked. "You look a little pale."

"I'm fine. I'm just a little surprised by the party and everything. I didn't expect anything like this."

"Well, I just wanted to congratulate my baby brother on his big victory." Ginny gave me a tight hug and a kiss.

"It wasn't a victory," I explained for a second time. "It was just a settlement."

"Whatever. The money is still green, isn't it?" Ginny commented as she playfully punched me in the upper arm.

She seemed very happy, almost giddy. She was being really friendly. *Overly friendly*, like when a salesman you just met acts like he's been your best pal since first grade. At first, I couldn't understand why she was behaving like this, but it soon became perfectly clear.

"Speaking of money," Ginny continued. "I was wondering, you know, since you're doin' okay, if maybe you could spare a few bucks for a while?"

With that, she was done. *That* was Ginny's entire pitch, and, to be honest, I was quite disappointed with her effort. This wasn't the first time Ginny had hit me up for money. Not even close. Previously, she at least would put on a show, really *earn* her handouts. She'd say she was about to lose her apartment. She'd claim she couldn't afford to eat, which always cracked me up because she was about thirty-five pounds overweight. She could mooch with the best of them.

That night, she didn't give me much of a story. Maybe she was off her game. Maybe she thought I was euphoric from my "victory" or maybe she truly thought her baby brother was so flush with cash that he could just toss it around. Whatever her thinking was, she figured dead wrong.

"Are you fucking high?" I asked incredulously.

"What's the problem? It would just be for a little while until things settle down a bit for me and Ian, and then we'd pay you back."

"First of all, Janine and I are hardly '*doin' okay*.' The money I made today? All it does is let me float the firm for a few more months at best."

"But Rob … "

"But nothing, Ginny. Where the hell is Ian? He doesn't have the balls to hit me up for the money himself? He has to send my sister?"

"He's embarrassed."

"He should be. Unlike you and me, he has a rich daddy he can go to. Maybe he should be doin' a little more with his life than making minimum wage in a mail room."

"It's just until his music takes off, Bobby. He's really talented and if he could just catch a break then maybe …"

"Jesus H. Christ," I barked. "I've heard this fuckin' story too many times. Ian's a bum. And he's a little too old for rock-and-roll fantasies, if you ask me."

"Rob, we just need a little help and you know Mom and Dad don't have the kind of money …"

"Don't you dare ask them for any money," I warned.

"I won't. I promise," Ginny said sincerely, looking up at me with those big, green eyes of hers.

They were hopeful eyes. They'd always been hopeful eyes, even as a kid. Hopeful that the kids on the playground wouldn't make fun of her for being overweight, but they always did. Hopeful that someone would ask her to the high school prom, but no one ever did. Hopeful that Ian would truly love her but, so far, he showed no sign that he really did. The poor girl had never gotten a break her entire life and mostly it was because she was sweet and kind and trusting—and that made her a big, heavy, doe-eyed target for bastards like Ian.

"Listen," I softened. "If you or your baby ever needs anything, *anything*, I promise I'll do all I can to help."

"Thank you."

"But with God as my witness, I can't give you so much as a dollar if even one penny is going in that guy's pocket."

I was trying to do the right thing but that wasn't good enough for my sister.

"You can be such a son of a bitch sometimes, you know that?" Ginny stormed off toward the private room, blowing past Roland just as he approached me with two beer bottles.

"What the hell was that all about?" Roland asked, as he handed me one of the bottles.

"Nothing."

Roland raised his beer up high to toast me.

"To you, my friend," he said.

We clinked our bottles together. I took a long pull from my beer.

"This probably seems pretty silly to you, huh?" I asked.

"What?"

"My family making such a big deal over a hundred fifty grand case. You probably settle two or three cases like this every month."

"More," Roland grinned before swigging from his beer

He eyeballed me. He could tell I was doing the math in my head.

"You can make that much, too, you know," he added. "You're a much better lawyer than I am."

"How many beers have you had?"

"Seriously, man," Roland continued. "You're smarter than I am. You know the law better. And you're great with a jury."

I mimicked Roland's mantra: "*I just need to stay as aggressive as I can within the boundaries of the law.*"

Roland smiled. "That's the whole trick, Prince."

"But not an easy trick," I added.

"Hey, if it was easy, everyone would do it. But it's not impossible. You can *bend* the law like a pretzel, man. You just can't *break* it."

"But how do you know if you've bent it too far?" I asked.

"If you wind up in jail, you've bent it too far."

TWENTY-TWO

"THERE HE IS, Johnnie Cochran!"

I shuddered when I heard Jackie's voice. The case had been settled for all of four hours and he was already looking to collect. I turned to find him charging toward me, like a little bull in cheap clothes. He drove his shoulder into my gut, wrapped his arms around my waist, and lifted me high into the air. Jackie may have been short and squat but he was damn powerful. He spun me around and around, laughing like an idiot the entire time.

"Put me down," I said, making it clear that I wasn't enjoying it nearly as much as he was. Jackie obliged. "What are you doing here?" I asked, trying to hide my anger that he had shown up at Umberto's.

Jackie turned to Roland. "Can you believe the welcome this guy gives me?"

Jackie tapped both of my cheeks with his hands. "I came to

congratulate you, you ballbuster. On the settlement."

"Oh, okay. Well, thanks for coming by, but I'm just going to grab a quick bite with my parents and then I've got a bunch of stuff to do tonight …" I trailed off, trying to give Jackie the hint that I wanted him to shut the fuck up and leave. He didn't take it.

"I stopped by the office this afternoon to say hi and Joey told me the good news," he said.

"This guy stops by your office?" Roland joked. "What, are you branching out into criminal law now?"

Jackie playfully tapped Roland a few times in the stomach. "Hey, now," he said, "you better watch it, Cozzolino. You're bigger than I am but I'm feisty." Jackie turned back toward me. "I don't want to interrupt your party here, which, by the way, I notice I wasn't invited to …"

"Jackie, it's just a little dinner," I explained.

"Take it easy. I'm just bustin' your balls. I don't want to bother you during your dinner party, but I need to ask your advice on a legal matter. Can I talk to you alone for a minute?"

I was well aware of the legal matter Jackie wanted to discuss with me, and I sure as hell didn't want to talk to him about it in a public restaurant with my family in the next room. But I knew Jackie too well. He was there for one reason—to find out when he'd get his money. And he wasn't going to leave until he had his answer.

"I'll be back in a second," I said to Roland.

Jackie and I walked to the other end of the long oak bar, out of Roland's earshot.

"What the hell are you doing here?" I said quietly but firmly.

"I lied before," Jackie said excitedly, oblivious to my anger. "I really went by your office to see how the deposition went.

I shit myself when Joey told me the case settled. You're a helluva lawyer, cuz."

"We agreed you wouldn't come by my office."

"I know, I know. But I was too excited. I remembered what you said about how important the deposition would be to the case. So I just had to know. Man, I feel like a kid at Christmas."

I didn't respond. How do you respond to a guy who equates stealing a hundred fifty thousand dollars to the birth of Christ?

"So, when do we get the money?" Jackie asked, finally getting down to the real reason why he came by the restaurant.

"About three weeks."

"Three weeks! Why so long?"

"New York law allows an insurance company three weeks to process and send a settlement check. Once I get it, I'll deposit it in an escrow account. I'll take my fee and then write a check to Mr. Tangelino for the rest. How you get the money from him is between you guys and, frankly, I don't want to know a thing about that."

"Beautiful!" Jackie said, as he slapped his hands together. "I'm gonna go see Big Louie tonight to give him a full update. He's gonna be very happy when he hears about this. *Very* happy."

Jackie gave me a hug and patted me hard, three times, on the back. He pulled back and looked at me from arm's length.

"There's one other thing. I want to be there when you give the check to Tangelino. I don't want him gettin' any ideas about takin' the check and runnin' off to Canada or Bora Bora or some shit like that."

"No way," I protested. "That'll look way too suspicious if you're there."

"No it won't. I'll tell Tangelino I want him to meet me at

Patsy's so I can get the money. He does whatever I say; he's scared shitless of me. I'll tell him to ask you to hand deliver the check to him there. He's your client; you have to do what he says. He won't suspect you of anything. He doesn't even know you're involved in this thing."

I wasn't happy about Jackie's request but I caved.

"Alright," I said. "If that's what it takes to get this thing over and done with, fine, I'll do it." I pointed my index finger at Jackie and tried my best to let him know I was serious. "Just don't come by my office again."

Jackie laughed at the very sight of me trying to intimidate him. He pushed my finger out of the way and gave me another hug and a kiss.

"You worry too much, Prince. You know that?"

Jackie grabbed two matchbooks from a bowl on the bar and walked out of the restaurant, giving a respectful nod and wave to Roland as he went. Roland walked over to me and we watched Jackie leave.

"You're not representing him on a case, are you?" Roland asked incredulously.

"No. What do you think, I'm crazy? He's looking to buy some property and he had some real estate questions."

"Did you tell him that there are ordinances against burying bodies in his backyard?"

"I told him he could dump them in your new pool, wiseass."

"Seriously, man. Don't take this the wrong way. 'Cause I know he's your cousin and all. But you don't want to get involved with Jackie Masella. He's a real piece of shit."

TWENTY-THREE

"I JUST DON'T LIKE that he was there. He's a real piece of shit," Janine said as she changed for bed.

She had been riding my ass about Jackie showing up at the dinner since we got in the car and left Umberto's. She had hated Jackie since the first time they met. She knew what he was all about and didn't want to have anything to do with him. She wasn't shy about expressing her feelings about him either, whether it be to me or to Jackie himself.

Once at a family barbeque, Jackie got all bent out of shape. While Ginny was grilling a burger, she pressed down on it with the spatula and some blood squirted on his tacky polyester-blend shirt. He made a real big deal about it and he made Ginny feel like crap. She kept apologizing but Jackie kept on bitching that the shirt was ruined.

Janine came to my sister's defense.

"C'mon Jackie," she said, "I'm sure by now you're an

expert on getting blood stains out of your clothes."

Everyone at the barbeque clammed up. Even the birds stopped chirping. No one said anything for a few minutes, not even Jackie. In fact, I don't think anyone even moved except for Janine, who just sat at the table eating her burger like nothing had happened. She's one tough woman, my wife. And I love her for it.

"It's a public restaurant," I countered. "I can't stop him from coming in. Besides, he's my cousin. He just wanted to congratulate me." I sat on the edge of the bed and removed my pants.

"Roland said you were giving him legal advice."

I walked into our bathroom in my boxer shorts and T-shirt and brushed my teeth.

"He had a real estate question," I mumbled while working vigorously on my molars.

Although I had lied to Janine for the very first time earlier that day, I had already become quite adept at it. So much so that I found I could do it while performing everyday tasks like brushing and flossing without a problem. It bothered me that I found it so easy.

"What is he bothering you for? You don't even do real estate law. You don't know a damn thing about it," Janine very accurately pointed out.

I spit into the sink so that I could respond.

"You know Jackie. He's always looking to save a buck. He thought he could get some free legal advice. Could you please stop breakin' my shoes now?"

I put more toothpaste on my brush and began brushing again—not because I was really into dental hygiene, but because I thought that if I stayed in the bathroom long enough Janine would just drop the whole conversation. I was wrong.

"I don't like you associating with him," she said.

Janine entered the bathroom and stood directly behind me, lifting up on her tiptoes and peering over my left shoulder so she could look at me in the mirror when she talked.

"He's a gangster and a thief and God only knows what else. And he's an embarrassment to our family."

Janine wrapped her arms tightly around my waist from behind. Her fingers linked together and rested on my stomach. She pressed her right cheek against my back. I could feel the warmth of her face through my T-shirt.

"I want you to promise me that you won't get involved with him, even if it's just a real estate closing."

"I promise," I garbled while still brushing.

Janine's hands moved to my hips and she spun me around so that we were face to face. She yanked the toothbrush from my mouth.

"I mean it, Robert. Look me in the eyes and promise me."

"I promise," I said, lying through my freshly brushed teeth. "Now let's get some sleep, okay? I'm exhausted."

"Okay," Janine responded.

She stuck the toothbrush back into my mouth and climbed into bed. I rinsed and joined her. We snuggled up together, face to face.

"Did you like your party?" she asked.

"Yeah, it was great. How much did it cost?"

"Couple hundred bucks. But we can afford it now. We're getting a check for fifty grand in a few weeks."

"Have you forgotten that we have a high six-figure mortgage, a law firm that's drowning in debt, eighty grand in law school loans, and a little critter growing inside of you who is going to want to go to college?"

Janine smiled devilishly and pushed me over onto my back.

She straddled me, leaned forward, and kissed me.

"If I remember correctly, it was a lot of fun making that critter," she reminded me.

"I don't know, honey. You're pregnant."

"So?"

"It's just …"

"Come on, baby," Janine persisted. "We haven't done it in weeks. Let's finish this celebration right."

"Well, it sort of freaks me out with the baby in there and everything. What if I poke him in the eye or something?"

"*Her*," Janine laughed and kissed me on the neck. "You're a moron, you know that?" she giggled.

I gently pushed Janine's head up from my neck so she was looking at me. I wasn't laughing.

"I have to ask you a serious question," I said. "And I need you to tell me the truth."

"Okay."

"Let's say this one settlement is it, and I've got no more money coming in and the firm has to close down. And we lose everything. The business. Our home. Everything."

"Yeah?"

"Would you still love me?"

Janine's eyes searched mine. I don't know what she was looking for in there. Perhaps the source of my concern? Or some depth of character that I just didn't possess? Her eyes stopped moving and they just looked sad. Sad for me.

"You don't get it, do you?" she asked. "We could be penniless. We could have nothing. And I'd always love you."

Janine kissed me again.

I held her tight. I was relieved. I knew she was telling me the truth because, unlike me, Janine would never lie to her one true love.

TWENTY-FOUR

I HAD BEEN IN PATSY'S a few times in my life, but I'd
never been in The Office. The Office was the stuff of urban
legend. Ask any kid in Bensonhurst and they'll tell you that the
wood-paneled door in the back of Patsy's with the plaque that
read "Office" was a portal to hell. Rumor had it that Sammy
"The Barber" Scala was sitting at Patsy's bar when he was
called into The Office. He climbed off his bar stool and walked
slowly toward The Office door, knees shaking, legs trembling,
knowing full well that a call into The Office was a death
warrant. He slowly turned the knob and entered, the door
closing behind him. No one ever saw The Barber again.

I was surprised as hell when I found out that The Office
wasn't really an office at all. It didn't have a desk, a file cabinet,
or a computer. It didn't have any of the things you would
expect to find in an office. It was a four-hundred-square-foot
room with hardwood floors, a leather couch, and a round,

marble-topped table in the corner next to a wet bar. The table was surrounded by four metal-framed chairs. There was a big-screen television across from the couch and in front of the couch was a coffee table with the same marble top as the round table. I know all this because, despite my better instincts, the day after my Umberto's dinner I found myself sitting at the round table watching the big-screen TV, waiting for Louie Turro to enter.

I had gone to Patsy's hesitantly, not sure if I should even be there, when Choo Choo spotted me.

"Hey, Prince," he called out, waving me over with his fat hand and sausage-link fingers.

I walked to the table where Choo Choo was polishing off a sausage-and-pepper hero that could have choked a donkey.

"You here to see Jackie?" he asked. "'Cause he's out making the rounds for Big Lou."

"No. Actually, I was hoping to speak to Mr. Turro for a moment if that's possible."

Choo Choo looked at me as if I had just asked if I could climb onto his table and take a dump on his sandwich.

"Big Lou's a very busy man," he said in between bites. "I don't know if he can see you, ya know?"

"I realize that. That's why I asked you," I explained, playing to the enormous ego that seemed to be standard issue with all wiseguys. "I figured if anyone could get me a two-minute meeting with Mr. Turro it would be you. I hear you're the man behind the man, if you know what I mean?"

Although I would have bet the ranch that it was impossible, Choo Choo actually got bigger—his barrel chest puffed out with pride. He put the rest of his sandwich down and stood.

"Tell you what," he said. "Why don't you wait in The Office. Big Louie should be here soon."

As soon as Choo Choo mentioned The Office, I wished I had never gone to Patsy's.

"No, no. That's okay. I don't want to bother him," I backpedaled. "I'll just come by another day and see if he's around."

"Don't worry about it," Choo Choo insisted as he opened the door to The Office. "Just have a seat and I'll give him a ring on his cell."

I reluctantly walked into The Office and felt the breeze of the door closing behind me. I slowly scanned the room. I know it sounds crazy but I think subconsciously I was looking for blood stains on the floor or bullet holes in the wall or some kind of evidence of prior hits that had taken place there. There was nothing. It looked like the tacky basement rumpus room of a suburbanite.

I sat at the table and watched *SportsCenter*, which had been playing on the television when I entered. I glanced around the room some more. There were no shovels, no buckets of ammonia, no plastic on the floor—nothing that would be used to clean up a "mess." Somehow that made me feel more at ease. I was actually able to relax for a few minutes and enjoy some football highlights. And then Big Lou walked in.

Lou stood about six-foot-two and weighed in at, conservatively, three hundred pounds but he wasn't fat. He had a round belly but this guy was solid. His broad shoulders slumped down into granite arms that led to meaty hands that looked like miniature baseball gloves, all worn and leathery. His legs were thick like tree trunks, and you just knew that this guy, despite his half-century age, could beat you into the ground if he was so disposed.

"Bobby Junior," he greeted me warmly. "Good to see you. Good to see you."

"Hello, Mr. Turro," I said respectfully as I stood from the table and extended my hand to meet his. We shook. His grip was surprisingly gentle, almost dainty.

"Please, don't get up," he said, motioning with his hand that I should return to my chair. So I did. "Choo Choo didn't offer you anything to drink?" he asked, a little upset.

"No, he did," I lied, not wanting to get Choo Choo in trouble. More importantly, not wanting to get him mad at me. "I just didn't want anything."

"Not even a coffee or something?"

"I'm fine, thanks."

"I'm gonna have a coffee."

As if on cue, Choo Choo entered with coffee and cookies. He carried them in on a wooden tray that had mother-of-pearl inlay in the handles and baroque-style hand carvings along the base. Choo Choo poured a cup for BLT and one for me. Mr. Turro lifted his cup in my general direction.

"Salute."

He held the cup there for a brief moment. He was testing me. He knew goddamn well that I didn't want any coffee. I had just told him that. But now he was toasting with me, and it would have been an insult if I didn't return the gesture. This was how these guys worked. They start off small, with little favors or tasks or gestures. They want to see how you respond. They want to see if they can make you do something you don't want to do, even if it's as seemingly irrelevant as having a cup of coffee. They want to see what kind of man you are. Lou quickly found out.

"Salute," I said, raising my cup and touching it to his. Then I took a sip of coffee that I didn't even want.

"That's a beautiful tray," I said, making small talk, scared to get to the reason why I was there.

"Thank you," Big Louie said, his face illuminating a bit but, strangely, his eyes growing sad at the same time. "My son Donnie made it for me."

So much for small talk. Donatello Marco Turro, BLT's only child, had died at the age of seventeen while playing in a football game. Donnie was the starting tight end for New Utrecht High School, where all the Italian kids in Bensonhurst went. And Donnie was good. Real good. He had gotten scholarship offers from Temple, C.W. Post, and Hofstra. The kid could really play. He was the pride of Bensonhurst.

Back in '97, Donnie was playing against Lincoln High, which the kids from Utrecht often called *"What Were You Thinkin', Abraham Lincoln?"* High, a derogatory nod to the fact that Lincoln was a predominantly black school. In the fourth quarter, Donnie ran a route across the middle. The pass sailed wide over his head but Donnie leapt for it anyway. He floated in midair for a few seconds, totally vulnerable, and then the impact came. Rondell Trace, a six-foot-five, two-hundred-sixty-pound monster of a linebacker shot through the air like a cannonball, landing a clean but vicious hit on Donnie that spun him upside down before he landed on the turf. People who were at the game said that they knew Donnie was dead when he hit the ground. They could tell by the way he landed—like a doll, one arm twisted behind his back, neck turned to the side, face down in the dirt.

Big Lou was there. He saw the whole thing from the stands. The Brooklyn gossips will tell you that even as people raced from the bleachers to check on Donnie, BLT stayed right where he was, staring down at his son's lifeless body. Folks say his face displayed no emotion, but instead showed a look of acceptance of the situation. That always made sense to me because Big Lou had been around death all his life. He'd ordered hits and killed people himself, I was sure of it. He knew that once someone was dead, there was nothing you could do about it. So I believed it when people told me about how he reacted that day.

The strangest thing about Donnie's death was what happened after the funeral. Word got back to Rondell that Lou Turro wanted his pound of flesh for his son's death, so Rondell got out of Brooklyn as fast as he could. Some people said he grabbed an Amtrak to Chicago out of Penn Station but got off in South Bend, Indiana, hitched a ride south to Bloomington, and pretended to be an undergraduate at Indiana University for a few weeks, posing as a transfer student and getting some free room and board for a while at a black fraternity.

Somehow a message got out to Rondell—Big Louie wasn't blaming him for what happened. On the contrary, he wanted to speak to Rondell and thank him for holding Donnie's hand down on the field and talking to him until the paramedics arrived. He wanted Rondell to come back to Brooklyn. He had given Rondell's grandmother his word that he would never hurt the last person who ever touched Donnie while Donnie was still alive. He believed in some way that Donnie's spirit lived on in Rondell; that it had somehow transferred from one player's body to another's on the football field that day.

So Rondell came home and Louie kept his word. He took Rondell under his wing—made sure he graduated from high school and sent him to summer football camps. He even paid for Rondell to go to college when Rutgers University only came up with a partial football scholarship.

Some people began to think maybe old Lou wasn't such a bad guy after all. But that kind of thinking stopped when Charlie Campo, the quarterback who threw the bad pass to Donnie, washed up underneath the Brooklyn side of the

Manhattan Bridge, two bullet holes behind his right ear. I guess that, in Lou's mind, it was okay for Rondell to hurt Donnie because that was Rondell's job. To put Donnie in the position that caused him to be hurt—that was inexcusable.

"Really? I didn't know he was an artist. He must've been very talented," I said, hoping this would be the last of any discussion about Donnie Turro and the tray he made.

"He was good at a whole lot of things. He was a very special boy." BLT took another sip of his coffee.

I used this as an opportunity to change the subject away from death.

"I really appreciate you taking the time to meet with me," I said.

"Don't be silly. You can come see me any time you want. My door's always open to you."

"Thank you. But I do know you're a very busy man, Mr. Turro …"

"Please, call me Lou or Louie. Just don't call me BLT. I hate that. I know some guys like to call me that, but I don't like it. I mean, who likes to be called a sandwich? Would you like that?"

"Me? No. I wouldn't want to be called a sandwich."

"See? We think alike. How's your old man doin'?"

"My dad? He's fine, thank you."

"You know I've known him since we were altar boys at Saint Joseph's. Your dad's the best carpenter in Brooklyn, you know that?"

"He's very talented, yes. He does excellent work."

"Do you have any idea how many times I tried to get him to come work for me? I want him to manage a few of my contracting companies. Son of a gun turns me down every time. I've told him, *'You'll make a hundred times what you make in the union,'"* Big Louie lamented. "He's still an altar boy, that one," he chuckled.

Louie grabbed an anisette cookie and bit into it, showering crumbs onto the table. "So, what can I do for you?" he asked.

I held my breath for a moment before I spoke. I wanted to make sure I sounded exactly like I had practiced in the bathroom mirror. I needed to sound confident and resolute, brave and secure. I needed to sound like I had some balls.

"I want out," I said. To be honest, it sounded pretty damn good, just like I had rehearsed. I was respectful but firm, just like the good guys in the movies. But then BLT threw me a curveball.

"Out of what?" he asked innocently.

That wasn't the response I expected. What did he mean, *"out of what?"* He knew damn well "out of what." Was he actually going to make me say it aloud?

"Out of our arrangement," I said, answering his question without actually giving any specific information—a typical lawyer's answer.

"What arrangement?"

Jesus Christ, this guy isn't going to make this easy for me! I thought.

"The arrangement with the lawsuit," I said. "Salvatore Tangelino. His case settled."

"So?"

"So you'll be getting your money in a few weeks. Once that's done, I want to end this."

"End what?"

"Our arrangement," I said, exasperated. I didn't know if Lou was dense or just fucking with me, but I was pretty sure it was the latter. "It's just too dangerous. I could be disbarred, or worse. I just want out."

"Oh, the *arrangement*. The thing with the accident on the job site," Lou said as if he barely knew anything about it.

This guy had turned playing dumb into an art form.

"Yes, that's what I mean by arrangement, Mr. Turro."

Lou waved his finger at me. "Uh, uh, uh. What did I tell you before?"

"Sorry, Lou. That's what I mean by arrangement, Lou."

"That's better. I hate formalities." Lou leaned back in his chair and sucked on his lower lip for a moment. "I can't say I'm not disappointed, Robert. I was really very happy with how things turned out. Tangelino owed us thirty Gs and you got us a helluva lot more. I made a few bucks, you took home a nice paycheck, and Tangelino, well, you can't put a value on what he got out of the deal. Everybody wins."

"Even so," I countered, "I've got a family to think about now. I can't take any more risks."

"You know, I've spoken to some people that I do business with. About this whole thing. And they were very interested with what you've come up with. They were hoping to meet with you and possibly set up a similar arrangement. It would almost be like you were ... I don't know ... *franchising* or something. There's a lot of money to be made here, Bobby. Why would you want to kill something with so much potential?"

"I ... I never used the word *kill*, Lou. That ... that's your word. I'm just saying this situation isn't really for me, that's all."

I pushed my coffee cup to the side and leaned in a bit closer to Lou, raising my eyebrows in an effort to use my "sincere look" that I used so often with judges. I swear I was so nervous I almost called him "Your Honor."

"I don't mean any disrespect to you or what you do for a living," I explained, "but I'm an Officer of the Court. I try to live my life according to the law, the Tangelino case notwithstanding. And I'm ashamed that I even did that. But I was desperate. And now that the whole thing is over with and I've got my head a little above water, I think it's a good time to stop. That's why I've come to see you today. To ask you if I can please get out of this thing."

Lou chuckled. I was clearly quite amusing to him.

"You want out, you're out," he said. "But there isn't really anything to let you out *of*. I told Jackie we'd do this thing on a trial basis. I'm disappointed by your decision, but I respect it. Look, you and I had an agreement. You honored your end of it and you don't want to continue the arrangement. That's your prerogative. I'm fine with that."

Lou reached across the marble-topped table, cupping my hand with his left hand while shaking it with his right. "I wish you luck in your future endeavors. And with your impending child. Do you know if it is a boy or girl?"

"We want to be surprised."

"Good for you. That's nice. A nice surprise. But between you, me, and the lamppost, I hope it's a boy. Having a son is like nothing you could ever imagine."

I smiled at him. I really felt bad for the guy, because of what had happened to Donnie. If I wasn't so scared of Louie, I would've stayed and talked for a while. But it was hard to just kick back and relax when you were in The Office.

"Take care. I guess I'll see you around the neighborhood," I said as I pushed my chair back and stood. I crossed the room and opened the door to leave.

"Rob," Big Louie called out.

"Yes?"

"Give my regards to your father."

"I'll do that."

"And if you ever change your mind and you want to do

business in the future, just come on by and we'll talk."

"Okay, Lou. But I don't think that's going to happen."

"Hey," Lou smiled, "like I said, it's up to you."

I closed the door behind me, walked through the bar where some ancient paisans were playing dominoes, and exited Patsy's. My feet floated along the sidewalk, as if the soles of my shoes were filled with helium. I was overcome by an intense desire to run. Not to anywhere in particular. Just to run for the sake of running. I felt unburdened for the first time in years and I wanted to sprint like a child. So I did. For the first time since I played high school basketball I ran as fast as I could, weaving in between pedestrians and spinning around light poles. After a block I stopped and doubled over, out of breath, an intense pain in my side. God, I was in such lousy shape but I felt great nonetheless. I had gone into The Office and lived to tell about it. It was all over.

TWENTY-FIVE

THE NEXT TWO WEEKS were relatively uneventful. I put all thoughts of Jackie Masella, Lou Turro, and Salvatore Tangelino out of my mind and directed all of my energies toward trying to reinvigorate my practice. I sent out a mass mailing to every person I knew, and I mean *everyone*. Cousins, colleagues, high school pals, friends from college, friends of friends, *acquaintances* of friends, my dentist, his friends, *anyone*. I wanted the entire world to know that there was a litigator in Brooklyn who was ready, willing, and able to fight for their rights. I must've sent out six hundred letters.

I received four responses—three envelopes marked "Return to Sender" because of improper addresses and a phone call from my Aunt Philomena who wanted me to draft her will for free. I started to get very depressed.

My spirits lifted a bit when the check came in, however. It was one of those large corporate checks that are about twice the size of a personal check. It was aqua green and had a watermark right in the middle—the Union Central Insurance Company corporate seal. The check's edges were so pristine, crisp, and sharp that I swear you could have cut a steak with it. The ink was dark black and the paper was thick, almost like a postcard. God, it was beautiful. The check was for one hundred fifty thousand dollars and it was made out to Robert R. Principe, Esq. but, trust me, I wasn't getting nearly that much money.

The public has been duped into thinking that if they get hurt and sue, they will be set for life and their lawyers will get rich. Nothing could be further from the truth. The average jury verdict in New York State is about fifty thousand dollars. In a case like that, after expenses and fees, the client is lucky to walk away with twenty-eight grand.

Take the Tangelino case—the expenses weren't that bad because there was no trial but they were still significant—two hundred ten bucks for the court filing fee just to start the lawsuit; ninety-five to schedule the preliminary conference with the judge so deposition dates could be set up; four hundred for copies of my client's MRI films; forty-five for copies of his medical records; and fifteen hundred dollars for a physical examination and narrative report from Dr. Bass. These expenses came out of the settlement, so now we're down to one hundred forty-seven thousand eight hundred ten dollars. I get one-third of that—forty-nine thousand two hundred seventy dollars—for my legal fee.

If this had been a normal case, Mr. Tangelino would have walked away with over ninety-eight thousand. Tax free. But this wasn't a normal case and Mr. Tangelino was lucky to be walking away at all.

I went through the forty-nine grand very quickly. About

twenty thousand dollars went to estimated taxes—God bless the IRS. Five grand went to office equipment lease payments on which I was late. Five grand for malpractice insurance. Twelve grand for a massive double-page ad in the Yellow Pages in the hopes of drumming up some *legitimate* clients and a few grand bonus to Joey because she'd been underpaid for years and I felt it was the right thing to do. Throw in office supplies, bar association dues, backed-up telephone and electric bills, and computer technical support fees, and I had committed full-blown insurance fraud so that I could pocket about six thousand bucks, which was just enough to keep the bank off my ass about the mortgage payments, at least until next month when it was due again.

I called Mr. Tangelino and told him the check had come in. He said he wanted to meet at Patsy's to get it from me. He claimed he didn't trust the mail but I knew that Jackie must have given him his marching orders like he said he would.

When I entered Patsy's, Jackie and Mr. Tangelino were sitting at the same table where I first hatched the scheme. It seemed fitting that the same place would be where the money changed hands. I approached them and politely said hello to both men. I purposefully acted surprised to see Jackie there.

"Sit. Have a drink," Jackie offered, like we were all old friends who were just there to shoot the shit.

"No, thanks. I've got to get back to work."

I reached inside my suit jacket, pulled out an envelope, and handed it to Mr. Tangelino. He opened it. His eyes grew wide upon seeing the amount of the check—ninety-eight thousand five hundred forty dollars.

"Good luck, Mr. Tangelino."

I shook his hand, and then Jackie's, and turned and headed for the exit. I had literally put the whole thing behind me. Or so I thought.

TWENTY-SIX

WITH BUSINESS still in the toilet and most of the money from the Tangelino case going to cover expenses, I was reduced to taking per diem jobs from Roland and a few other ham-and-eggers I knew—fifty bucks to cover a compliance conference, a hundred bucks for a deposition, that sort of thing. It's not that I thought I was too good for that kind of work, but it was a step backward, not forward. I would have done pick-up work for the rest of my life rather than get involved with Jackie again. Not that he didn't try to change my mind.

Despite my protests, he'd come by my office almost every day and try to convince me that I should go back into business with him and BLT. I remember one of these conversations in particular—not so much for its substance, but because it was the last time Jackie would plead with me to bring the scam back to life.

"Why are you being so fuckin' thick?" Jackie harassed me

that day, tapping his index finger to his temple.

"There are about a thousand lawyers in Brooklyn," I answered. "There are two dozen on this block alone. Why don't you go bother them?"

"Because they're not my fuckin' cousins, that's why. We're blood, Prince. Nothin' would make me happier than for you and me to profit together from this. Besides, Big Lou really likes you, man. He trusts you. He told me that himself. He doesn't want to do this with anyone else."

I stood up and grabbed a law book from a shelf. I didn't really have to look anything up. I just wanted Jackie to think that I was busy so he'd leave.

"Not a chance. I'm not taking any more risks. Have you ever heard that pigs get fat but hogs get slaughtered?"

"What the fuck are you talking about?" Jackie asked, totally confused.

"It means we should be happy with what we got and not get greedy," I explained.

I sat back down at my desk and flipped through a text on federal civil procedure. I had never tried a federal case in my life and most likely never would, but Jackie didn't know the difference between a law book and a phone book. Since I just wanted him to think I had a lot of work to do, the book served as a fine prop. But Jackie wouldn't leave. He sat across from me and spoke softly.

"Look," he said, darting his eyes back and forth as if there could have been someone else in the office trying to listen to our conversation. "I didn't want to tell you this because I don't want to put any more pressure on you than you already got, but I ain't earnin' so well. Louie's been far from impressed with my performance this past year. But he was real happy with me when I brought in this project of ours and he was very disappointed when you wanted out."

"So?" I said pointedly.

"So, you sort of made me look bad, Robert," Jackie said as if I owed him something.

"Made you look bad?" I laughed. "You want me to violate about two dozen state and federal laws so you can score points with your boss?"

Jackie contemplated my question a moment and then answered, "Yes," without any sense of irony.

I didn't respond as there is no point in trying to reason with unreasonable people. I closed my prop book, grabbed my suit jacket, and walked toward my door.

"I promised Janine I'd be home for dinner," I said as I passed Jackie. "I gotta go. Joey's gonna lock up in a few minutes so, well, I'll see you later."

I walked home that night confident that I had successfully given Jackie the brush-off for the last time. I wanted him to become the kind of relative you only saw at weddings and funerals. I hoped our relationship would be like when you get drunk and hook up with a girl you've been friends with for a long time; whenever you see each other you politely say hi and never discuss or acknowledge what you did together.

The air was crisp that night, no humidity. I breathed it in deeper with each step I took as if the clean air could get inside me and cleanse my soul. I convinced myself that it was working; that with each breath I was getting closer to a new beginning, that each step took me further from the sins of my very recent past. I was feeling quite good about myself and my future when I climbed the stoop to my front door. But after I turned the key in the lock and entered, all those good feelings instantly disappeared.

TWENTY-SEVEN

FROM THE FOYER I saw Ginny crying uncontrollably at my kitchen table. Janine sat next to her, holding Ginny's head, stroking it gently in a vain attempt to console her sister-in-law. Janine looked up at me. I could tell by the look on her face that something was terribly wrong. My stomach kicked into high gear.

"What's going on?" I asked, rushing over to my sister's side.

Ginny buried her head into Janine's shoulder. She couldn't stop crying. Janine answered for her.

"She got some tests back today from the doctor. The baby has Down syndrome." She was barely able to say the words.

"Oh, my God," I said. I leaned my back against the refrigerator, using the appliance to hold me up.

"Ginny, sweetheart?" Janine whispered to my sister. "Rob and I are going to go talk in our bedroom for a second but we'll be right back. Okay?"

Ginny lifted her head up and looked at Janine and me. Her eyes were swollen from hours of crying. She slowly nodded her head once.

Janine walked toward the bedroom and I followed. As I passed Ginny, I placed my hand softly on her back and rubbed her gently for a moment.

"I'll be right back," I muttered.

Janine closed the bedroom door so that Ginny couldn't hear us. I sat on the edge of the bed and rubbed the left side of my chest with the palm of my hand in a circular motion, as if doing so could mend my aching heart.

"I can't believe this," I said, my voice weak. "All she ever wanted was a healthy baby."

"There's more," Janine said ominously.

"What do you mean?"

"That asshole Ian took off as soon as he found out."

"What?!"

"He told Ginny it was her family's *defective guinea genes* that gave her a *retard baby*."

I sprang from the bed. "I'll kill that son of a bitch!" I shouted.

"Shhh, she'll hear you," Janine hushed. "Besides, you can't kill him if you can't find him. He packed up a bag and he's gone. Even his parents don't know where he is."

I grabbed the closest thing to me, a Mary Higgins Clark novel from Janine's nightstand, and threw it across the room. Then I kicked a shoe box as hard as I could and a new pair of sling backs Janine had just bought flew into the closet door, leaving a dark scuff mark just below the doorknob.

"Calm down," Janine said, taking me gently by the wrist.

I pulled away.

"My sister's facing a lifetime of raising a sick kid on her own and you want me to calm down?"

"You don't have the luxury of being angry right now. Ginny needs you and if you're out of control you're of no use to her."

Janine was right. I took a deep breath and tried to calm down.

"Okay," I said, sitting back down on the bed. I took Janine by the hand and looked up at her. "We have to take care of her."

"Of course we will," Janine responded matter-of-factly. "We're a family."

Ginny was wiping her eyes with a sheet of paper towel when Janine and I re-entered the kitchen.

"You were right," she said. "You always told me Ian was a piece of shit. I really thought he loved me. How could I have been so stupid?"

I wrapped my arms around my sister. She cried into my chest as I rocked her back and forth.

"Who's gonna want me now?" she continued. "I'm a broke single mother with a sick baby."

Ginny looked up at me. This time, all hope was gone from her eyes.

"The doctor said he'd need special schooling. I can't even pay my rent. Mom and Dad are barely getting by on Social Security; I can't ask them to help. How am I gonna take care of my baby?"

Ginny placed her cheek against my chest and took the short shallow breaths of exhaustion that come from a long, hard cry. She was wiped out. I stroked her hair like she used to do to me when I was little.

"Janine and I want you to move in with us," I said. "You'll stay in the spare bedroom. Don't worry about the doctors or the schooling; we'll take care of that."

"But Rob ..." Ginny interrupted.

"You just worry about caring for that baby inside of you.

All this crying can't be good for it, right?"

"But the spare room is *your* baby's room."

"When our baby comes, we'll put the crib in our bedroom," Janine said.

"You can't fit the crib …" Ginny argued.

"We'll return it and get a bassinette," Janine shot back. "We'll be fine."

Ginny continued to protest.

"I can't ask you guys to do this. Rob, you just told me at your party that you guys are strapped for cash. You can't afford to take me and a baby into your home."

I kissed my sister on the cheek and looked into her frightened eyes.

"Don't you worry about that," I reassured her. "There's a solution to every problem."

TWENTY-EIGHT

A COOL MORNING BREEZE passed through the backyard of Big Louie's brownstone. A few leaves fell toward the ground, spinning the entire way, eventually landing in a meticulously maintained carp pond.

The mesh-iron garden chair I was sitting on was quite cold. I could feel the chill of the metal on the back of my thighs, right through my suit pants. I suppressed the urge to let my teeth chatter because I thought it would have been perceived as a sign of weakness. I sipped down the hot coffee Choo Choo had poured for me before he went inside the house to get his boss, but it wasn't really helping me keep warm.

I heard a door open behind me. In the stainless steel of the coffee pot I saw the distorted reflection of Louie, Choo Choo, and Jackie approaching me from behind. Louie wore a thick terry cloth robe and leather slippers. He had the robe pulled so tightly I couldn't tell if he was wearing anything underneath it.

I assumed he must have been because he didn't seem to be cold at all.

Big Lou sat down across from me. Choo Choo promptly poured him a coffee. He drank about half of it before he even acknowledged that I was sitting two feet from him. I did not know if he wanted me to start speaking first, but I figured it was best to keep my mouth shut. Jackie didn't say a word either. He just stood next to Big Lou with a satisfied look on his face, giving me a slight smile whenever our eyes met. Finally, Big Lou spoke.

"I'm sorry we're not meeting inside, but I'm having my kitchen redone and the whole place is a mess. I thought it was best if we spoke in the garden," he explained.

"That's fine. It's very beautiful back here. You could never tell from the street that there was so much property behind the house."

"That's why I like it here. It's quiet. Private. Secluded."

I noticed another reflection in the coffee pot. Tony was just a few yards behind me. Had he come out of the house with the others and I hadn't noticed him? Or was he trying to sneak up on me quietly?

I decided my best move was to let him know I knew he was there. I turned a bit in my chair and faced him.

"Hey, Tony," I said, giving him a slight wave. "I didn't see you there or I would've said hi sooner."

Tony didn't say anything. He just gave me a slight nod of the head. Man, he was one scary motherfucker.

"So," Big Lou started, as I turned my attention back to him. "Jackie said you wanted to talk to me about something."

"Yeah." I looked up to Jackie. He gave me a reassuring nod, which didn't reassure me at all. "I want back in," I said and then shut the hell up.

Lou thought about my statement for a moment and then he laughed.

"You know," he said, "you remind me of this girl that I took to my junior high prom. Bernadette Casuto. She was a beauty. Long black hair, dark brown eyes, and big tits. Only fourteen, but with God as my witness she had the tits of a twenty year old. So, anyway, after the dance she and I were in the back seat of my old man's Caddy, steamin' up the windows, you know what I mean?"

I nodded that I understood.

"At first," he continued, "she said she didn't want to do it. Then she changed her mind and said she did. Then she changed her mind again and said she didn't. She was a very uncertain kid."

Louie lifted his coffee cup to his lips and took a long, deliberate slurp. He put the cup back down and looked at me.

"Just like you," he said, making his point crystal clear.

"Well, I'm certain now. I want to do this," I said, trying to sound as committed and sure of myself as I could, which was no small feat considering how unsure I actually was.

Lou stared at me intently, searching my face for any sign of doubt. He couldn't have looked too closely because he smiled and clapped his hands together loudly.

"This makes me very happy," he said. "Same arrangement as before. We supply the clients, you get your fee, and we get the rest."

"Alright," I said as I rose from my chair.

"Except for one small change," Louie added.

I sat back down.

"I want Jackie to spend some time in your office. You know, to keep an eye on things. Make sure everything runs smoothly. Help you out a bit."

I couldn't believe what I was hearing. Big Lou wanted me to let Jackie Masella set up shop in my law firm. *Was he crazy? No way*, I thought, *this is a deal breaker.*

"Lou," I said in a tone that was respectful but at the same time resolute, "I can't have that."

Jackie erupted. "What the fuck is your problem?" he shouted, arms waving around like a crazy man. "What are you, ashamed of me?" Jackie slammed his fist on the table.

"Hey, take it easy," Lou said, raising his hand to indicate to Jackie that he wanted him to shut the hell up.

Jackie instantly shut the hell up.

I was taken aback by Jackie's reaction because I saw more than just anger or hurt feelings in his eyes. I saw violence. He was my cousin. We had grown up together. He showed me my first *Playboy*. I invited him to every birthday party I ever had. I loved him, and I was pretty sure he loved me. But I'm certain that if Lou had let him, Jackie would have jumped across the garden table and torn me to shreds.

"Jackie," I explained, trying to calm him down, "this has nothing to do with you personally."

Jackie just stared through me. I could tell he wasn't listening to a word I said, so I turned my attention to Louie.

"Lou, my clients can't know that I'm involved in any way. They have to think that their arrangement is solely with you and that Jackie sends them to me only because I'm his cousin. If Jackie is camping out in my office, the clients will know he's involved with me somehow. I have to protect my reputation. With all due respect, Mr. Turro, on this issue I cannot budge."

I looked to Jackie to see if my explanation had soothed him at all. It hadn't. He was still steaming.

"And with all due respect to you," Louie countered, "if you had a reputation worth protecting, you wouldn't be here right now doing business with me. My men *will* be in your office keeping track of things. On this issue *I* cannot budge."

Lou stared at me, eyelids half open, unblinking. We were at an impasse. I knew arguing my position was futile so I sat silently. Several seconds passed with Lou and me just looking at each other. Jackie broke the tension.

"Come on, Prince," he cajoled, much calmer now, as if he hadn't just wanted to kill me moments earlier. "We'll stay out of your way. You can tell people I'm your paralegal or something. I tell ya what, I'll even get a briefcase."

I don't know if I really believed Jackie when he said that things would work out or if I just wanted Big Lou to stop staring at me with that dead look in his eyes, but I acquiesced.

"Okay," I said, "but you'll have to keep a low profile."

"I'll keep *no* profile," Jackie promised, grinning with pride at his mediation skills.

"So, we're agreed," Lou said.

"I guess so," I responded as I stood. "You know where to reach me."

I shook hands with Lou and headed for the backyard gate. I thought I had made a clean getaway when Lou spoke up again.

"Rob, one other thing," Louie called out.

I stopped and turned back to him.

"Just like last time, you gotta see each case through to the end. If you get cold feet or a sudden case of legal ethics, that's your problem."

"Understood," I said, resigned to my predicament.

I reached the gate and clumsily tried to open the lock. My mind was too clouded from anxiety and self-hatred to figure out the mechanism that would free me from the backyard prison. While I fumbled with the lock I thought about the desperation I had felt the night before.

I had tossed and turned in bed, unable to sleep, thinking about how I was going to take care of my own family and Ginny's, while saving my firm and my home. I had convinced myself that the only way out was reviving the scheme with Jackie. I figured if I only did it a few more times I would never have to do it again. With the money from just a few cases, everything would be all right.

As I tried desperately to open the gate, I was amazed at how preposterous my plan seemed to me in the daylight. I knew how dangerous these people I had just teamed up with were. I knew what they were capable of and I knew what they would do to me if I didn't follow through with my promises. I had just climbed back into bed with them anyway. I was cuddled up under a big down comforter with Big Louie Turro and Jackie and Choo Choo and Tony. I had made the bed and now I was going to have to sleep in it. I just hoped it wasn't my death bed.

A hand reached over my shoulder and grabbed the gate lock.

"You have to press here and here at the same time," Louie said.

The gate sprung open. I was free to go but I didn't. There was something I had to know. I turned to Louie.

"What ever happened to that girl from the prom?" I asked.

Lou grinned.

"Eventually," he said, "she got fucked."

TWENTY-NINE

I HADN'T UNLOCKED the spare office in years. I was surprised that I still had the key for it. The door opened to reveal to Jackie and me a shit-hole of a room, covered with almost a decade's worth of dirt and dust. The room was so full of refuse that you could only take a few steps inside. There were boxes piled from floor to ceiling. They were overflowing with brochures and promotional materials from the travel agency that had occupied the space before I moved in. A few old desks were stacked on top of each other and some chairs and shadeless lamps were resting on top of them. There was even a huge globe sitting on top of a bookcase that was missing two of its three shelves. It was a nice globe except someone had drawn a big X on a bunch of countries—Greenland, Ecuador, Nigeria, Lebanon, and a few others. I'm not sure if the destinations were places the person had already visited or places they wanted to visit. Or maybe they were places they wouldn't visit for a million dollars. My bet was on the latter.

"What a dump," Jackie snorted.

"It was like this when I moved in," I explained. "I figured that I would have to clean it out eventually, you know, when my practice grew, but well ..."

I didn't finish the excuse. I didn't have to. The fact that Jackie was moving into my office was evidence enough that my career hadn't exactly turned out like I had planned.

"It'll do," Jackie said with an air of contentment.

Over the next several hours Choo Choo and Jackie moved almost all of the items from the room and left them out on the curb. The only things left in the small office were one of the desks, an old lamp, and three chairs, one for Jackie's desk and two chairs for guests.

Jackie stood outside his office, next to me, and placed his arm around my shoulder. We looked at his newly established place of business.

"It looks just like yours," Jackie noted, beaming with pride.

He was right. Our offices were almost identical. There was no difference between us anymore. I had made Law Review at Columbia, Dean's List every semester. When Jackie was nineteen he was kicked out of Earl's Barber College for stabbing Earl in the neck with a pair of scissors. Now we were partners. And there was nothing I could do about it.

"You have to call Sanitation," I reminded Jackie.

"What for?"

"For all the crap you left outside. You can't just leave it there. You have to make arrangements with Special Pick-Up or the City will fine me."

"What Sanitation?" Jackie patronized. "The moulians will have that pile picked clean by midnight."

"Jackie, come on. A lot of my clients are black. You can't talk like that in here."

"Oh, sorry," Jackie mock apologized. "*Moulian-Americans.*"

Exasperated, I went back to my office and closed the door. I needed a break from Jackie and Choo Choo and all things stressful. I collapsed into my chair and closed my eyes. My break lasted all of ten seconds.

"Do you mind telling me what the hell is going on around here?!" Joey demanded, slamming my office door behind her.

"What?" I played dumb. I wasn't very good at it.

"Why the hell is Jackie Masella moving in here?"

"He needed some office space so I'm renting him the spare room for a couple hundred a month. We could use the money, or haven't you noticed?"

"Since when does someone need an office to break kneecaps?"

"That's not fair, Joey," I said, trying to sound insulted. "Every time an Italian makes a little bit of money in this country people automatically assume he's mobbed up. Does your brother Hector steal hubcaps for a living?"

"Bullshit," Joey shot back. "I *think* he's mobbed up because he *is* mobbed up. And you know it. And so does everyone in the neighborhood. And now he's gonna work outta our office."

Joey stared me down. Her Puerto Rican blood was boiling.

"*My* office," I reminded her. That was a real bullshit thing for me to say because Joey and I had been working together, trying to build up the firm together, since Day One.

"*Your* office? Okay, fine."

Joey spun and stormed to the door. She flung it open so that it smashed against the wall.

"And fuck you, too," she added before leaving. "My brother is in dental school."

Normally, Joey being angry with me would bother me enough that I'd take her out to lunch and try to smooth things out over a burger and fries. But once Jackie moved in, my attitude toward things started to change—I started to not give a fuck anymore.

I didn't care if Joey was angry with me. I didn't care that some mornings I'd show up at the office and find Jackie waiting for me with coffee and bagels and a litany of questions about how much money we were going to make and how soon we were going to make it. And I sure as hell didn't care about the law anymore, either. The same guy who used to scold his clients for merely exaggerating was now telling them to outright lie. The same guy who had to be lectured by Roland Cozzolino to not let his ethics get in the way was now flushing his ethics down the toilet.

Deep down, I knew that I was fucked. I had gotten myself into a situation that had no chance of working out for me. Even if I got away with it, and that was the best case scenario, I'd still be a felon—just not a *convicted* felon, and that distinction didn't really mean that much to me. I would have to look myself in the mirror every morning and know what I had done, what I had contributed to. So I decided that if I was going to jump off the cliff, it might as well be headfirst. At least then, I figured, as soon as I hit the ground I'd be out of this filthy business forever.

I realized I had hit rock bottom with the Oppenheimer deposition. Mrs. Gertrude Oppenheimer was eighty-two-years old and had fractured her hip in the New York City Public Library while attending a senior citizen's reading group. A fractured hip is a pretty good injury and the case would have been worth a lot if Oppenheimer wasn't so old. The actuary tables that the insurance carriers reference basically claim that a woman like Oppenheimer is living on borrowed time. Therefore, she shouldn't get much money for future pain and suffering because she doesn't have much future left. The older a client is, the less a case is worth.

Still, Oppenheimer's was a case you could settle for a quarter million dollars in New York, despite my client's advanced age, if you have a good liability argument. But, since Mrs. Oppenheimer was *my* client, naturally the liability against the city was for shit. So on the morning of the deposition, I took it upon myself to persuade Mrs. Oppenheimer to rethink what exactly happened to her the day that she fell.

"But I don't know how long the water was there," she kept telling me. "I just walked into the library, went to the fiction section, and slipped and fell. That's all I remember."

We had been at it for fifteen minutes and she wouldn't play ball. So I decided to play *hard*ball.

"Then you know what, Mrs. Oppenheimer? I'm going to cancel the deposition and you can find yourself another lawyer. Or you can listen to the lawyer you have now and go into this deposition and say you were in the library for an hour, went back into the fiction section, slipped, fell, and, while you were on the ground in *agonizing* pain, you realized that you had slipped on the *exact* puddle of water you had seen an hour earlier when you first went into that aisle to get your book. You say that, you have a case. You say anything else, you're wasting your time and mine."

"But isn't that dishonest?"

"Mrs. Oppenheimer, you're suing the City of New York. Do you have any idea how much money the city has? The city had a billion dollar surplus last year but there's the mayor on

TV saying he has to eliminate the senior citizen bus pass discount because of budget constraints. Don't you think *that's* being dishonest? You're just returning the favor."

At the time, I couldn't believe the words that were coming out of my mouth. This sweet old lady could have been my grandmother, for Christ's sake; she even sort of looked like her, well a German version of her anyway. Here I was, pressuring her to walk into a deposition, raise her right hand, swear to God that she would tell the truth, and then lie her ass off. I couldn't have been too disgusted with myself, though, because I let her do just that. I sat next to her during the deposition and watched a pretty, young court reporter type every lie Mrs. Oppenheimer told as if it were the Gospel truth.

I let it happen. I *caused* it to happen. And, at the time, I was glad it was happening. Like I said before, I had stopped caring and I just didn't give a fuck anymore. It had gotten that bad.

THIRTY

I RETURNED to my office after the Oppenheimer deposition and soon discovered that things were about to get substantially worse.

"Anyone call?" I asked.

Joey reached and pulled a half dozen phone message slips from a cubby hole. I sorted through them. One was from my father, one from Ginny, and four from Janine.

"Janine's not feeling well today," Joey offered. "I think her hormones have been having their way with her. I know when I was pregnant for the first time, some days I'd just sit on the couch and cry for hours. For no reason. I didn't even know what I was sad about. I just felt like crying."

I raised my eyebrows and gave a phony nod that was supposed to indicate some level of interest on my part and then continued on toward my office.

"I ran down to the corner and picked up some flowers. For

Janine. They're in your office. They'll make her feel better."

"You didn't need to do that."

"I didn't do it for you. I did it for her."

Joey was obviously still pissed at me. There was no use trying to reconcile until she cooled down, so I turned back toward my office. Joey stopped me again.

"Oh, and Mrs. Guzman called again today," she said, as she tore a phone message slip from her call log book.

I took the slip from Joey.

"God, she's a pain in the ass. Five friggin' calls a day," I muttered in a tone that was nastier than I intended.

"Maybe she wouldn't be such a pain in the ass if you called her back once in a while," Joey snipped.

"And maybe you haven't realized that I'm trying my best to keep this place afloat and don't have the time to return every goddamn phone call," I snapped.

I wasn't really mad at Joey, but she had picked the wrong day to play Latin Jiminy Cricket.

"And in case you have forgotten, Joey, I'm still the boss around here. And I expect to be treated like it."

I entered my office and slammed the door behind me but my troubles were squarely in front of me. Jackie was sitting behind my desk, smelling the flowers that I was supposed to give to my wife. The two chairs in front of my desk were occupied by a dark-complexioned man, who was clearly Italian, and a pasty-white redhead, whose ethnicity I could not immediately determine.

"What the hell is this?" I blurted out, not caring who I insulted.

Jackie jumped from my chair, full of energy, and practically ran over to me.

"Rob," he smiled, "I want you to meet Pino Finizio and

Patrick Higgins. They both fell from a scaffold at work, and they need legal representation."

I knew Jackie was lying and Higgins and Finizio knew he was lying. I also knew that Higgins and Finizio would, within the next few minutes, lie to me about their accidents and their injuries. Then I would soon lie to the court when I filed fraudulent complaints. And so on and so on, until we had created a chain of lies so vast, and so complex, that no one would be able to tell where one lie ended and another began.

"I told these guys," Jackie continued, "that they had to go see my cousin Bobby. That he's the best lawyer in Brooklyn. Didn't I say that, fellas?"

"That he did," Higgins confirmed in a thick Irish brogue, giving away his country of origin.

"Jackie told us you're the best," Finizio added.

I looked to Jackie. "Can you give us a little privacy, please?" I said, but I wasn't really asking him to leave.

I was telling him. If I was going to risk my ass, I decided, it was going to be on my terms. Jackie was already set up in my office, and there was nothing I could do about that. But I'd be damned if I was going to let him sit in on my meetings with clients. I still had some pride. At least that's what I was trying to convince myself of.

"I thought I'd stick around," Jackie challenged me. "I'm curious about the law. It might be interesting to watch you work."

Jackie sat down on the windowsill, arms crossed in a position of defiance. But I wasn't going to lose this battle. I'd lost too many recently. My conscience, my ethics, my soul— they had all lost battles to my fears, my insecurities, my greed. I wanted to win for once, just to see if I remembered what it felt like.

"I appreciate your interest but this is a confidential conversation with my clients. I'll come get you when I'm done," I fired back sternly.

Jackie stared at me for a few moments, furious that I had defied him in front of men who were supposed to be afraid of him. But he gave in. He had to. As long as the clients thought I wasn't involved in the scam, Jackie couldn't boss me around in front of them.

"Yeah, sure," Jackie said trying to save face. "I got a few things I need to take care of anyway."

Jackie stood and walked behind Higgins and Finizio. He put a hand on each of their shoulders and bent down so that his head was wedged between theirs.

"Now remember what we talked about, boys. All you gotta do is tell my cousin here *exactly* what happened. Just like you told me. And he'll take care of everything. And all your problems will be over. Got it?" Jackie shook each man playfully and then gave them both a hard slap on the back.

"Be good, Prince," Jackie said as he exited my office.

That was a strange parting command—*be good*. It had been so long since I had been good I wasn't even sure if I remembered how. At that point in my life, I didn't know if I could have been good if I tried.

I sat in my chair and opened my desk drawer that contained all of my preprinted forms. I pulled out two Retainer Agreements and handed them to Finizio and Higgins. This time I didn't experience nearly the hesitation I had felt when I signed up Tangelino as a client. Breaking the law had become much easier.

The two men handed the signed retainers back to me and I placed them in a folder. I was now a *serial* felon.

I didn't like it. I would have preferred to make my money

legitimately, but I had tried that and it didn't work. And every time I felt like I wanted to end the whole thing, I thought of Ginny and her situation and Janine and our own unborn child. Whenever I did that, I convinced myself that what I was doing was only temporary; that the people I was dealing with weren't really all that dangerous and that insurance fraud didn't really hurt anyone other than faceless corporations. I lied to myself like that all the time. And it worked. I had become quite adept at lying.

So it had come time to hear the lies of Higgins and Finizio. I was curious to see if Jackie had become any better at coaching his witnesses, because Tangelino had been horrible. I grabbed a yellow legal pad and a pen from a small ceramic jar Janine had made for me when we were first dating. I asked my new clients a few simple background questions about their accidents and injuries. But I didn't write down anything they said. I wanted to. I had planned to. But I couldn't because I was in shock. I couldn't believe what they were telling me.

THIRTY-ONE

JACKIE WAS AT his desk reading the sports section of the *New York Post* when I flung his office door open so hard that it bounced against the wall and slammed back closed behind me.

"Answer me one simple question," I shouted at him, face red with anger, spit shooting from my lips. "Are you fuckin' stupid?"

"Whoa, whoa, whoa." Jackie stood and cocked his head. He wasn't used to anyone, especially me, talking to him like this. "What did you just say?"

"Both of these guys you sent me just happened to fall down on the same exact job site as Salvatore Tangelino? Are you fuckin' crazy? Do you *want* to get caught?!"

Jackie walked out from behind his desk and approached me.

"First of all, calm down before you say something you'll regret," Jackie said calmly as he flipped an unlit cigarette between his lips. "I figured that the Tangelino case went so well, I'd send these guys to the same construction site as him. We already know that the foreman ain't too sharp because he filled out an accident report for Tangelino, no questions asked. And we know that the insurance company for that site likes to settle. I was using my head. I'd think you'd be grateful I thought it through."

Jackie lit his cigarette, breathed in deeply, and exhaled a stream of smoke that rose just above my head. He had a very satisfied look on his face, as if he had it all figured out. But what he didn't know could have filled a warehouse.

"Insurance companies aren't run by fuckin' morons, you jackass," I yelled. "Three accidents within five months of each other?! All of them fall from scaffold cases?! All of them hurt on first day on the job?! And to top it off, they're all represented by the same goddamn attorney?! You don't think the carrier will look into this?!"

"If anyone starts askin' questions, we'll say these guys knew Tangelino from the neighborhood and they asked him which attorney he used when he got hurt," Jackie pooh-poohed me.

"It's not that simple; we could get caught!"

"We won't get caught."

"Can you promise me that?!"

"Lower your voice," Jackie warned.

"Fuck you!" I shouted. "You can forget this entire thing! I'm not representing these guys. It's too goddamn dangerous!"

I turned and went for the door but, before I could reach it, I felt a force lift me off my feet and drive me face first into the wall. I was spun around, totally dazed, to find Jackie holding me by the lapels of my suit jacket. He had me jacked up against the wall so the tips of my toes barely touched the floor.

"Now you listen to me, you miserable little fuck!" Jackie whispered in my ear. "You can piss and moan all you want, but you're gonna represent those two guys or I'll fuckin' kill you! I am not fuckin' around! I will stab you in the heart until you are fuckin' dead! Do you understand me?"

I nodded silently. Jackie glared at me. I could see my reflection in his brown eyes—I looked scared as hell. I was finally, after all these years, seeing the side of Jackie I had only heard about.

"You think I give a shit about you and your stupid law license? You think I care about your fuckin' firm? All I know is that these two guys owe my boss money, and I told him that me and my cousin would get him that money and then some! So if you think you can just walk away now, think again, Counselor! Because if you fuck things up with me and Louie Turro, I will fuckin' kill you without thinking twice about it!"

I didn't dare move. I just stared back at Jackie, my eyes searching his for any trace of the kid I flipped baseball cards with in the alley behind Genovese Drug Store, the kid who used to race Schwinns with me up and down Bay Parkway. But that Jackie was gone. His eyes were lifeless; they had changed; they were dead, sort of like when a shark's eyes roll back and turn white before it attacks its prey. I stared deep into my cousin's soul, and I did not see a single remnant of the Jackie I knew.

His breath shot from his mouth in short, hot bursts against my face. The scent of Aqua Velva and cigarettes filled my nostrils. He said nothing else. He knew he had made his point. He unclenched his hands and the soles of my shoes fell hard against the floor. He took two steps backward, away from me, but he never let his eyes stray from mine.

I straightened the lapels of my jacket and tried to flatten

the creases Jackie had caused. I noticed Jackie's cigarette smoldering on the carpet. He must have dropped it when he charged me from behind. Jackie's eyes followed my gaze to the cigarette. He took a step and ground the butt into the carpet.

He was marking his territory. He might as well have lifted his leg and taken a piss on the floor. The charade was over. This was his office now. It was his firm. He was the alpha male. He knew it and I knew it. There was nothing left for me to do but leave. So I did. But I was hardly done with Jackie. Not by a long shot.

THIRTY-TWO

THE OFFICE was much more intimidating the second time around. When I got there, the television wasn't on. The first time I had met with BLT, I found it very comforting that I could hear Chris Berman's voice rattling off rushing and passing stats in the background. It was as if the television was a lifeline to the world outside the dimly lit Office. This time, The Office was quiet—no television, no radio, no sound at all.

It also didn't help that Jackie was there. When I entered The Office that afternoon, my cousin was already sitting at the marble-topped table. It was the first time I had seen him since he had pushed me around about a week earlier. I purposely had been avoiding my office during the times when I knew he'd be there.

"Hey," I said, unenthusiastically.

He didn't even look up at me. He reached into his pocket, took out a nickel, and spun it like a top by flicking his thumb and forefinger. I knew he'd be pissed at me for asking Big Lou for this meeting but Jackie had left me no choice. He had caused the meeting to take place as much as I had.

I sat down next to him at the table. He still wouldn't acknowledge me. He just watched the spinning nickel, hypnotized by its movement. Sometimes the coin would spin for almost two minutes before it came to a stop. When it did, Jackie would snatch it up and spin it again. This continued, without a word spoken between us, for about fifteen minutes, until BLT entered with Choo Choo lumbering behind him.

"Bobby Junior," Big Louie called out. "How are you?"

Jackie snatched up the nickel and shoved it back in his pocket.

"Good. Thank you. How are you?" I stood and extended my hand. BLT once again served up a soft handshake.

"Couldn't beat my life with a stick," he joked.

Jackie stood as well but his boss just gave him a slight nod and then sat down across from me.

"So, how are those two new cases I gave you coming along?" he asked, getting right down to business.

"The complaints were served yesterday."

"Already? That's pretty fast, no?"

"Well, it was fairly easy drafting the documents. The facts of each case were pretty much identical. Same location, same injuries. All I had to do was change the names."

I glanced quickly at Jackie. He was staring at me. If looks could kill, I'd have fallen dead to the floor right there.

"I understand this was a problem for you," Louie noted.

"It's a problem for all of us. Such similar cases, they make us vulnerable to detection."

"I agree." Louie looked at Jackie, clearly displeased. "I'm also unhappy with how this was handled, but I've dealt with it.

I can assure you it won't happen again."

Jackie looked down at the floor, like a scolded child. Big Lou turned his attention to me just as Choo Choo was placing a white cereal bowl full of cashews on the table. Lou stuck his thick hand into the bowl and came up with a grasp full of nuts. He tilted his head back, unclenched his fist, and let the cashews pour like a waterfall into his open mouth.

"You want some?" he asked after he had swallowed.

"No, thanks."

"I can't get enough of these things," he said as he grabbed another handful. "A lot of people think that nuts are bad for you. Too much fat. Too many calories. But, you see, nuts have the good kind of fat. Saturated. Or is it unsaturated? I'm not sure. But it's the kind your body needs. I love 'em."

Lou threw another dozen cashews into his mouth. He seemed to swallow them without chewing.

"So, if that's all ..." Louie concluded in a tone that sounded like he had just wrapped up a shareholders' meeting or some other legitimate business venture. He pushed back from the table and began to rise.

"Actually, that's not all," I said, causing Lou to sit back down.

"What else is there?" he asked, a bit annoyed I hadn't let him get on to wherever he was going.

"We need to stay away from construction for a while."

"Why?"

"Because insurance carriers talk. They share information. They've got computers loaded with statistics and data on everything from accident probability to the success rates of every law firm in the state. If a small firm like mine starts getting big numbers on identical construction cases, it'll turn some heads. And then we'll be in trouble."

"What do you suggest?"

"Laying low. I'll see all your cases through to the end like I promised. And then that's it. We end it before we get caught."

I waited for his response. I wanted so badly for him to agree with me. I prayed silently that he would smile, tell me to just discontinue the cases I had already filed, and move on with my life. But he didn't. Instead, he scratched himself behind his right ear and scrunched up his face like he was thinking. Then he lowered his hand and rubbed the side of his neck while he looked at me, squinting his eyes, as if he was really considering my proposal. I knew he wasn't.

"That isn't possible," he said. "Because we have a bit of a situation."

"What kind of situation?" I asked, knowing that whatever situation it was, it was the kind of situation I'd want no part of.

"About a year ago, the Falzone brothers borrowed some money from me to start a bricklaying business. You know them?"

"Dom and Frankie-boy? Yeah. They used to live across from the school yard."

"Still do. They're good boys. But bad businessmen. They've had some difficulties meeting their payment schedule. So Jackie approached them recently with two options. The first option dealt with the arrangement we have set up with you, and the second option, well, let's just say they had no interest whatsoever in the second option," Louie laughed.

Choo Choo chuckled along with him like a big fat parrot.

"But we can't do any more of these construction cases. I just told you why."

"You're a smart boy," Big Lou patronized. "I'm sure you can come up with something else. Something that doesn't raise any more suspicion."

"But Lou ..."

"I gave these guys an option, Bobby, and they took it. I can't go back on my word. Just like you can't go back on yours."

Big Lou shoved another handful of nuts in his mouth and stood.

"Feel free to stay and watch the game on the big screen if you want. I gotta run."

He was so full of shit. He didn't care about keeping his word. He was a criminal. He probably broke his word a dozen times a day before breakfast. All he cared about was getting a lot more money than the Falzones actually owed him. And I was the guy who was supposed to get him that money.

Instead of leaving The Office with no obligations to Big Lou, I had somehow managed to pick up two more. And he wasn't going to let me lawyer my way out of it. Besides, I couldn't. I had given him my word, remember?

THIRTY-THREE

"WHY DON'T YOU turn a light on or something?" Louie asked.

"Bulb's burnt," I lied. "The streetlights shine through the windows, though. You'll be able to see fine at my desk."

The truth was I didn't turn the lights on because I didn't want anyone working late in one of the buildings across the street to see me meeting with Lou Turro and Jackie Masella in my office.

The few days since my last trip to The Office had been exhausting. Ginny was due in a couple of weeks and her doctors had basically confined her to strict bed rest. Janine and my parents did all they could for her but my wife was feeling run down herself and my parents were getting on in years and could only do so much. I found myself coming home to two very pregnant, very unhappy women who needed my care.

Late night runs to White Castle had become commonplace

and I'd rubbed more swollen feet than a podiatrist at a fat farm. To make things worse, I wasn't getting any sleep. Sleeping with a pregnant woman was something for which I was totally unprepared. Actually, it's probably more accurate to say *not sleeping* with a pregnant woman was something for which I was totally unprepared.

Every night was a production. Her back hurt. Her sides hurt. Her legs hurt. And when she finally did doze off, all she'd have to do was roll over half a turn and I'd wake up to find myself holding onto the side of the bed for dear life, trying to prevent a very unpleasant three-foot fall to the floor.

On top of all this, since construction cases had been ruled out, I had to come up with a new way to defraud the legal system that would satisfy BLT. Amazingly, I thought of something quickly. For a guy who never planned on breaking the law his entire life, I was finding that I had quite an affinity for it. That was why I had Lou and Jackie come by my office that night, so that I could present my new plan.

I walked behind my desk and pushed the chair out of the way. Lou stood to my left, Jackie to my right. From my top drawer, I took a large piece of paper that had been folded up several times and placed it on my desk.

"What's that?" Jackie asked.

Those were the first words he'd spoken to me since the day he pushed me around in his office. I was actually startled to hear his voice. I had figured he was going to give me the cold shoulder for the rest of my life.

"It's a *Big Apple Pothole and Sidewalk Protection Committee* map."

"What's *that*?" Jackie repeated, growing a little impatient.

I turned to my cousin. Standing next to him like that, in the dark, felt strange—to suddenly be in such a close, intimate situation with him after I had been avoiding him for the prior two weeks.

"Remember when we were kids?" I asked him. "When my grandpa would tell us how he stowed away to America in the boiler room of that ship, living for weeks on nothing but rice and water a deckhand would sneak down to him?"

"Yeah? Uncle Ralph was an illegal, so what?"

"What did he always say whenever we asked him why he did it? Why he went through all that just to come to this country?"

Jackie smiled. I could tell he was thinking about my grandfather—picturing his big nose; square, handsome jawline; bald, shiny head; and the warmest chocolate-colored eyes in the world. He had no blood relationship with Jackie—he was my mother's father. But he lived down the street from me and around the corner from Jackie, and Grandpa treated us both like his grandsons. We both loved him very much. And we were both devastated the day he died.

"Yeah, I remember," Jackie grinned. "He'd say: *In America, the streets were paved with gold.*"

"He was close," I said. "But the gold isn't in the streets." I unfolded the map and tapped it with my finger. "It's in the sidewalks."

Lou and Jackie looked down at the map laid out in front of them. It covered a four-block area of the Bronx, on Grand Concourse, just east of the County Courthouse. There were all kinds of markings on the map—squiggly lines, arrows, circles with slashes through them—like some kind of urban hieroglyphics.

"I don't follow," Lou chimed in.

"If you trip and fall on a crack in the sidewalk, you can sue the City of New York," I said.

"Get the fuck out of here. I'll go outside and fall down right now," Jackie cracked.

"It's not that easy. You've seen the sidewalks; it looks like fucking Beirut out there. If people could sue every time they fell because of a crack, the city would go bankrupt. So the city passed a law saying they aren't responsible for any injuries unless the city had fifteen days prior written notice of the defect that made the person fall."

"Who the hell is gonna write a letter to the city to tell them about some crack they saw in the sidewalk?" Big Lou asked.

"That's what the city was banking on," I explained. "They figured if they passed this bullshit law, they'd be home free; no one could sue them. But what the legislators didn't count on was the response they'd get from the only group of people scummier than them."

Jackie and Lou stared at me. Their blank expressions conveyed their lack of understanding.

"Plaintiff lawyers," I explained. "They didn't count on plaintiff lawyers. After the law was passed the plaintiff's bar organized the Big Apple Pothole and Sidewalk Protection Committee."

"You lost me again," Jackie confessed.

"They're the group who made this map. They pay college kids to take a map of a couple of blocks of any one of the five boroughs and mark it up with every goddamn crack in the sidewalks."

I pointed to some of the markings on the map.

"A circle means a hole in the sidewalk; a squiggly line means the sidewalk is raised or uneven. This thing here means that a chunk of curb is missing. When the map is complete, Big Apple Pothole sends it to the city and says, 'Here's your friggin' fifteen days prior written notice, now choke on it.'"

Lou grabbed the map and held it up to the window. The streetlights' illumination made it almost glow in the dark. His eyes darted up and down and across the map, scanning all of the intricate markings and symbols. Jackie looked along with him.

"You gotta be shittin' me," Lou snorted.

"I'm telling you the truth. I've got dozens of these maps. And I can get one for any section of the city that I want. They're public record. All I gotta do is make a Freedom of Information request or I can just buy 'em from the committee."

"So, every one of these marks is a potential gold mine?" Lou asked, almost drooling.

"Well, not a gold mine, but a chance at some nice money, yes."

"I shoulda gone to law school," Jackie said quietly to himself, eyes wide, staring at the map.

Lou let the map drop to the desk.

"How do you see this playing out?" he wanted to know.

"All we have to do is take a map, find a big hole in the sidewalk, have the Falzone brothers walk by, and they both trip on it and fall down. We'll pick a nice public spot with lots of pedestrian traffic. That way we'll have totally independent witnesses who will think they saw a legitimate accident. Dom and Frankie will roll around on the ground in pain, holding their backs or their knees or whatever, and I'll send them over to see Dr. Bass. And the city won't be able to claim they didn't have prior notice of the hole because we'll know they already had a map that informed them of that very defect—a defect we handpicked ourselves. It'll be open and shut."

"But what about the insurance companies?" Lou asked. "Don't we still have to worry about them catching on?"

"That's the best part," I said. "There are no insurance companies. The city is self-insured."

Lou happily clapped his huge hands together. It sounded like someone had dropped a dictionary onto a wooden table. He kissed me on the cheek. Jackie watched, grinning.

"I love this guy!" Lou shouted.

"He's a smart guy, my cousin. I told you he'd hook us up," Jackie added, trying to score points with his boss while he was in a good mood.

"He is smart. Maybe you can learn something from him," Lou said as he headed for my door.

Jackie's grin instantly disappeared.

"Okay, boys, it's late. I'm headin' home. Jackie, you'll keep me posted."

"You got it, Big Louie."

Big Lou gave a quick wave of the hand and walked out of my office. An incredibly awkward silence filled the void left by his departure. I folded up the map and slipped it into my desk drawer. Jackie stood silently watching me. I pretended to sort through some paperwork that was in my in-box in the hopes that Jackie would just leave, but he didn't. Instead, he put his hand on my shoulder.

"Prince, about the other day," he started. "I just want to say, I may have been a little out of line."

"A little out of line?" I asked incredulously, suddenly emboldened by Jackie's act of contrition. "Jackie, you threatened to kill me."

"I may have misspoke."

I shook my head and blew some air through a small crack in my lips as a sign of my disbelief in Jackie's sincerity. I grabbed my jacket and took a few steps.

"I gotta go."

"No, wait," Jackie pleaded, grabbing my jacket from my hands and throwing it back onto my chair. "You gotta understand where I'm coming from, man."

"And where's that?" I shoved my hands into my pockets and waited for an answer, stone-faced. If Jackie was looking for my forgiveness, he was going to have to earn it. Mob or no mob, Jackie was family, and when he attacked me he crossed a line.

"This scam, Bobby, it's my baby. *I* brought it in to the crew. Not Choo Choo. Not Tony. *Me*. Ya know, I've never really been a favorite of Louie's. The best that can be said is that he tolerates me because I don't mind doin' some of his dirty work for him. But if this thing we got here, if it works out, and we all make money on it, I'll get my button."

I stared at Jackie, unmoved.

"You know what that's like, Bobby?" he continued.

Jackie tilted his head up and looked at the ceiling, as if divine intervention would help him answer his own question. After a moment, he lowered his head.

"That's like Law Review for the Mafia," he said wistfully.

"Good for you. I hope you get it," I said, unimpressed.

I wasn't giving this guy an inch. I wasn't going to let him off the hook that easily. I probably would have held my ground except I was totally unprepared for what happened next. Jackie started to cry. Right there in my office. Right in front of me. A few tears at first and then a steady stream. Within seconds he was sucking in his breath and wiping his nose with his sleeve.

I'd never seen him cry in my entire life. I didn't think he even possessed the basic human emotions necessary to enable someone to cry. But there he was, crying his eyes out. And there I was, standing two feet away, watching him. Just me and Jackie Masella, one of the soldiers of the Turro crime family, and he was bawling like a baby. I would have been less surprised if he had bent over and pulled a pelican out of his ass. I didn't dare say a word. For all I knew, now that I'd seen him bawl, he'd have to kill me. As it turned out, I didn't have to say anything. Jackie did all the talking.

"You think it was easy for me when you went away to college?" he shouted between sobs. "Huh? It was real hard on me. I bet you didn't know that, but it was. Not only did I lose my cousin, my *friend*, but all I heard every fuckin' day from everyone in the family, everyone in the neighborhood, was '*Why don't you go to college like Bobby? Why don't you make something of yourself like Bobby?*'"

Jackie grabbed a tissue from a box on my desk, blew mightily, and continued.

"Never mind that I can hardly fuckin' read, they want me to go to college. And then, when you moved back to New York to go to Columbia, it got even worse. '*Bobby's in the Ivy League; Bobby's gonna be a rich lawyer, what are you gonna be?*'"

"I'm sorry. I had no idea it was like that for you," I said.

"I'm ashamed to even say it," Jackie confessed. "But when I heard things at your firm weren't goin' so good for you, there was a part of me that was glad."

Jackie sat on the edge of my desk and looked down at the floor. He pinched the bridge of his nose with his fingers and sobbed into his hand some more, but more violently this time. When he looked up, his face was red and his mouth was open but when he cried, no sound came out. A line of saliva stretched from his upper lip to his lower. He had trouble getting the words out between sobs. Jackie was making his penance, which was fine with me, except I had somehow become his priest.

"There were times, in the past, when I wanted you to fail so bad," he continued. "So our family would shut the fuck up about you already. But that made me hate myself. Because I shouldn't have wished bad things for you. I love you. Like you're my brother."

"That's alright" was all I could think of to say. I mean, God, what could I have said?

"No, it isn't. But when you came up with this plan, I was so goddamn excited. I figured we could make our fortunes *together*, show everybody, ya know? That's what I wanted. That's why I got so upset when you said you were gonna bail out. That's all."

Jackie took a step closer to me and put a hand on each of my shoulders. I looked at his eyes. They were red and swollen. His face was wet.

"You gotta know I'd never really hurt you, don't ya Bobby? You're my little cousin. I love you. I'd never hurt you. My dad would be so ashamed of me for saying what I said to you that day. Please, you gotta forgive me."

Jackie hugged me tight, his head hanging over my shoulder. I thought that maybe he truly felt bad for attacking me or maybe he was in the middle of a nervous breakdown. I didn't really care what the reason was for his sudden emotional outburst. I just wanted it over. I just wanted to get away from him and go home. I had never been so uncomfortable in my entire life.

"Please forgive me," Jackie said again.

"Sure, Jackie. Sure. I forgive you."

I patted my cousin on the back. He let go of me, his head hanging. He softly said "thanks" into his chest and left my office. I watched him from my window as he walked down the dark, empty Brooklyn street by himself. When he got to the corner he turned and looked up at my office. I thought about stepping back into the shadows so he couldn't see me, but I was too slow.

Jackie raised his hand and gave me a slight wave. It was a bizarre gesture, considering what had just happened between us. Jackie just stood under the streetlight, looking up at me, waiting for a response. I didn't want to acknowledge him, but I knew I had to. So I lifted my hand slowly, palm facing out toward the window.

Even from that distance I was able to see Jackie's eyes brighten. He smiled widely, the moonlight making his teeth look fluorescent.

A city street sweeper rumbled down the deserted block, right in front of my cousin, blocking my view of him. It passed, and Jackie was gone.

THIRTY-FOUR

LIKE MOST sane young men, I never desired, at any point in my life, to see my sister's vagina. But there it was, staring me in the face like some terrifying vortex to another dimension. I thought I was going to faint.

"Pretty amazing, isn't it," Doctor Berman asked, as he held my wrist with one hand and pointed to Ginny's crotch with the other.

I couldn't answer. I was afraid that if I opened my mouth I'd vomit into my surgical mask. I also think I was partially hypnotized by the bloody, contorted, and persistently growing mess that was somehow a combination of my sister's genitalia and her soon-to-be-born child, because I wanted nothing more than to leave the delivery room but for some reason my feet wouldn't move.

"I thought you should get a good look at the miracle of birth," the doctor continued. "So many fathers are afraid of the process, but it's really quite remarkable."

"Oh. No. I'm not the father" was all I was able to muster.

"The father's an asshole!" Ginny shrieked, one of six dozen ear-piercing screams she had let out in a five-minute period.

"Jesus Christ, Doc, what the hell is that kid doing to her?" I asked.

"She's doing fine. She just needs to push real hard next time."

"Fuck you! You push!" Ginny offered.

Dr. Berman looked up at me from his position between my sister's legs.

"Go on up there and talk to her," he whispered. "Encourage her."

I gladly left the junior high health-class film that was taking place below Ginny's waist and stood next to her. She grabbed my hand tightly, rolled her head to the side, and looked at me.

"I can't do it anymore," she said.

"Sure you can."

"No, I can't."

"Yes, you can. Remember when we were kids, at the beach, and those rich bastards from Nassau County bet you couldn't hold your breath underwater for two minutes? And you did it? And afterward you said your lungs hurt like hell."

"So?!" Ginny was in no mood for a trip down memory lane.

"So this is gonna hurt a hell of a lot more. But it will take a lot less than two minutes."

What do you want from me? That was the best I could come up with. Ginny looked at me like I was crazy.

"You've never backed away from a challenge, Gin," I reminded her. "That's all this is. I know you can do it. I believe in you. Always have."

Ginny smiled. Not with her mouth, but with her eyes. They were hopeful again. I knew she was about to give it another go. She gave Dr. Berman a nod.

"Okay, push," he commanded.

I have never in my life seen the shade of purple that my sister's face turned at that moment. She tried with all of her might to not only push that kid out of her body, but I swear I think she was trying to shoot it across the room and through the goddamn wall. Ginny gripped my hand tighter. Her fingernails dug into my flesh. She actually drew a little blood.

A monstrous, high-pitched wail filled the room and most likely, the entire floor of the hospital. One of the nurses actually covered her ears. It was at least ten seconds until I realized that I was the one screaming.

"Okay, Mommy," Dr. Berman beamed. "You're done."

Like a magician, the doctor popped out from behind a stirrup-framed white curtain with my niece in his arms. She was bloody and slimy and screaming her freaking head off. And she possessed the facial features commonly associated with a Down syndrome newborn. She was the most beautiful baby I had ever seen.

A short Samoan nurse handed me a pair of surgical scissors.

"What are these for?" I asked.

"To cut the umbilical cord. It's customary for the father to do it."

"I told you, I'm not the father. I'm the uncle …"

"You do it, Bobby," Ginny said. "I want you to do it."

In her weakened state, my sister was able to manage a small smile. How could I say no? So I made the cut. Blood squirted from the cord and splattered onto my face. Twenty seconds later I had my first encounter with smelling salts.

THIRTY-FIVE

THINGS COULDN'T have gone any better after Michelle was born. I was handling the four bogus clients for Lou Turro, but I had also started getting some incredibly valuable cases through the new Yellow Pages ad I had taken out. It had the heading "Accident Lawyer" in huge type with my picture next to it. Under my picture I listed all of the various cases I handled: Automobile, Construction, Medical Malpractice, Trip/Slip & Fall, Worker's Compensation, and so on. Granted, it wasn't the most tasteful ad but it was working like a charm.

Case after case started coming in and each one was better than the last. They all had the three things you need in a personal injury suit—bad injuries, good liability, and insurance coverage up the ass. Janine said the ad was so effective because I looked so handsome in my picture. However, others disagreed.

"Holy shit, look at the size of your forehead," Roland

mocked one afternoon while checking out the ad. "You're really losing it up there, aren't you?"

"I can get a hair piece, but you'll always be as ugly as homemade sin."

"Seriously, man. Your forehead's gigantic. You could play handball off it."

"Alright, that's enough."

I snatched the phone book from Roland and tossed it in the corner.

"Picture might be ugly but the ad's damn effective. Look what's come in just the past few weeks."

I grabbed three new files from my desk and dropped them in his lap. I sat and watched Roland read through the first file. His eyes grew wide with excitement, possibly even envy. I loved every minute of it.

"Fractured leg with open reduction, internal fixation surgery." Roland whistled. "That's a good injury."

"Check out the next one," I taunted.

"Fractured skull with thirty-six stitches!" Roland nearly jumped out of his chair.

"They only get better."

Roland scanned the last file. "Six fractured vertebrae!" he shouted like a kid who just discovered his favorite player's baseball card in a newly opened pack. "These are all from your stupid ad?"

"My picture can't be that bad, can it?"

"I don't get nearly this much action from my ad," Roland lamented.

"Why don't you rent some space on my huge forehead," I joked. "I'd be like a big walking billboard for you."

Roland laughed.

"I'm happy for you, man," he said. "It's been a long time coming. You deserve it."

I sat behind my desk and took a sip of lukewarm coffee, not remembering that it had been sitting out all morning. I was in such a good mood it didn't even bother me.

"I can't explain it," I smiled. "I can barely keep up with the work. That's why I wanted to talk to you."

"About what?"

"The per diem work I've been doing for you. I can't take it on anymore. I'm just too damn busy."

"Good, I'm glad. You're above that shit, anyway."

"I just want you to know how much I appreciate you sending the work my way when I needed it." I extended my hand to Roland. We shook.

"Hey, it wasn't charity, pal. You're a damn good attorney. Everybody seemed to know that but you. Glad to see you're finally coming around."

Roland turned to leave but his path was blocked by Joey. Roland had always had the hots for my secretary. The feeling wasn't mutual. She thought Roland was the kind of sleazy lawyer who made the whole profession look bad. If she only knew the kind of guy she was working for.

"Hey, sweetheart. When are you and I gonna get that drink we've been talking about?" Roland grinned.

"You've been talking about it. Not me," Joey said as she skirted past her suitor and into my office. "We have a walk-in. Construction accident. Crushed right-hand injury with surgery. Said he saw our ad in the Yellow Pages."

Roland looked at me in disbelief.

"Un-fuckin-believable!" he shouted. "What did you do? Make a deal with the devil or something?"

"When it rains it pours, my friend. When it rains, it pours. Bring him on in, Joey."

Roland flashed an unreciprocated smile at Joey as she

passed him on her way back into the reception area. He looked at me, shrugged, and followed her out.

I couldn't help but laugh. I was married to the greatest woman in the world. I was my own boss. I had the kind of job where my best friend could stop by in the middle of the day for a visit. And seven-figure cases were falling from the sky like raindrops, and I was about to sign up another one. Life was so damn good I couldn't stand it.

And then Mr. Luongo walked in and everything turned to shit again.

His right arm was in a cast and in a sling. There were at least a half dozen screws and pins sticking out of his hand and wrist in all directions. I almost burst into tears of joy when I saw him.

That's the problem with the personal injury game. You need your clients to be badly hurt because the worse off they are the more money you stand to make. You find yourself praying for rain so roads get slick and wishing for snow storms so ice patches form on walkways. You spend your career hoping for human pain and suffering to take place. It's a miserable way to make a living.

I extended my hand. He weakly grabbed it with his left hand and made no real attempt to shake it. His hand was very soft for a construction worker.

"Nice to meet you, sir. I'm Rob Principe."

"Giovanni Luongo."

Luongo was in his late forties, about five-foot-eight, one hundred sixty pounds. He wore his salt-and-pepper hair slicked back with the aid of some kind of medicinal-smelling hair gel. He was neatly dressed, but his worn shoes and the frayed cuffs on his shirt and pants made it clear he didn't have a lot of money.

"Seems like you have a pretty bad injury there." I figured stating the obvious was the best way to get the ball rolling since Mr. Luongo didn't seem to be a talkative fellow.

"Yeah, it's pretty bad."

"Why don't you sit down and tell me what happened?"

Mr. Luongo sat very gingerly, taking care not to strike his cast on the arm of the chair.

"Well," he began, "I was working on a construction site, when my hand, it was busted when …"

"I don't mean to interrupt," I apologized, "but do I know you from somewhere? You look very familiar."

"No, I don't think so."

"Are you sure? I could swear I've met you somewhere before."

"No, I'm pretty sure we've never met."

"I'm sorry. Please, go on."

Mr. Luongo proceeded to tell me how he had been working on a construction site, on his hands and knees picking up scrap wood for the foreman, when a dumpster keeled over and landed on his hand, breaking every bone except his thumb. His wrist was broken in two places, as well. He said the dumpster was missing a wheel, and that it had tipped over because it was unbalanced.

He was lying to me. I knew this before he was even half way through his story. Finally I had figured out where I had seen him before—at Patsy's. The same day I got the call from Paul Stevens about the late mortgage payments. The same day I first got the idea for the con. The same day I saw Jackie standing in Patsy's doorway slapping a man whose face was partially obscured by the glare of exterior sunlight. But I was able to make out enough of his face that day. Enough to know that the man sitting across from me, lying about how the bones of his hand were turned to dust, was the man I saw that day at Patsy's getting cracked across the face by my cousin.

Jackie had broken Mr. Luongo's hand, not some defective dumpster. Mr. Luongo knew that. And so did I. But we could never tell each other what we both knew.

I felt queasy. Not the normal stomach problems I experienced from anxiety. This felt more like sea sickness. My face became beaded with sweat. I took a tissue and dabbed at my brow. Luongo kept talking but I was no longer paying attention. I steadied myself and stood from my chair.

"Excuse me," I said.

"You okay?" Luongo asked.

I must have looked as pale as I felt.

"Yeah. I just need to take care of something. I'll be right back."

I left my office and walked down to Jackie's. His door was closed. For some strange reason, that really pissed me off. It was as if by closing the door, Jackie was somehow shutting me out from part of my own firm. My nausea quickly changed to anger. I entered and slammed the door behind me.

Jackie was at his desk, kicked back in his chair, nonchalantly reading the *New York Jury Verdict Reporter*, a legal trade publication.

"Hey," he scolded, looking up from his reading. "Take it easy on the door."

"You broke Giovanni Luongo's hand!" I accused.

Jackie knew that I was angry as hell because he didn't even try to lie his way out of it.

"Was that wrong?" he asked glibly.

"You think this is funny, you idiot?!" I shouted. "Are you insane? I'm not gonna represent people after you beat the shit out of them! I will not be an accessory to criminal assault!"

"Yeah, I figured you'd react this way so I took the liberty of keeping you in the dark these past few weeks," my cousin explained unapologetically.

"What the fuck are you talking about?"

Jackie swung his legs off his desk and stood up. He laughed condescendingly.

"Prince, you can't possibly believe all these great cases that have been coming in have been from the pathetic ad you took out in the phone book."

Instantly, one of my knees buckled and my temples started pulsating rapidly, like there were mosquitoes trapped under my skin that wanted to break through to freedom. It felt for a moment that the floor was turning to Jello and it would swallow me whole. If that had happened, I probably wouldn't have struggled against it. At the time I would have welcomed the finality of a sticky, gelatinous coffin. I reached behind me blindly and felt for the chair. I found it, pulled it closer, and sat.

Jackie walked out from behind the desk and sat next to me. He placed a hand on my knee.

"Don't take it so hard," he said. "Who cares where your business comes from as long as business is brisk, right?"

"Which ones?" I asked softly, staring at the ground.

"What difference does it make?"

"Which ones?" I repeated.

"I think it best you don't know."

"Which ones, damn it?"

Jackie searched my eyes. I believe he really didn't want to tell me, as if telling me would hurt me even further. The strange thing is, to this day, I believe Jackie truly cared for me in his own dysfunctional way.

"All of them," he said.

My heart sank.

"Mr. Kress?"

"The broken leg with surgery? That one was mine. Except instead of a cinder block falling off the back of a flatbed truck, it was Choo Choo whackin' him with a sledgehammer."

"Mr. Cappabianco?"

"Fractured vertebrae case. Crowbar to the back. Batter up!" Jackie took a swing with an imaginary baseball bat.

"Not Mr. Trokey?"

"Cracked skull, thirty-six stitches. Now that one was messy."

I couldn't believe what he was telling me. Instead of four fake cases that I was hoping to wrap up in a month or two, I now had over a dozen that were just starting up. And in each of these cases I was representing someone who had been beaten or maimed or worse, all because of an idea I had come up with. I was no longer a white-collar criminal. I was a thug. Just like Jackie.

"You're not gonna get away with this. You'll get caught," I said.

Jackie put his arm around my shoulder and pulled me in tight, like a big brother giving a little brother a hug.

"No, we won't. I listened to what you told me, and I set these accidents up so we *can't* get caught. I made some calls and got these guys workin' on all different job sites. I also had 'em all work a few days before they got hurt, no more of that first-day accident bullshit. I learned my lesson on that. And they're not all fall from scaffold cases. I got crane hooks whackin' guys in the head, broken dumpsters tippin' over. The whole shebang. I'm tellin' you, I got this thing down to a science."

"You're assaulting people!"

"They don't mind! They're happy to do it! Trust me, they'll take a broken leg to the alternative any day of the week."

I couldn't stand Jackie touching me anymore. I pushed his hand off my shoulder, stood up, and walked over to the window. As I stared down at the street, Jackie walked up behind me and patted me on the back.

"If you're thinkin' of jumping, I wouldn't recommend it," he said. "Two stories isn't high enough to kill a guy. Trust me, I learned that one the hard way."

My cousin stepped between me and the window so we were face-to-face.

"Prince, I know you're a little upset. But trust me when I tell you I know what I'm doing. These cases are worth a helluva lot more than the Tangelino case. A while back I grabbed one of these things you got lying around, so I'd have somethin' to read in the can."

Jackie plucked the *Jury Verdict Reporter* from his desk.

"So I was flippin' through it," he continued. "I couldn't believe it when I saw the money these people get when they have a bad injury. So I started thinkin' that we're being too generous with these dead beats. We're lettin' 'em off the hook just so long as they fake a neck and back injury, which ain't worth more than a couple hundred grand at best. That's crazy."

Jackie flipped through the *Reporter* to demonstrate his point.

"Look at this," he cried, pointing to a page. "Fractured ankle with surgery, seven hundred and fifty thousand. Here. Fractured arm with surgery, five hundred twenty-five thousand. Loss of arm, four point three million. Ooo, I gotta make a note of that one."

He pulled a pen from his shirt pocket and circled the loss-of-arm entry in the *Reporter*.

"I can't do this anymore, Jackie."

Jackie got right up in my face, his nose an inch from mine.

"You *can* do it and you *will* do it! What I did to Luongo's hand is nothing compared to what I'll do to you if you fuck this thing up!"

I had nothing to say in response to Jackie's threat. He'd threatened me before and I knew debating the issue with him would only make him angrier. I knew what I was going to have to do, and trying to reason with Jackie was not part of the solution.

"I'm going for a walk."

As I walked toward Jackie's door, I held my breath and tensed all of my muscles. The last time we fought, Jackie had charged me from behind and slammed me against the wall, and I suspected that he'd do it again. To my surprise he didn't.

I walked out to the reception area without turning around to look at my cousin. As the door closed behind me, I could hear him call me a son of a bitch under his breath.

THIRTY-SIX

MY PLAN was to walk a few blocks and try to clear my head, maybe stop by the river and sit and watch the boats go by for a while. There was something about watching boats that always calmed me. Like most of my plans, this one fell apart as well. I didn't even get through the reception area.

"Oh, wait a minute," Joey said into the phone. "He just walked by. Let me put you on hold."

Joey pressed a button on the phone and turned to me.

"Mrs. Guzman wants to talk to you about her husband's case …"

I don't know why I did what I did next. I think it was because I knew I was in a situation I couldn't get out of and I knew it was one hundred percent my fault. And I needed to take it out on somebody. Like a kid at school who gets picked on, instead of fighting back against the bully who

I knew I couldn't beat, I went after someone smaller and weaker than me.

"Guzman again!" I shouted. "Do me a favor, tell her that her case isn't worth shit because her husband was a welfare case who was worth nothin' when he was alive and is worth even less dead! Is that clear enough for her? Maybe then she'll leave me the hell alone!"

Joey froze. Her light-brown skin drained of most color, almost turning white. I knew I had just said something terrible, but I had no idea how terrible it actually was.

"I was about to tell you that Mrs. Guzman is waiting for you. Your *wife* is on the phone," Joey said softly.

My stomach tied in a knot. I slowly turned toward a file cabinet that walled off part of the waiting area. It was metal and the shelves were rusting, and I'd been meaning to replace it for years but didn't want to waste the cash. Now I was wishing like hell that I had sprung for the extra hundred and fifty bucks because my eyes had just locked on a pair of black, orthopedic women's shoes peeking out from behind the cabinet's metal frame. They belonged to Mrs. Guzman.

My thoughts had been so focused on Jackie's revelations that I hadn't noticed her sitting there. She stood and stepped out from behind her hiding spot—the look of hurt on her face made it clear she not only heard but had taken to heart each and every insensitive word I had shouted.

I stood motionless next to Joey's desk as Mrs. Guzman approached. Each step she took toward me seemed to take forever. It was the longest two seconds I'd ever experienced. By the time she got to me, I felt like I'd aged five years. The entire time I was praying that when she reached me she'd just haul back and slug me in the gut. I wasn't so lucky.

"I told you that I didn't care about the money," she said, eyes filled with tears, but too proud to let me make her cry. "I just wanted the doctors to apologize."

I thought of responding, possibly trying to apologize myself. But I knew anything I said would have sounded insincere. There are just some things you can't apologize for, so I didn't say a word.

Mrs. Guzman shuffled past me and out the door. I remained where I was. Silent. I felt so incredibly sick that I was afraid to move. I was dazed, like I had been tagged with a right-left combination from a prize fighter. I almost didn't notice Joey cleaning out her desk.

"What are you doing?" I muttered.

"I don't know what the hell's happened to you or what's going on in this office, but you're not the same man who hired me eight years ago."

Joey grabbed the framed pictures of her kids from her desk and shoved them into her oversized purse.

"You used to care about your clients. I admired you. Looked up to you. Now you just make me sick. I quit."

I tried to think of something to say to change Joey's mind. The problem was that I cared for Joey. She was a great woman, a hard worker, a loving mother, and a fantastic friend. As her employer, I'd never want her to leave. But as her friend, I wanted her to get as far away from me as possible because I was sinking like a stone and I didn't know who else I might take with me. So I said the only honest thing I could think of to say.

"I don't blame you," I told her.

Joey didn't respond. She stormed past me and left the office.

I looked down at the phone. The button was still blinking. Janine was still on hold. I picked up the receiver and pressed a few buttons, but that just made the blinking light shut off. I had disconnected her. Joey had always worked the phones and I had no idea how to use them.

God, was I fucked.

THIRTY-SEVEN

SAINT JOSEPH'S CHURCH was one of the true beauties of Brooklyn. It was built in the 1840s, almost exclusively by European immigrants. The Roman Catholic Church, seeing the immigrant influx into New York as a way of helping Catholicism get a stronghold in America, spared no expense in making the church as grand and majestic as possible. The exterior steps were solid marble, as was the foyer. There were five steeples, four boxing in a larger one that was crowned with a gold cross that pierced the clouds. Each pew was hand-carved oak and the chandeliers, over a thousand pounds each, hung from gold-plated chains attached to thick wooden rafters.

My father's father was one of the masons who worked on the renovation in 1946. He helped craft the twenty-five foot Jesus on the back wall of the altar that was made out of Italian ceramic tile. If you looked closely at Jesus's right ankle, a handful of dark tiles were arranged to spell out his initials,

"RP." You had to really look close to see it, but it was there.

When my grandmother found out about this she threw a fit. She was certain the son of God would never let my grandfather past the pearly gates after he desecrated his body like that. My Grampa wasn't worried; he said when he died he'd just tell Jesus that Ronnie Pastore, the foreman for the job, did it. When he did pass away, my grandfather's funeral Mass was held on that same altar, right under "Grampa's Jesus," as Ginny and I called it growing up. I was glad Michelle was being baptized in the same place. I found it comforting, but that comfort didn't last too long.

As I stood on the altar with Janine and Ginny, I scanned the pews of the crowded church. My parents were there. Aunt Edith and Uncle Vinny sat beside them. Roland was recording the whole thing on some new digital camera toy he just bought. I kept looking.

I couldn't find him but I knew he was out there. Jackie was out there somewhere mixed in with the nieces and nephews and aunts and uncles and family friends. I knew he'd show up. A sharp elbow to the ribs interrupted my search.

"Pay attention," Janine chastised, as she passed baby Michelle into my arms. Janine expected whomever we chose to be godparents to our child to take the responsibility seriously, so she was quite earnest about becoming Michelle's godmother.

Janine wanted her sister Donna and Donna's husband, Chris, to be our kid's godparents. I was totally against it. They were a couple of flakes. He was an acupuncturist and she was an aroma therapist, and they went to some communal hippie church where all they did was sing for three hours and then go home.

I wanted Roland to be the godfather and Janine could pick whoever the hell she wanted for godmother, but Janine wouldn't have it. She didn't feel comfortable leaving the immortal soul of our child in Roland's hands. She may have had a point, but I was still lobbying hard for the Cozzolino ticket.

I held my niece carefully in my arms. The priest gently poured a trickle of holy water over Michelle's forehead. She barely even stirred. She was such a good little girl.

I looked up to smile at my parents, so they'd know Michelle was okay. That's when I spotted Jackie. He was sitting by himself way in the back of the church.

Sunlight shone through a stained glass window next to him, causing his face to bear a fiendish, reddish color. It was as if the devil himself was sitting right there in the back of old Saint Joe's.

We made eye contact but I didn't acknowledge him. Instead, I stood on the altar, holding my newly baptized niece in my arms and silently cursing my cousin in a way that would surely keep me out of heaven.

THIRTY-EIGHT

MICHELLE'S BAPTISM party was, of course, catered by
Umberto's. As usual, the food was delicious and plentiful—
ziti, lasagna, steak with peppers and onions, and chicken
cutlets. And that was just what Janine had Umberto's set up in
the kitchen. In the dining room there was even more.

But I didn't feel like eating. Despite a house full of relatives
and friends, I didn't feel much like socializing either. Instead,
I stood by myself at my front door and stared outside.

I watched cars drive by. I waved to Mr. and Mrs. Pinnisi as
they walked their pure-bred boxers, Beau and Blackjack. I even
found myself rooting for a small kid playing basketball against
what appeared to be his older brother in the dead-end street
across from our house.

When I saw Jackie come up our walkway, my first impulse
was to close the door and lock it. It was supposed to be a day
of celebration for family and friends, and I didn't want him

there. I didn't consider him family anymore, blood or no blood, and I sure as hell didn't consider him a friend. But I knew I just couldn't close the door. I knew I had to confront him.

Jackie opened the door and entered. He actually had the balls to act as if everything was okay.

"You ran out of the office so quick yesterday," he said. "I wanted to make sure you were alright."

"Don't pretend to give a shit about me, Jackie," I shot back.

Jackie knew right away that I wasn't in the mood to play games, not in my own home.

"Hey, whether you believe it or not, I do give a shit about you. And you'll see, I'm right about these cases."

"No, I won't see. Because I'm not taking any more cases from you. I'm gonna go talk to Big Louie tomorrow."

If we were in my office, Jackie probably would have punched me for even mentioning the fact that I might talk to BLT. He would have at least slapped me again. But he couldn't in my home, not that day. Not with my parents and Aunt Edith and Uncle Vinny and half the branches of the family tree in the next room.

So he did all he could to intimidate me. He poked me hard in the chest with his index finger. He got up real close to make sure no one would overhear him.

"Like hell you will," he threatened. "I'm in charge of this thing and I'm not gonna have someone who works for me goin' directly to my boss. I speak for Louie and I say you're seein' these cases through."

Now it was Jackie who was lucky there was family nearby because I came as close as I ever had to knocking his lights out.

"I do not work for you, Jackie," I said slowly and deliberately through clenched teeth.

"Like hell you don't."

Jackie pushed open the door and left. Across the street, I could see that the small, overmatched kid had just lost the game. Man, I had really wanted him to win.

"Godfather," someone behind me said in a horrible Marlon Brando impersonation. "I ask for a moment of your time."

I turned to find Ginny, smiling. I wasn't.

"What?" she asked. "That wasn't funny?"

"No, it wasn't."

"Man, lighten up. It's a party. Here, I made you a plate."

Ginny pushed a plastic plate covered with at least three pounds of food under my nose.

"Thanks, but I'm not hungry."

"You sure?"

"Yeah, I'm sure."

"You feeling okay?"

"Yeah, I guess."

"Something bothering you?"

"Not really."

I sat on the landing of my staircase and looked outside again. A new game had started and the older brother was just kicking the crap out of the little kid now. The small kid couldn't even get a shot off. It wasn't even close anymore. Ginny sat next to me.

"I really wanna thank you for the party, Rob. And for being Michelle's godfather. And for letting us stay here. I know it's tough on you money-wise."

"You two can stay here as long as you want," I told her, and I meant it. "Don't worry about the money. I'll find a way to make it work, I promise."

"Thank you."

Ginny gave me a kiss on the cheek, rested her head on my shoulder, stared out the front door, and watched the ball game with me. We didn't say anything for a while but then Ginny asked me a question.

"Remember Billy Fertig?"

"Billy Fertig? Yeah, why?"

"Remember when we were kids and he was tellin' everyone at school I let him touch my boobs?"

"You did let him touch your boobs."

"Yeah, but you didn't know that. He was three years older than you and twice your size but you jumped him at lunch."

"That Fertig kid deserved everything he got," my father interrupted.

I don't know how long he had been standing behind us.

"*Everything he got?* Dad, he kicked the shit out of me. I had to have my jaw wired shut for two months," I reminded my old man.

"You got in your shots," my father insisted, despite the fact that he didn't see the fight and that I had already told him a hundred times since the seventh grade that other than my original sucker punch, my fist never came within a foot of Billy Fertig.

"Dad," I corrected. "The fight lasted two minutes. For one minute and fifty-five seconds I was a punching bag."

"That's my point," Ginny said, ignoring our father's delusions. "After all these years, you're still willing to take one on the chin for your family. You're the best person I know, Rob. You always do what you think is right, even if you know you'll get hurt."

Ginny gave me a kiss and walked back into the kitchen. My dad took her spot next to me on the landing and we watched the game.

"Man," he said, "the small kid is really getting his ass handed to him."

"Yeah."

"You know," he said, "what you're doing for your sister ..."

"It's no big deal," I cut him off.

"Yes, it is. It's my job. To take care of my kids, that's my job ..."

"Dad, you did your job already. You raised us. Ginny and I never did without. You and Mom sure as hell did. But we never did without."

"Yeah, but ..."

"But nothing. Now you get to be a grandfather. You don't have to worry about your kids anymore. We'll be fine. Just enjoy your grandchildren. I'll take care of everything. Ginny and Michele will be just fine, I promise."

My dad took this in. He didn't say anything for a while. He just stared out the door. Then he put his hand on top of mine.

"I raised a good man."

I didn't respond. I didn't want to call my dad a liar.

THIRTY-NINE

"I NEVER AGREED to anything like this!" I shouted, which was pretty brave considering the guy I was shouting at was Lou Turro.

I quickly peeked over my shoulder to see if anyone had heard me. They had. Choo Choo and Tony were sitting at the end of Patsy's bar playing gin rummy. Tony put his cards down and gave me a long, hard eye-fuck. It was obvious he didn't like me yelling at his boss.

"You said to give you clients and we gave you clients. We upheld our end of the bargain, now you uphold yours," Lou said.

I jumped from my seat, causing my chair to skid back behind me. I pointed my finger at Lou, trying to look as tough and threatening as possible.

"I never agreed to crowbars and broken legs!"

This time I had pushed the envelope a little too far. Choo

Choo and Tony were up in a flash. Lou raised the palm of his hand to his men to indicate that he was alright.

"Shut the fuck up right now," Big Lou warned me. "Take a look around. There are four people in this club. Which one doesn't belong? Anyone even know you're here?"

I swallowed hard. Lou had made his point.

"You better remember where you are and who you're talking to," he said. "Now, I'm telling you again, and for the last fuckin' time, you asked for clients and we gave you clients. So shut your cry-hole and do your fuckin' job."

"But I want out," I pleaded. "You let me out after Tangelino, why won't you let me out now?"

"Because we have several outstanding cases with your office. We hurt a lot of people and told them their debt has been forgiven. *Their* debt is now *your* debt. And *your* debt is not forgiven."

Tony walked across the room to a seat a few tables behind his boss. He turned his chair around and sat on it backward, so that his arms rested on the top of the chair's back. He glared at me, giving me the stink eye again. If he was trying to intimidate me, it worked.

"Now, if you know what's best for you and your family," Lou said, "I suggest you get back to the office and draft pleadings or file complaints or do whatever the fuck it is you do."

Lou stood, signifying that he was through talking to me and I couldn't have been happier. I couldn't wait to get the hell out of there. I stood, too. I should have just walked out but, like most lawyers, I had to try to get in the last word.

"I'll see these cases through, but no more," I said, hoping I sounded firm in my conviction. Deep down I know I sounded like a wimp.

Lou's fist shot out from his side like a cannonball, striking me right in the middle of my chest. For a big guy, he was pretty damn quick. I didn't even see the punch coming. I'd never been hit so hard in my entire life. I could have sworn I heard my sternum crack. The blow pushed me backward, causing me to fall down hard onto my ass. I grabbed my chest with my hand and gasped for breath.

"You don't decide when it's over!" Lou shouted.

Lou was in real bad shape because the punch made him almost as winded as I was.

"There's one more guy," he said. "Jackie's meeting with him tomorrow, some Polack. You have to represent him, too. After that, I'm done with you. You're too much of a goddamn headache. Now get the hell outta here."

Lou didn't have to tell me twice. Fighting the excruciating pain, I stood up and walked past Choo Choo and out the door. It was dark out. The air was cold and it hurt like hell when I breathed it in. I unbuttoned the first few buttons of my shirt and examined my chest. I already had a huge red welt. I'd seen enough car accident photos over the years to know that it would be dark purple by morning.

During the walk home I decided that I'd wear a T-shirt to bed the next couple of weeks, so Janine wouldn't see the bruise. I was getting real tired of lying to her. I was getting very tired of the whole damn thing. But Lou Turro had given me my marching orders, so there was nothing I could do … except go back to work.

FORTY

SO I PUSHED BLT's cases through. I scheduled preliminary conferences, exchanged discovery, and treated the false claims as if they were as legitimate as any other. I had to do this. I found that if I at least pretended the cases were real it wasn't as hard for me to work on them. So now I had truly come full circle—I had lied to everyone else and now I was lying to myself.

Problem was, the lie was about to be exposed. It was at the deposition of Finizio that the scam started to fall apart.

The deposition had just ended and it had been pathetic. Finizio testified almost exactly as Higgins had the week before, which was of little surprise considering that Jackie had the two workers stage identical accidents at identical locations. I had tried to prep both men to alter their stories a little bit, but it was next to impossible. The accident reports had already memorialized what had happened—they had fallen from the same scaffold on the same job site and had suffered the same injuries and hired the same lawyer. There wasn't much wiggle room. I had Finizio say that his neck hurt more than his back and Higgins say that his back was worse off than his neck. Other than that, one's testimony was a carbon copy of the other's. This fact wasn't lost on Kent Reilly.

"We could've saved everyone a lot of time and effort and just cut and pasted Finizio's name into Higgin's depo transcript," he said pointedly, after the deposition had been wrapped up and everyone else had left the conference room. "Come to think of it, we could've just used Mr. Tangelino's transcript as a template."

I had been going up against him for years and this was the first time I had seem him legitimately angry. He had feigned annoyance before, when I had made a settlement demand he thought was too high or when he thought I got a little too rough while questioning one of his clients. But that was always for show—part of the dance that makes up litigation. This time Kent was really pissed. He wasn't shouting or raising his voice, but I knew he was truly upset with me because his language wasn't colored with his usual flavoring of profanity. In fact, he wasn't cursing at all. He wanted me to know he wasn't playing around. I tried to cover my ass.

"You don't expect guys who get hurt on the same job site to have similar information for you when you question them?"

"Please," Kent said, not wanting to hear my bullshit. "It was as if they were reading from the same script."

Kent walked toward the door. For a moment I thought he was going to leave. But he shut the door and sat next to me at the conference table. He spoke in a hushed tone.

"I'll deny I ever told you this. And the only reason I'm saying anything is because we've known each other a long time and I've always thought you're a pretty straight-up guy."

"Okay. What?"

"I could lose my job over this," he said.

"Jesus, what the hell are you talking about?"

Kent took a deep breath, exhaled, and leaned forward. He spoke even softer.

"The Fraud Division of the New York State Department of Insurance is looking into these cases."

I instinctively moved my hand to my stomach, waiting for the knifelike pains to come. But they didn't. Not a twinge, not even a gurgle. Nothing. I think deep down I always knew that this moment would come, the moment where I learned that someone else was on to what I was doing. And I guess my body had prepared itself for it. Because, amazingly, despite finding out that the State of New York was now investigating my fraudulent cases, my stomach felt absolutely fine. I tried my best to play it cool.

"Why would they do that?" I asked.

"A *first day of work* accident usually sends up a red flag. So does a neck and back injury. And so do multiple accidents on the same job site. You've got all three here. Throw on top of that the fact that all these guys are from the same neighborhood with the same attorney and we've got more red flags than Moscow."

"I have accident reports confirming every ..."

"I don't care what your accident reports say, man. Your clients are liars."

That was the first time anyone had ever told me that. I had obviously known it all along but it was hard to hear someone actually say the words. I didn't know what to say, so I fell back on the first thing you learn in criminal law class—when accused, Deny, Deny, Deny.

"No, they aren't. You have no proof of that."

"You don't actually believe them?"

"As an attorney I have an ethical duty to believe my clients and zealously advocate for them."

To this day I can't believe I had the audacity to make an ethical argument in my defense.

"You also have a duty not to perpetrate a fraud before the court," Kent pointed out.

"I'm not perpetrating a fraud," I said.

More untrue words have never been spoken. They go right up there with "I did not have sexual relations with that woman" and "Read my lips; no new taxes."

"Look, Rob. I'm not saying you personally are doing anything wrong. I'm just saying you might be getting played by your clients and not even know it. And now that the government is involved, you could get in some real trouble."

I closed my briefcase and stood.

"Hey," Kent added. "I'm the one who paid you a buck and a half on Tangelino. If this whole thing's a scam, I look like an asshole. I could lose my job, too."

I opened the door to leave.

"There's no fraud here," I lied again.

"I hope you're right," Kent said as I exited. "For both our sakes."

FORTY-ONE

AFTER THE DEPOSITION I called Jackie on his cell phone but I got his voice mail. I left him a cryptic message that we needed to speak right away, that there was "a problem" but I didn't elaborate.

When I got to the office he wasn't there. It was six thirty. I spent the next five hours calling him every fifteen minutes. I was frantic. He and I needed to discuss what Kent had told me and figure out what to do. I had called Janine earlier and told her I was trying to catch up on some paperwork and that I'd be home around midnight at the latest.

By eleven thirty I was jumping out of my skin. I hadn't heard from Jackie and my mind was racing with horrible scenarios of what had happened to him and what was about to happen to me.

I opened the bottom drawer of my desk and pulled out a bottle of Jim Beam that a client had given me as a Christmas gift about three years earlier. It was covered with dust. I unscrewed the top. The smell of Kentucky bourbon whiskey rose up and smacked me across the face. I'm not much of a drinker, never have been. At high school parties when everyone was getting wasted, I'd more often than not suck on the same bottle of Michelob all night.

But I had never in my life been so certain that I needed a drink than I was that night in my office waiting to hear from Jackie. I filled a Styrofoam coffee cup halfway and took another sniff. The smell made my throat tighten a bit. I stood and put the cup to my lips, swung my head back, and let the alcohol fill my mouth in one big wave. I swallowed it in a single gulp. My throat became hot. The liquor warmed my belly as well. I instantly felt better. I poured some more, this time filling the cup almost to the top. I hesitated a moment, held my breath, and downed the Beam again. I sat back down at my desk and poured myself another. I drank it.

I turned off my desk lamp, which was the only light on in the office, and rested my head on my desk, using my hands as a pillow. The whiskey had done its job calming my nerves. I just wanted to close my eyes for a while.

FORTY-TWO

WHEN I WOKE UP I had no idea what time it was. I walked to the window and looked at the Colgate clock that hung above the awning of the corner pharmacy. Three forty-five in the morning! I reached for the phone to call Janine. The message light was blinking. I pressed speakerphone and the voice mail button.

A robotic voice said, "You have two new messages. First message." It was from Janine.

"Rob, sweetie, it's twelve forty-five and you're not home yet and I'm a little worried. I'm going to wait up for you. If you get this, please call me right away."

Second message.

"Rob, it's me again. It's one thirty and I have no idea where you are. I had Roland drive by your office. He said all the lights are out. Where are you? He's coming over here. Please be alright."

I knew Janine must have been worried sick. I picked up the receiver to call her when the lights in my office went on. I looked up. Jackie and Choo Choo were standing in my doorway. I hung up the phone and rushed over to them.

"Where the hell have you been?" I asked. "I've been trying to get in touch with you for hours. We have a major problem."

Jackie's punch landed hard on the left side of my nose. I know he only used his fist but it felt like he had belted me with a brick. I stumbled back and grabbed onto my desk with my hand. He hit me again. This time my left eye took the brunt of it. As soon as I hit the ground I felt Jackie's shoe connect with my stomach. That hurt worse than the punch. I could taste blood collecting in the back of my mouth. It was making it difficult to breathe. I tried to spit the blood out but a shoe smashed into the bottom of my chin, slamming my mouth shut. So I swallowed the blood. Jackie kept kicking me. Most of the shots hit me in my stomach. I was too dazed to defend myself. I curled into a ball and covered my face with my forearms.

"What did I tell you?" Jackie yelled as he beat me. "Huh?! I told you not to go to Louie, you motherless prick. I told you to keep your motherfuckin' mouth shut!"

I could tell Jackie was getting tired because his kicks were losing their ferocity. He grabbed me by my shirt collar and lifted my upper torso from the floor. Even from my knees and through swollen eyes I could tell he was looking at me with disgust.

"Look at you," he said. "You are so fuckin' stupid."

He punched me hard in the face with his free hand. My head bobbed around like a newborn's. I don't know if it was that last punch or the kicks to the stomach or the mixture of blood and Jim Beam that was sloshing around inside of me, but

I vomited all over Jackie's left shin.

"Son of a bitch!"

Jackie let go of me and I dropped to the floor. He grabbed some papers from my desk and tried to wipe the vomit from his leg. He pulled some flowers from a vase and poured the water on his pants, as well. If it was possible, he looked at me with even more contempt now.

"Pick him up," he told Choo Choo.

Choo Choo lifted me by my armpits and propped me up against my desk. I was barely able to stand on my own. Jackie stood in front of me.

"You gonna listen to me from now on?" he asked.

It hurt to move my mouth. I was barely able to mumble "Yes."

Jackie grabbed a letter opener from the ceramic pen holder my wife had made me and pressed the point deep into my temple, almost breaking the skin.

"I can't fuckin' hear you!" he shouted.

"Yes," I said louder. I wasn't aware of it at the time, but I had started crying.

"Good. Put him down."

Choo Choo dropped me in a chair. Jackie walked behind my desk and sat in my chair. He put his feet up on my desk and lit a cigarette.

"You fucked up, Prince. You got Louie questioning your dedication to this thing. He's afraid that you might turn tail and run. I told him, 'Not Bobby. Not my cousin.' But thanks to you, my word don't hold any weight with my boss any more."

I didn't know how Jackie wanted me to respond, so I said what I thought he wanted to hear.

"I'm sorry."

"Don't apologize. 'Cause I'm gonna give you a chance to prove to everyone how devoted you are to our little project," Jackie smiled.

He stood, took a last drag from his cigarette, dropped it into my bottle of Jim Beam, and walked out the door. Choo Choo grabbed me by the arm, yanked me from the chair, and we followed my cousin.

When we got outside Jackie was standing next to a black Lincoln Town Car. The back door was open. Choo Choo pushed me in the direction of the car. I didn't get in. I looked at Jackie, but he gave me nothing back. I knew from the way he looked at me that, in his mind, I wasn't his cousin any more—I was just another son of a bitch trying to screw him out of a buck.

Choo Choo's meaty hand shoved my shoulder. I knew that if I didn't get into the car that the next shove wouldn't be so gentle. I climbed into the backseat. Choo Choo got in and sat next to me. Tony was at the wheel. Jackie sat shotgun. Tony looked at me through the rearview mirror and I'll be damned if that bastard didn't smile.

His face scared the shit out of me because Tony LoBianco never smiled. Even in '94 when he beat an extortion charge, he didn't so much as curl his lip when the jury came back with its not guilty plea, even though the prosecutor had been asking for twenty years—the guy was ice. So I knew that Tony was really looking forward to whatever Jackie had in store for me, because that sick fuck was grinning from ear to cauliflower ear.

Tony drove through the quiet streets of Brooklyn and over the Brooklyn Bridge. All of Manhattan was asleep. We got on the FDR and headed north. We drove in silence. Choo Choo actually fell asleep and softly snored for about ten minutes. We took an exit that read Triboro Bridge–Bronx. I had no idea where we were going, but I knew it wouldn't be good.

I kept thinking of Janine. That I might never see her again. That she might never know what happened to me. I thought about how I might end up as one of those sensationalist news stories that makes the cover of the *New York Post* for about a month. Then, after a while, when the body is never found, interest fades and no one cares any more. I thought about our child being born without a father, and how I had managed to hurt my baby before it was even born. I thought about my parents, especially my dad—how angry and frustrated he'd feel never knowing what had happened to me.

But more than anything, I thought of Jackie in his suit mourning me at Tucci's Funeral Parlor with my family— hugging my father, consoling my mom, kissing my wife on the cheek, playing the grieving cousin. I almost threw up again.

FORTY-THREE

IT WAS ALMOST SUNRISE when the Lincoln pulled into a construction site about fifteen blocks north of Yankee Stadium. It looked like another set of low-income housing was going up in the Bronx but it was hard to tell because the project was only about a quarter complete. Ten-story scaffolds embraced steel girders that stretched upward forever until they melted into the grey sky.

The car crept between various incomplete structures on the site, bouncing us around due to the potholes and scrap lumber that littered the ground. About thirty yards ahead I saw the outline of a figure standing next to one of the scaffolds.

Maybe this is the guy who is going to kill me, I thought. *Maybe Jackie doesn't have the nerve to do it himself.*

Tony drove closer and then stopped the car. Choo Choo opened his door and got out. Tony and Jackie followed. I stayed where I was. I figured if they were going to kill me,

I sure as hell wasn't going to make it easy on them and walk to my own damn execution. Besides, thanks to Jackie, I felt like two-hundred pounds of recycled shit so I was trying to move as little as possible.

The door next to me opened. Jackie grabbed me by the collar and yanked me out of the car. The person I had seen from the car was still standing next to the scaffold. He was a young, blond kid—couldn't have been more than twenty-five-years old, twenty-six tops. He looked as scared as I felt. I could tell that my bloody and bruised face wasn't making him any more comfortable.

"Luke Kozzowski," Jackie said to the kid. "I'd like you to meet your attorney."

Luke didn't say a word and he didn't move an inch. He also never took his eyes off me. He looked at me as if I was his own personal Ghost of Christmas Future and it was midnight Christmas Eve.

"I know he don't look like much," Jackie told Luke, "but he's a real-life Ivy Leaguer. Ain't that right, Bobby?"

I opened my mouth as much as I could but the pain was excruciating. My jaw felt as if it had been cemented shut.

"What are you doing, Jackie?" I could barely speak so I had to get right to the point.

"Introducing you to your new client," he answered. "You see, Luke here has a taste for the ponies. And even though he never won, he kept on bettin', day after day, week after week. With our money. Which goes to prove what, Luke?"

"That Polacks are stupid," Luke answered with no hesitation.

It was clear this was not the first time Jackie had asked Luke that question. It was also clear Luke knew the degrading answer that Jackie wanted to hear.

"Very good," Jackie encouraged. "But you see, Prince,

Polacks ain't that stupid, or at least this one ain't. 'Cause he figured out a bad injury is better than a good funeral."

"Don't do this," I mumbled.

I wasn't exactly sure what "this" meant, but I had a pretty good idea, and I knew I didn't want it to happen.

Jackie ignored me. He approached Luke and kept talking.

"While negotiating his debt with me, Luke mentioned that he happened to be working as a carpenter in the Bronx. 'What a fortunate coincidence,' I told him. 'That'll make everything so much easier.' Isn't that right, Luke?"

"Yes," Luke answered, his voice shaking almost as much as his legs.

"So, Counselor," Jackie continued. "When you draft your complaint, you might want it to read as follows: *On the date of the accident, the Plaintiff was ascending an unstable scaffold ...*"

Jackie grabbed the scaffold and rattled it.

"*And was caused to fall.*" Jackie stressed that last part for my benefit.

Tony handed Jackie a small leather bag that was already unzipped. Jackie reached inside and took out a nail gun. It was a Black & Decker. My dad had one exactly like it at home. I got it for him for his sixtieth birthday.

Jackie pointed the nail gun at Luke—the tip was less than an inch from the kid's eye. Jackie summed up his proposed Complaint.

"*Upon hitting the ground, the Plaintiff's nail gun discharged, imbedding a nail into Plaintiff's right eye.*"

Luke shut both his eyes tight. Jackie pressed the end of the nail gun against Luke's eyelid. His finger fondled the trigger, traced its curve, up and down, very slowly. Once, twice, and then a third time. Then his finger stopped. He slowly pulled back the trigger.

"No. Don't!" I shouted.

Jackie lowered the nail gun and turned to me and smiled.

"Don't worry. I won't."

My cousin walked over to me and shoved the nail gun into my right hand.

"You will," he whispered into my ear.

I instinctively dropped the gun to the ground. Jackie punched me hard in the stomach. I doubled over, my head hanging at my knees, and spit up blood.

"While you're down there, pick it up," Jackie ordered.

I had to do what he said. I could have shot him in the leg or the face or whatever with the nail gun, but then I might as well have just pointed the gun to my temple and fired. If I had shot Jackie I wouldn't have gotten more than five feet away before Choo Choo and Tony unloaded half a dozen rounds into my back.

I stood there holding the nail gun, my mouth bleeding, my eyes tearing. I said the only thing I could think of to say.

"You're sick."

Jackie laughed.

"You're thick as a brick, you know that?" he smirked. "But it's really my fault. I haven't given you proper incentive."

Jackie nodded to Choo Choo who took two steps toward me, pulled a gun from his jacket, and pressed the muzzle hard against the left side of my head, about an inch above the ear. Tony pushed Luke from behind so that he was standing a foot in front of me. Jackie put his hand over mine and forced my arm to rise so that the nail gun was pointed directly at Luke's eye again.

"Put your finger on the trigger," Jackie commanded.

I couldn't.

"Put your finger on the mutha fuckin' trigger!"

Choo Choo cocked his gun and pressed it deeper into my skull. I slowly curled my index finger around the trigger. Jackie stood behind me, his chest pressed against my back, his mouth right next to my ear, whispering encouragement, like a father teaching his son how to shoot his first bow and arrow.

"Don't be scared," he whispered.

Jackie placed his finger on top of mine. He applied a little bit of pressure, causing the trigger to move a fraction of an inch, but to me it seemed like Jackie had pulled the trigger all the way back to Brooklyn.

"I'll see the cases through, I promise! Just let him go!" I pleaded.

"Let him go?" Jackie asked. "But he doesn't want to go. Luke, did I force you to do this?"

Luke didn't say a word. His eyes were pressed shut and he was trembling. My nose picked up a whiff of the distinct smell of feces. I'm pretty sure Luke had shit himself. It was a miracle I didn't as well.

"Luke! Answer me!"

"No."

"Didn't you have choices?"

"Yes."

"What were they?" Jackie prodded.

"I could pay you the money, or … or …"

"Or what?" Jackie was getting impatient.

"Or I could take the nail gun," Luke stammered.

"And what was the third choice?" Jackie coached.

"You could kill me for not paying," the kid said between sobs.

The poor guy was ready to snap.

"See, Bobby. Luke had *three* options to choose from. He chose giving up an eye, which, considering how much he owes us, is a fuckin' bargain. Besides, these are small nails. They won't even go all the way through."

Jackie pulled his hand and mine closer to Luke's eye. The nail gun was now pressed hard against the eyelid. It felt like we were going to pop his eyeball back into his head.

"I'm beggin' you, Jackie. Don't make me do this," I said, barely able to get the words out.

Jackie didn't say anything for a few seconds. We stood motionless, both of us pointing the nail gun at Luke, but only one of us willingly. I felt Jackie's lips press against my ear.

"Okay," he whispered, softening, "that's enough."

He lowered my hand and his so that we were holding the nail gun at my side. Luke exhaled audibly. Choo Choo took the gun away from my head. Jackie took a small step to my right. I looked partially across my shoulder at him. His expression had changed. He gave me a half smile.

"Bobby, you're my cousin. I love you. If you can't do this, I understand."

Now it was my turn to exhale.

"But maybe you just need to see one done first," Jackie sneered.

In one swift motion he jerked my hand up and fired the nail gun.

Luke immediately fell to his knees. He clutched his hand to his eye. The nail protruded between his fingers, which were covered with blood flowing down to his wrist. He screamed like a wounded animal, a primal wail that rose out of the depths of his body and lingered above us, stuck in the thick predawn mist.

"No!" I shouted and tried to rush to Luke's aid.

Jackie grabbed me by the arm and I could not break free.

"Don't worry about him," he said. "The site opens in a few

minutes. One of the workers will find him."

I kept pulling toward Luke.

"We gotta get outta here!" Jackie yelled.

I could barely hear him over Luke's cries.

Choo Choo wrapped his hairy forearm around my neck and dragged me ten feet to the Lincoln. He pushed me inside and then climbed in behind me. Jackie hopped in next to Tony and we were off.

FORTY-FOUR

I DIDN'T SAY ANYTHING on the ride back to Brooklyn. I rested my head against the window, taking comfort in its coolness, and watched garbage barges float down the East River. Jackie turned around in his seat so he could see me.

"I'm proud of you, Prince," he said. "You did a good job. You really *nailed* that guy."

Jackie laughed at his joke. Tony and Choo Choo joined in. I didn't respond. I just kept staring out the window, trying to understand how a conversation on a school yard bench could turn into a maiming in the Bronx.

"I know you don't think so now, but this was a very good thing, what happened today," Jackie said. "Now I can go tell Louie that we're all on the same team. That he's got nothin' to worry about."

I could tell Jackie wanted me to say something. Or at least he wanted me to nod in agreement. I wouldn't even look at him. My nose was so swollen that I had to breathe through my mouth and that made the window fog up. I couldn't even see the barges anymore.

"Christ, you look like shit," Jackie said. "Try to get some rest. You'll be home soon."

Never before did I want to go home so badly. Never before had I needed to be there like I needed it that morning in the Lincoln. I needed to be in my own house. In my own bed. I needed to be with Janine, to touch her, to smell her hair, to hold her tight in my arms. All the things I had thought, just moments earlier, I'd never get to do again.

I was going to tell her everything, I decided. Once she saw me and what I looked like, I'd really have no choice anyway. But I wanted to tell her the truth. I wanted to tell her and then beg for her to forgive me. If I was lucky, she would.

As we crossed the Brooklyn Bridge for the second time that morning I began to silently pray. I asked God to give me one more chance. It was a chance I didn't necessarily deserve, but I asked for it anyway. I prayed for a solution to the mess I was in. I prayed for Luke, who was hopefully already in an ambulance, but I had no way of knowing. I prayed for all the people who had been hurt by Jackie—all the people who had been hurt by me. But I prayed hardest that God would just get me home. Because I really missed my wife.

FORTY-FIVE

TURNS OUT GOD has a pretty sick sense of humor. Or maybe I just wasn't specific enough in my prayer. He let me get home, but I still didn't get what I prayed for.

Tony stopped the car in front of my house. Aluminum siding and brick had never looked so appealing. I opened the car door and slowly climbed out. My body still hurt all over, but I wasn't bleeding anymore and most of the throbbing in my head was gone. Choo Choo reached over and pulled the door closed. I had taken less than two steps from the Lincoln when Tony pulled away from the curb, leaving me alone in the middle of the street.

I gingerly maneuvered the three steps leading up to my stone walkway. I was twelve feet from my front door, only four yards from home, a mere one hundred forty-four inches from Janine. A relieved smile crept across my sore face.

"Mr. Principe?"

I turned my head toward the voice coming from the sidewalk. My smile disappeared.

"Robert Principe?" a tall redhead in a dark blue suit asked me.

Next to him stood a shorter black male, a bit younger than the redhead, also wearing a dark suit. He had a neatly trimmed moustache that was an obvious attempt to look older, but it didn't work. The black guy was thirty, thirty-one tops. I pegged the redhead at thirty-seven or so.

"Who wants to know?" I asked, but I already had a pretty good idea.

The redhead flashed a badge, just like in the movies. Whenever I saw that in a film, I always wondered why someone would believe a person was a cop or a fed simply because a small piece of metal was shown to them for two seconds before being snapped back up into a wallet. I always wondered why no one ever checked the badge to see if it was authentic or called police headquarters to see if the guy is really who he says he is.

But in real life, when you're the one getting flashed, you don't ask those questions. Especially when you know you've done something that would make the FBI go out looking for you. I knew right away that the redhead and the black guy standing in front of me were the Real McCoy.

"Special Agent Christian McLean, Federal Bureau of Investigation. This is Agent Townsend. We'd like to ask you a few questions if you have a moment."

"Now's not a good time," I said.

"I strongly suggest you cooperate, Mr. Principe," Townsend said. "We're here to help you." Townsend gave me the once-over. "And from the looks of it, you could use all the help you can get."

"And I strongly suggest you kiss my ass," I shot back. "I'm no fuckin' dummy, pal. I know my rights."

McLean smiled.

"I would hope so," he said, "considering you were tops in your class at Columbia Law. Summa cum laude at Penn undergrad. Hell, you even got a 1420 on the SATs."

Townsend whistled as if he were impressed.

"Better score than me," he said. "But that test is racially biased."

"The point I'm trying to make," McLean continued, "is that we've obviously taken the time to learn all there is to know about you. I know how you did in school. I know where you buy your coffee in the morning. I know how often you spank it and who you think of when you're doing it."

"You know I think of your mother?"

Townsend unsuccessfully tried to stifle a chuckle at his partner's expense. Aside from a disapproving look to Townsend, McLean ignored my comment altogether and kept up with the hard sell.

"You wanna know the most interesting thing I learned about you? You're not a piece of shit. But it looks like you've got yourself caught up in some pretty *severe* shit. Now I recommend you believe my partner when he says we're here to help and that you should cooperate."

I didn't know what to do. I looked back at my house. The front door was so close. I could have told them to fuck off and walked inside. But if they had reasonable belief that I had just been involved in a violent felony—and from the looks of me they wouldn't have any trouble convincing a court that they thought I was either the victim of, or participant in, something pretty violent—they could follow me into my own home. They didn't need a warrant to tear the place up under the "hot pursuit" exception to the Fourth Amendment. I didn't think that's what they wanted to do, but I wasn't going to take that chance. Not with Janine in the house.

"Five minutes," I said. "Let's talk in your car."

"Good decision."

McLean led me to a standard government-issued black sedan. Townsend got into the driver's seat. McLean sat behind him. I sat next to McLean who flipped open a folder that he retrieved from the front seat. He held it at an angle so I couldn't see what was in it. This was done very intentionally, and I was sure the folder was just a prop to make me nervous and there was nothing in it but random pages torn out of some magazines.

"We've been keeping tabs on Louie Turro and his crew for over a year now," he said. "Insurance fraud is only one of his many hobbies. He also dabbles in loan sharking, gambling, drugs, prostitution …"

"He's a real Renaissance Man," Townsend added.

"What does this have to do with me?" I asked.

"You tell us," McLean continued. "During routine surveillance, one of our agents notices Jackie Masella making frequent trips to a certain law office. We check out the office, the lawyer who runs it, and we find out he's a stand-up guy who just happens to be cousins with a scumbag."

"We didn't think much of it," Townsend said.

"Until we see these men walk in with Masella."

McLean removed an eight-by-ten black-and-white photo from the folder and handed it to me. So much for my theory that the folder was a prop.

The photo showed Jackie walking into the street-level entrance of my firm with Patrick Higgins and Pino Finizio. I handed it back to McLean, trying to appear unimpressed.

"We recognized Higgins and Finizio as men we had seen placing dozens of bets with, and borrowing thousands of dollars from, Masella over the past year," Townsend explained.

"I don't know what you're talking about or how any of this has anything to do with me or my firm," I said, resorting right back to the old reliable Deny, Deny, Deny defense.

"We learned that within a week of this photo being taken, lawsuits had been commenced on behalf of both men by your law office," McLean pointed out.

"You went and talked to my clients when you knew they were already represented by counsel?" I tried to sound outraged. "That's unlawful."

"We didn't need to speak to anyone. It's public record. Took us about five minutes."

McLean took a pack of Juicy Fruit gum from his coat pocket, unwrapped a piece, and popped it into his mouth.

"You want a piece?" he asked.

"No. I like spearmint. Juicy Fruit's for assholes."

For a guy who was sitting in the backseat of a car with a couple of pissed off feds, I had a hell of a lot of nerve.

He put the pack back in his pocket and continued.

"So the thing is, the complaints were almost carbon copies of each other. I mean practically identical. We became a little suspicious so we contacted the Fraud Division of the New York State Department of Insurance."

I've played cards my entire life, ever since my Uncle Phil taught me how to play poker when I was nine. He also taught me how to keep a pretty damn good poker face. But when McLean mentioned the Fraud Division, my face was easier to read than a billboard, despite Uncle Phil's training. Townsend noticed this.

"What?" he laughed. "You thought the insurance carrier or

the State made the connection here? They don't know shit from pound cake."

McLean took a plain white business envelope from the folder.

"And to their surprise, but not really ours, they found that Higgins and Finizio's cases were not only identical to each other, but they were also identical to a case you settled for Salvatore Tangelino a few months back. We knew Tangelino as a small-time numbers runner for Louie Turro until he started placing some bets himself. It's funny how all these men made a career change into the construction industry right before they came to you."

"Mr. Tangelino had a legitimate case. I don't know of any association he has with Jackie," I lied.

"Then how do you explain this?"

McLean removed a check from the white envelope and handed it to me. It was the check I had given Mr. Tangelino when his case settled.

"Turn it over," McLean said.

I did. What I saw made me sick to my stomach. On the back of the check was written "Pay to the Order of Jackie Masella." Underneath that, Salvatore Tangelino had signed his name. That's when I knew I wasn't going to get to go home.

"Masella was so worried Tangelino would take off with the money that he made him sign the check right over to him. So much for not leaving a paper trail, huh?"

"But don't feel bad," Townsend mocked. "I mean, who the hell looks at the back of checks when they get their bank statements, anyway?"

"Where'd you get this?" I demanded.

"Your office," McLean answered. "Got a warrant early this morning."

He plucked the check from my hand and put it carefully back into the envelope and then placed the envelope back into the folder. He handed the folder to Townsend.

"We got you, Mr. Principe," he said smugly.

"If you had enough," I countered, "you would have arrested me already."

"We have enough, trust me. We just wanted to see if you'd cooperate first."

"Fuck you."

"That's not the kind of cooperation we were looking for."

McLean removed handcuffs from his waist and placed them tightly around my wrist. It was the first time I had been handcuffed since Dean Giannone's birthday party magic show when I was seven. This time wasn't nearly as much fun.

McLean exited the car and got back in the front seat. Townsend turned the key in the ignition and we drove off.

As we pulled away from the curb, I turned and stared at my house through the back windshield. Janine was in there, worried, waiting for me. I had been so close to being with her.

Behind me, either Townsend or McLean flipped on the radio. I listened to John Denver's "Sunshine on My Shoulders" as my home got smaller in the distance. When I could no longer see it, I turned around, faced front, and Townsend drove me to jail.

FORTY-SIX

I HAD BEEN in the Metropolitan Federal Detention Center in Brooklyn before. When I first started out, I signed up this case, Juan Rivera, some guy who had been hit by a city bus and broke his arm. By the time his deposition came around, old Juan had been locked up. He was doing federal time for drugs. So I worked it out that Juan be transferred to the Detention Center in Brooklyn for a day so his deposition could be taken.

He turned out to be a pretty good witness and I wound up settling the case for fifteen grand. After expenses, I took in around forty-five hundred dollars. Three years of work to earn just a forty-five hundred dollar fee. The case would have been worth a hell of a lot more if my client wasn't a scumbag criminal, but that's the kind of luck I've been blessed with when it comes to my practice.

The center was pretty much the same since the last time I'd been there, except now I was on the other side of the glass partition. I immediately asked for my phone call. I know that the first thing you're supposed to do is call your attorney. I'm well aware of that. But I didn't. I called Janine.

The phone only rang once before it was answered.

"Hello?"

It was Ginny and she was worried as hell.

"It's me."

"Oh, thank you, Jesus," Ginny shouted. "Where the hell are you? We've been freakin' out all night over here!"

"It's a long story. But I'm okay. Just put Janine on."

"She's at Mom and Dad's. They're callin' everyone they know. Roland and I were stayin' here in case you showed up."

"Roland's there? Put him on."

"But where are you …"

"Put him on!"

I waited while Ginny handed the phone to Roland.

"What's going on, Rob?" he said seriously.

He had known me long enough to know that when I don't come home and don't call anyone, that I must be in some serious trouble.

"Listen to me carefully. I'm in Metropolitan Federal Detention. The one in Brooklyn. I need you to get here immediately. Got it?"

"Got it."

The phone went dead. I wasn't worried. I knew Roland as well as he knew me, which was pretty damn good. He was probably in his car before I hung up the receiver.

It was time for me to get processed—photos, fingerprints, and an inventory of my personal belongings, which consisted of a subway token, forty-three dollars, my house keys, and the Columbia Law School ring my dad had given me.

When I was done Townsend took me to the men's room

and let me clean up a bit. He gave me a bar of Ivory soap, a washcloth, and a small tube of antibiotic ointment for my cuts. I had a long gash above my left eyebrow that wasn't too wide and probably could've used a few stitches. I didn't ask for medical attention, though. If I had, by law, they would have had to send me to a doctor and that would've just meant several more hours before I could speak to Roland. And I couldn't have that. I knew time was of the essence.

After I was done with the ointment, Townsend looked me over. He applied a butterfly to the cut over my eye and a small Band-Aid over the bridge of my nose. The other cuts and scrapes had stopped bleeding, and we both felt it was best to let them breathe.

"As my momma used to say," Townsend offered, "the sooner they scab, the sooner they heal."

He gave me a plain white T-shit to change into because my dress shirt was stained with blood, dirt, and vomit. I was hoping Townsend would be dumb enough to throw the shirt away but he put it in a sealed evidence bag.

I spent the next forty minutes or so in my holding cell. I lay on the floor and tried to let my body heal its wounds. Townsend came down to check on me every once in a while. He brought me a turkey sandwich, which was pretty good, and every ten minutes he'd bring me a small paper cup of water. He said that all the water would hydrate my body and keep my bruised muscles, especially in the abdomen, from cramping up. I don't know if he knew what he was talking about, but I sure as hell knew what he was doing. The ointment, the Band-Aids, the clean shirt, the food—he was being the Good Cop.

Eventually, when they tried to force me to take a shitty plea and rat on Lou Turro, McLean would play the Bad Cop. And good old Townsend would be there to protect me. Good old

Townsend, who had given me food and water and medical attention, would tell me that he had my best interests in mind all along and that he knows that I should take the deal they're offering, because he really wants what's best for me. It was so transparent that it was pathetic. But if Townsend wanted to be my buddy, then there was something he could do for me.

"Hey," I said during one of his water runs. "I need a copy of the two-sided check you showed me in the car."

"I'll have to see."

"See about what? You have to give it to me," I corrected. "I'm an attorney and I'm representing myself in this matter with the assistance of Roland Cozzolino, who should be here any moment. And I need to start preparing my defense immediately."

"We'll get it to you eventually."

"The government has to disclose, *in a timely manner*, all documents that might possibly be used against me. If you guys don't give it to me, I'll be forced to make a motion to have that particular piece of evidence suppressed. And without that check, you guys have no case against me, Jackie, Louie, nobody. The whole case vanishes because you won't give me a photocopy of something you've already shown me. Not a good career move on your part. I mean, what the hell do you think I'm going to do with it, make an origami file and bust out of here?"

Townsend chuckled.

"Let's not make this a big thing, Townsie. I just want a photocopy of the check. No big deal."

"I'll have to ask," Townsend said.

"Ask away. But if I don't get it, you'll get my motion to suppress tomorrow from Mr. Cozzolino."

Fifteen minutes later I had a copy of the check in my hand.

I sat in my cell and stared at it.

I started thinking about the working man's curse. The working man wants his son to never have to make a living the way he did, so he works long and hard for years. Eventually, proudly, he sends his boy out into the world to make his fortune, a fortune that is not dependent on a strong back and good knees.

What the working man doesn't know is that he is pushing his child into an unknown world—a world where his son doesn't know the rules. The other sons in that world, the fifth-generation white-collar kids, the kids whose grandparents captained the *Mayflower* instead of stowing away in the boiler room, those kids knew the rules. They knew how the game was played in the world of suits and cigars, of polished shoes and sit-down lunches.

The working man's son was often lost in this new world. Before he knew it, despite all the sweat and blood spilled by the working man for his son, the son would still find himself far behind the others. And some sons believe the only way to make up the ground is to cheat. That's what I did. I didn't know the rules and when I realized I was losing the game, I decided to cheat.

As I sat in my cell, the more I thought about the working man's curse the more I realized that it was nothing more than a big fucking excuse for my actions. When I found myself falling behind everyone else in the race, I shouldn't have cheated. I should have just done what the working man would have done, what my father would have done—I just should have run faster.

I heard Townsend's keys in the door. He told me to come with him. He was getting me out of my holding cell just in time because after an hour I was beginning to get a little stir crazy.

Not a good sign for a guy who was looking at a minimum of ten years.

He walked me down the same white corridor as before. Except this time McLean was waiting by the conference room door. He glared at me as he opened it. Bad Cop.

"You have ten minutes," McLean fumed.

"I might need twenty," I said defiantly.

The door swung open to reveal Roland sitting alone at a wooden table. He took one look at me and jumped up.

"Did you do this to him?" he shouted at McLean.

"Settle down, counselor," McLean responded. "Why don't you talk with your client? I'm sure he can explain everything."

Roland looked at me, his eyes a mixture of confusion and concern.

"They didn't do this," I said.

Roland locked eyes with me. He knew me well enough to know when I was lying, or if I was being forced to lie, and he could tell I was being truthful. He backed off.

"Okay," Roland said. "But I'm stating for the record that I am here as Mr. Principe's legal counsel. Any attempt by the government to record or monitor this conversation is a violation of federal and state law and an infringement of the attorney-client privilege and any information gathered through such improper activity is wholly inadmissible and will result in swift civil action against the agents involved in this matter as well as the federal government."

I was impressed. When my boy wanted to, he could really lawyer his ass off.

McLean just laughed.

"Settle down, Matlock. We know the law. Besides, we're not about to do anything to jeopardize this case. We already got everything we need on your pal here."

McLean closed the door and he and Townsend walked away.

"Bobby ..."

"Just sit down, man."

Roland sat, never taking his eyes off me.

I pulled a chair away from the table and sat as well. I left my handcuffed hands in my lap, out of Roland's sight. I was ashamed of them.

"Roland," I began. "There's a lot I have to tell you."

FORTY-SEVEN

"WHAT DID I TELL YOU?!" Roland shouted. "Huh?! What did I tell you again and again and again?"

I didn't respond so Roland answered his own question.

"*Within* the law! Within the motherfuckin' law!"

"I know, I know. But I never in a million years thought that …"

"Shut up! I can't stand to even look at you right now, let alone hear your stupid fuckin' excuses!"

So I shut up. And it was quiet, very quiet. Roland paced, running his hands through his dirty-blond hair, seething. I had expected him to be angry after I told him my story but he was a hell of a lot more than just angry—he was furious.

I wanted to say something so badly, something to let him know how sorry I was for doing what I did. But I knew that whatever I said would sound like a weak excuse, because that's what it would be—a weak, pathetic excuse. I really wanted to just shout out my pleas for forgiveness because the silence was driving me mad.

Roland grabbed his chair and threw it across the table with a cry of rage and frustration. The chair bounced off the wall and landed in the corner with a loud crash. At least the silence was over.

About five seconds later the door flew open.

"What the hell's going on in here?" Townsend asked.

"I leaned back on my chair and it slipped out from under me. Why don't you get some real fuckin' furniture in this cage. My back hurts now. You're lucky I don't sue your ass," Roland shouted.

Townsend smirked and closed the door. I could hear his footsteps as he walked back down the hall.

Roland picked up the chair and sat down next to me. He got right in my face.

"When my grandfather came to this country, he changed our name from Cozzolino to Casey. From Cozzolino to Casey! You didn't know that, did you?"

I shook my head.

"You wanna know why? Because of guineas like Jackie Masella and Louie Turro. Because of guineas like you."

Roland made no effort to hide his disgust with me. I accepted it. I embraced it, even. It was what I deserved.

"My grandfather said it was better to lose a little of our heritage than for people to think that we were somehow associated with that Mob bullshit. But my dad, he changed our name back. He figured that in a city *built* by Italians, how much longer could the Mafia be all that people think of when they hear a last name that ends in a vowel? Thanks to you, Rob, I don't know the answer to that question. You're as bad as your fuckin' cousin."

I couldn't argue with him, for two reasons. First, he was right. Second, from the moment I had been arrested my mind had been racing, desperately trying to figure a way out of the mess I was in. And I had come up with something. It was dangerous and had little chance of working, but I had to do something. I knew if I stayed in prison long enough, Lou Turro would eventually be able to reach out and get me, even if I was inside. So, even if I had wanted to defend myself against Roland's verbal assault, I knew it would have been a waste of time. And at this point in my life, time could not be wasted.

"I know I fucked up," I said. "And I can fix it, but I'll need your help."

"You need my help?" Roland asked incredulously. "You drag me and Tim Bass and God knows who else into this mess with you, and now you're asking for my help? Go to hell."

"Roland, please," I pleaded. "You're not implicated. I haven't mentioned your name and I never will. You know I wouldn't do that."

"What about Bass? He's got two kids, Prince. You even think about that?"

"He didn't know anything about this. And I'll say so. The most he can get in trouble for is finding herniations that may not have been there. But like you told me, everyone sees something different in the films. He's got a defense. Besides, they don't give a shit about you or Bass. The feds don't care about me, either. We both know who they want."

"Big Lou Turro," Roland said.

"Big Lou Turro," I confirmed. "I can fix things. Maybe. But you have to bail me out. Get me the fuck out of here as soon as possible and let me try to make things right."

Roland stood and began pacing again. He wasn't delaying for dramatic effect. And he wasn't doing it to make me sweat it out a bit to teach me a lesson before he eventually agreed to help me out. Roland was actually considering whether or not he should help me get out of federal lock-up. I was panic-stricken waiting for his decision. He knew I didn't have the money to make bail and he knew my parents didn't either. Roland was well aware that he was the only person in the world who could help me.

Cozzolino and I had been best friends since Mrs. Kadet's first-grade class. In 1983, when we were confirmed at Saint Joseph's, I chose "Roland" as my confirmation name and he took "Robert," even though my sponsor was Uncle Vincent and Roland's was his cousin Gaetano. And when I was sixteen, even though I was a virgin with raging hormones who would have stepped over his own mother to see a bare breast, I refused to fool around with Rachel "Score On" Voron because I knew Roland had a crush on her. We were as close as brothers. I loved him, and I knew he loved me. While I sat there watching him, it hit me—the true magnitude of what I had done. What I had done was so bad, so horrible, it could possibly turn my own brother against me.

Roland stopped pacing. He silently turned and walked to the door.

Oh, my God, I thought, *he's just going to leave me here.*

"Roland ..."

He looked back to me.

"Why should I do anything for you?" Roland asked. "After what you've done?"

I could have pointed out that Roland had already told Townsend that he was representing me. Once he took on that responsibility, he had to do so zealously, as per the Rules of Ethics. I could have told him that the clock was ticking and that if he didn't help me now I might be beyond help in a few days. Instead, the only answer I came up with was the best reason I could think of.

"Because you're my best friend," I said, "and you're the only chance I've got."

FORTY-EIGHT

ROLAND CALLED in a few favors with some friends he had in the court system and was able to swing me an early arraignment in front of a federal magistrate. Otherwise, I would have been stuck waiting for a bail hearing until sometime that afternoon.

The federal prosecutor assigned to the case was Saul Seymour, a veteran of the Eastern District. I had actually seen him prosecute a few drug cases when I was in law school. Back then I was still mesmerized by the law—it was still pure to me, still about fairness and justice. It wasn't a contest over who could make the most money.

I loved sitting in the courts all day when I didn't have class. I'd watch motions get argued, settlements get negotiated, people win and lose millions or get sent to prison for life. I was a real trial junkie for a while, and I saw some of the most notorious cases litigated just ten feet in front of me. It was more of an education than Columbia could have ever given me. While sitting in those courtrooms on Centre Street in downtown Manhattan, I saw attorneys at the top of their game. I saw the artistry in argument, the poetry in negotiation—the dance that takes place between skilled adversaries who go head-to-head before bench and jury. It was the dance that sucked me in.

My problem was that Seymour could dance with the best of them. He was good. In fact, he was great. Hell, he was fuckin' Fred Astaire with a government job. He had been receiving offers for years from all the big private firms in Manhattan but he never considered leaving the public sector. He liked putting people in prison way too much. He got off on it. It was what made him tick, and I was his next project. Seymour was the topic of conversation as Roland drove me home.

"You pulled Seymour of all people. Talk about your shit luck."

"Yeah, I know."

"You're fucked."

"Yeah, I know."

I stared out of the window, exhausted, as the landmarks told me we were getting closer to home, closer to Janine.

"Guy's a goddamn bulldog," Roland continued. "You see him fighting me on bail? He was being reasonable and all until that asshole McLean whispers in his ear and all of a sudden he goes from agreeing on a hundred grand to opposing your release."

"Well, you got me out, so it doesn't matter now."

"Barely got you out. Quarter million bail. It's ridiculous. I mean, you've got a home in Brooklyn, a pregnant wife, a niece who is basically your responsibility, and a New York law license that you'll try to keep if you can get out of this mess. I mean, come on, where the hell does this guy think you're going to disappear to?"

Roland's words hit me like a slap in the face. My mind instantly raced back to the courtroom and the arraignment. Roland was right. Seymour had been more than willing to let me out on bail. He was a seasoned prosecutor; he knew I wouldn't jump bail—I had too much to lose.

But then McLean hurried into the courtroom and whispered something to him. Something that changed Seymour's mind. It was appropriate that we were passing Tucci's Funeral Parlor when I realized exactly what McLean had told him. I needed a bathroom. My stomach was going to explode.

"Something wrong?" Roland asked, picking up on my discomfort. "I mean, other than the fact that you're looking at a double-digit sentence?"

"I know what McLean said to Seymour."

"What are you talking about?"

"I know why Seymour changed his position on bail."

"What? Why?"

"Jackie knows."

"Jackie knows what?"

Roland was totally confused.

"Jackie knows I've been arrested. After I refused to talk and lawyered up, the FBI must have gone to Jackie. Told him I had been picked up. Probably told him I talked or was about to talk. They were trying to pressure him to turn on BLT, the only guy they really care about."

"Fuck."

"That's what McLean told Seymour. That's why Seymour changed his bail recommendation. I get bailed out, Jackie can get to me and shut me up for good. They wanted me inside to make sure I don't get killed. I disappear, they got no case."

"Wait a minute," Roland stammered. "If they were trying to play Jackie like that, why didn't they just tell you they were going to go to Jackie, try to scare you into talking."

"Because they know I won't say anything. I made that clear to them. I'm looking at ten years. Tough time, but doable; nothing I'm gonna risk my life over by flipping on Lou Turro. But Jackie is looking at federal time and state time. He's committed violent felonies. And then there's RICO on top of it, so he's spending the rest of his life in lock-up if he's convicted. If they can get anyone to flip, it's him. And the best way to get him to flip is to keep me in jail without bail, so Jackie will think I'm in there spilling my guts, implicating him and everyone else in Bensonhurst before he gets a chance to cut a deal. That's what they told him. And now that I'm out ..."

I didn't even bother to finish the thought. Didn't need to. Roland and I both knew the end to that sentence.

"You sure you're right?" Roland asked.

My cell phone rang, as if in answer to Roland's question. I answered.

"*Hey, cuz.*"

I looked to Roland. From the look on my face he knew exactly who was on the other end of the line.

"Hey, Jackie," I answered.

"I called your cell because I didn't want to wake the family this early, ya know."

"Thanks," I said. "Appreciate it."

"You home?" Jackie asked.

That's when I knew for certain the feds had gotten to him. Just a few hours earlier, Jackie had dropped me off at my house, battered and bruised and an emotional wreck. Where the hell else could he have possibly thought I'd be except home? Why would he even bother to ask that question unless he had some reason to believe that I had somehow been prevented from staying at my house?

"Of course," I said. "Where the hell would I be?"

"I don't know," he countered. "Thought maybe you went to get some breakfast or something."

"Nope, I'm home."

"I'm coming over."

My guts tightened into a small fiery ball.

"Now? It's early."

"I'll pick you up. We'll get something to eat."

"Jackie, I'm tired."

"Yeah, yeah, yeah. All you do is complain. Come on. I want to talk about what happened this morning. I feel bad about it. I'll be there in half an hour."

I couldn't say no. If I fought him too hard, he'd know I was on to him. He would rush over, and I couldn't have that because my sister and Michelle were at the house alone. I needed some time. I had no choice but to agree.

"Okay," I said. "See ya in half an hour."

My cell phone beeped, signaling the battery was low and was about to shut off.

"What's that sound?" Jackie asked, suspicious.

"My cell's dying."

I knew Jackie thought the call was being dropped on by the FBI. He was wrong, but he was clearly paranoid and scared. I could hear it in his voice. And nothing was worse than a cornered and scared Jackie Masella, because he would do anything to anyone to protect himself.

"Alright," Jackie said, unsure. "We'll go get eggs at Junior's."

Liar, I thought. *You have no intention of taking me to Junior's. I don't know where you plan on taking me, you son of a bitch, but it sure as hell isn't to Junior's Diner.*

"Okay," I said. "But just give me some time to get ready, okay?"

The cell phone battery died on me before I could get a response.

"Fuck!" I shouted.

"What's going on?" Roland asked.

"My cell died. Give me yours. I have to call my house."

Roland patted his pockets.

"Shit. Mine's at your place. I rushed out after you called and must've left it on the table."

"Dammit!"

"What's goin' on?"

"Jackie might be heading to my house right now. And if I'm not there …"

"… your entire family's there."

"What do you mean, my entire family?"

"When I left to bail you out, Ginny was calling Janine to tell her we found you. I think your parents were going to take her back to your house."

"Shit!" I slapped my hand against the car door in frustration.

"We'll pull over and find a pay phone," Roland suggested.

"We're on the BQE, where the fuck is there a pay phone?!"

I was starting to panic. My mind raced with the horrible things Jackie was capable of doing to my family if he got there and thought they were hiding me or somehow stalling him.

"We can pull off at an exit."

"And spend twenty minutes trying to find a working pay phone in Brooklyn? Just get me home. Now!"

I didn't have to tell Roland twice. I think he'd been waiting since he bought that Mercedes to have a reason to open her up on the highway, and now he had as good a reason as any. At that point, we were a solid fifteen minutes away from my house. We got there in eight.

FORTY-NINE

JANINE DIDN'T SAY a word when Roland and I walked in the back door. She just ran to me and wrapped her arms around me, pulling me against her as tight as she could. She buried her head into my chest and sobbed. In the kitchen, Ginny sat holding Michelle in her arms. My mother and father stood behind her. They all just stared at me. They knew something horrible was happening but they weren't sure what that was.

"I'm okay, sweetheart. I'm okay," I said as I stroked her chestnut brown hair.

She looked up at me, her face wet with tears.

"You're in trouble, aren't you?"

I nodded. "Yes."

"What kind of trouble?" my mother asked.

I didn't answer. I couldn't. I didn't have enough time and, besides, I just couldn't. My father approached, his eyes wide.

He placed his hand against my bruised face.

"Who did this to you?" he asked, his eyes red with barely suppressed rage.

"It's not important. You need to get out …"

"*Who?*" he shouted.

It was the first time my father had yelled at me since I was a young boy and he caught me smoking one of Jackie's Chesterfields behind our garage. His voice boomed and echoed in the kitchen and caused baby Michelle to start wailing. I had forgotten how intimidating his voice could be when he was angry. It startled me.

"Everyone, please. Listen to me."

I took a deep breath and exhaled. I had tried so hard for so long to avoid this very moment. But I couldn't dodge it any longer.

"I messed up bad," I said. "I did some things. Real bad things. And now there are people who want to hurt me. And if they can't find me, they'll hurt you. So you need to get out of here as fast as you can."

"Jackie," Janine said almost to herself.

She looked at me and right away I knew she knew. There was no use in lying, not at this point.

"Yeah," I answered.

"What about him?" my father demanded. "You got into some trouble with Jackie? Well I'll go talk to that little bastard myself. Show him what happens to someone who lays a hand on my son."

My father grabbed his jacket from the back of the kitchen chair and stormed toward the front door. I chased after and grabbed him.

"Dad, no."

My dad spun toward me.

"No one touches my son!"

My father broke free of my grasp and opened the door. I slammed it shut, almost catching his fingers in the process. He pushed me and tried to open the door again but I wouldn't let him. I grabbed his shoulders and shoved him up against the door. Hard. *Real hard.*

"Listen to me!" I shouted.

I had never gotten physical with my father in my life. I think I scared myself more than anybody, but I had to let him know that I was serious—that the situation was serious.

"Listen to me!" I shouted again, my tear-covered face just inches from his. "I fucked up, okay?" I cried. "I fucked up bigger than you could ever imagine. Think of the worst thing I could have done and then think of something ten times worse. That's what I did. Get it? I'm the bad guy here, not Jackie."

"But he beat you," my father shouted, totally confused and enraged.

"This isn't about Jackie and I getting into a fight, Dad!" I shouted back between sobs. "This is about Jackie, and Choo Choo, and Tony, and Lou Turro, and the federal government!"

My father looked at me wide-eyed, shocked at what he was hearing.

"And *me!*" I yelled.

It was cathartic to say those two simple words. All of the lying and the deception were over with those two words. Forever. Now everyone knew that I was involved, that I was dirty, that I was to blame. I couldn't hide it anymore.

"I stole, Dad, okay? I committed fraud. That settlement you were so excited about, I stole it!"

My father looked at my face all red and wet. I looked back, hoping to find a sign that he understood what I was saying. He understood. I could tell from his expression that he knew exactly what I had done. He didn't understand the details, but he knew. Looking at his face, I never imagined that I could have caused him so much pain. It was the worst moment of my life.

"Robert …" My father couldn't even finish the sentence.

"Dad, I'm going to take care of this. But you have to get everyone out of here now. Understand? Right now. Jackie's on his way over and I won't be here but if you or Mom or Janine or anyone else is, there'll be a problem. Not a problem that you can solve by talking to Jackie and not a problem you can go to the cops with. It's a problem that Jackie will fix the only way he knows how. Okay?"

My father just nodded. I turned to Roland.

"Give Janine what you have in your wallet."

Roland opened his wallet without hesitation and handed my wife just under three hundred dollars.

"Dad, how much do you have on you?"

"I don't know," he said. "About sixty."

I reached into my pocket and pulled out forty-three dollars.

"Here, it's all I have. Get in the car and drive. Don't stop. Go over the Verrazano Bridge and get to the Pennsylvania Turnpike and just drive. Get off at the first exit after Harrisburg. At the end of the exit ramp, make a right and stay at the first motel you come to. That's how I'll find you. And pay in cash."

"Where are we going?" my father asked.

Janine grabbed my arm.

"I'm scared," she said.

"So am I. But you guys have to get out of here. *Now.*"

"What about you?"

"I'll be okay. I promise."

"How do you know?" Janine asked.

"Because I'm done lying."

Ginny quickly grabbed a diaper bag and some formula for Michelle, and my dad loaded up the family in the car. They were out the door in less than a minute.

I placed my hand on Janine's stomach to feel my baby. I kissed my wife softly.

"Everything will be alright," I said.

"This can't be happening."

"It's been happening for a while," I explained. "This is just the ending. And I promise you, it will work out."

"We love you," she said.

"And I love you more than you'll ever know. I'm sorry for all of this. But now you have to leave."

I kissed Janine again and helped her into the car where everyone was waiting except my father. He approached me. I handed him the car keys.

"Go."

"You be careful," he told me.

"I will. Listen, Dad. If something happens ... my kid ..." I didn't want to say the words.

"I won't let anything happen to your family."

"I know. What I meant was, just raise him like you raised me, okay? You were a great father. Don't ever think because of all this, that somehow you ... You were a great father. I just didn't listen to you growing up. About what's important. Now get out of here, please."

"You could get hurt."

I couldn't lie to my father. I just looked him in the eyes and nodded.

"Yeah, but I gotta do what I gotta do. To end this thing," I said.

My father hugged me tightly and kissed me on the cheek. He whispered softly in my ear.

"I love you, son. You're very brave. I'm proud of you."

He let go and got in the car without looking back at me. Seconds later, the engine started and the car pulled away.

As I watched my family drive away from me I realized two things.

First, this very well might be the last time I would ever see them because there were three possibilities—either the Mob would get to me, get to them, or get to neither of us—only one of which was good. So the odds were two to one against a reunion. I knew that.

Second, I had just confessed to my family countless crimes and sent them off to hide from an imminent danger that I had created. Despite all of that, my father's last words to me were *"I'm proud of you."*

I almost had to laugh at my stupidity. I mean, I had gotten myself into this situation for a million different reasons—fear, greed, and insecurity to name just a few. But my newly made promise to Janine that I was done with lying had had an interesting and unexpected side effect—I couldn't lie to myself any more either. And I knew then the real reason why I had done what I did. Why it had been so important to me to be a success, to make the big money, to be the personal injury king of Brooklyn. It was so simple and so pathetic. It was the same reason any boy does anything. I didn't ever want to be a disappointment in my old man's eyes. I just wanted my father to be proud of me.

Standing in that alley with Roland, watching the Taurus pull around the corner and out of sight, I realized that I was the dumbest guy in the world. "I'm proud of you," my father had said and, despite everything that had gone down, he meant it. All that time I had been trying so hard to get something that I already had, something that I couldn't have lost if I had wanted to.

FIFTY

"WE SHOULD GO," Roland said. "Jackie will be here in about ten minutes, assuming he doesn't get here sooner."

I looked at him.

"*We're* not going anywhere. *I'm going.*"

"Like hell you are."

"Roland, you're too involved as it is. You're not coming."

I grabbed Roland's keys from his hand and hurried toward his Mercedes. He hurried after me.

"Hey!"

"Get lost," I growled as I reached his car.

Roland leaned against the car, preventing me from opening the door.

"You think you can pull me into your little world of shit and then tell me to just walk away? Fuck you, Prince. I can help you. And you need help. You've got a family."

"Yeah, and you've got …"

"What?" Roland interrupted. "What've I got, Prince? Money? My lousy, goddamn law firm? You've got everything to lose, Bobby. I've got shit!"

"This isn't about you."

"Like hell it isn't!" Roland shouted, slamming his fist onto the hood of his Mercedes, leaving a small indentation. "You know what I did when you told me about Janine's pregnancy? I changed my will and left everything I got to your baby. How goddamn pathetic is that? I've got nothing but money, Prince. You're my family. That kid is the closest thing I'll ever have to a child unless I knock up a stripper some day. So don't tell me this isn't about me."

One look at Roland and I knew he wasn't going to let me leave without him.

"Get in," I said as I opened the door and slipped behind the wheel.

"Alright," he nodded with some satisfaction.

I turned the ignition key, and the car roared to life as I lowered the passenger window a crack.

"Prince, it's locked," Roland said through the window.

I turned to him.

"If this all goes wrong," I said, "help my dad take care of my family."

"Prince! Open the damn door," Roland said as he pulled frantically on the door handle.

I floored the Mercedes' gas pedal and peeled away from the curb, using every ounce of horsepower that German machine had in it. I didn't dare look in the rearview. I was so terrified at what I was about to do that I feared if I saw Roland in the mirror I would stop, turn around, and go pick him up … because I knew where I was heading was no place I should be going to alone.

FIFTY-ONE

RUMORS HAD A TENDENCY to spread like the plague in Bensonhurst. When those rumors concerned Big Lou and his crew, they spread like the plague riding on the back of wildfire.

I figured that as soon as the FBI lied to Jackie and told him I was selling him out, Jackie had fessed up to BLT and told him that everything was turning to shit. Lou probably then made it clear to Jackie, in no uncertain terms, that either he take me out or Lou would take out Jackie himself. Either way, Big Lou wanted to make sure my family was going to have to pay a visit to Tucci's Funeral Parlor as soon as possible.

Choo Choo and Tony were most likely there for this meeting because they never seemed to be less than ten feet from Big Lou's side. Choo Choo, who gossiped like a Long Island yenta, probably told his nephew Skinny what had happened while giving him the order for the morning breakfast run. And once Skinny knew something, the whole block knew.

The one thing you had to love about Bensonhurst was the predictability of its residents. I would have bet my last breath, which for all I knew would be exhaled within the hour, that there were a lot of people in the neighborhood who heard that morning that I was in a bad way with BLT.

I parked the Mercedes about two blocks away from Patsy's. I didn't want anyone in the neighborhood to see me driving it and link Roland to this thing. I made sure I hid the car behind a bunch of forklift pallets that were stacked up behind the 69th Street Warehouse. If I got killed over this mess, that was one thing, but I couldn't let anything happen to Roland. For all I knew, he'd be helping to raise my child.

I walked along New Utrecht Avenue, surprising myself with my quick pace—*rushing to my own funeral*. But I knew what I had to do, and I just wanted to get it over with. As I crossed Ovington Court, all I thought about was Janine.

Memories of our life together engulfed and warmed me even more than the sunlight that had broken through the clouds, shining right down on my face. Each memory came swiftly, touching me briefly and then escaping like an insect that lands on your arm and then quickly flies away.

I recalled our first date and how I had returned beer bottles to afford the thirty-one roses I sent her a month later, one for every day I had known her. I could hear my father as he leaned over the front-row pew on my wedding day to whisper to me "Bobby, she looks like an angel" when my soon-to-be wife started down the aisle. I remembered how I felt the first time I knew she really loved me.

The memories sickened me but I didn't try to shake them. On the contrary, I embraced them, invited more to escape the catacombs of my memory and invade my conscious mind.

I needed these memories to keep my feet moving along Ovington Court toward my final destination. The thoughts of Janine gave me the strength to not turn tail and run for my life, the strength to move forward and do what needed to be done.

Skinny spotted me just as I was beginning to cut across the Louis J. Turro Memorial Playground. He was on the corner, diagonally across from me, about fifty yards away. He had a bag of pastries and coffee from Ferro's Bakery.

We made eye contact and as soon as we did I knew my earlier suspicions were right. Jackie had run to Big Lou and now the whole crew and only God knows who else knew I was a marked man. Skinny, who wasn't skinny at all—he was a fat fuck but was just skinny compared to his bovine uncle—dropped the bag and ran from the corner to Patsy's as fast as his elephant-like legs would carry him. He disappeared through the front door. I didn't slow down. I just kept walking across the playground—past the swings and the sandbox and the water fountains—right toward Patsy's.

I was about thirty yards away when Skinny exited Patsy's and hustled down the street. His uncle probably sent him home and told him to stay there. Seconds later Choo Choo and Tony came out of the club. They stood on either side of the doorway and watched me approach. They each had a gun in their right hand—they didn't bother to hide the weapons because the street was empty. Also, they knew I would expect them to come out armed. For all I knew, they would wait until I got closer and then shoot me right there on the street. It wouldn't have surprised me. Even if a hundred people had seen what happened, no one would have seen what happened. That's the way things worked in Bensonhurst.

I figured the best thing to do was to not even look them in the eye, so I didn't. I stared straight ahead and walked past them, opened the door, and stepped into the club. They must have been expecting me to stop and ask for permission to see their boss because they were both pissed as hell a few seconds later. I was barely inside before Tony had me face down, bent over a table. He held me down by the scruff of my shirt collar while Choo Choo patted me down.

"Think you can just walk in here, you little fuck?" Tony whispered in my ear.

I heard The Office door open behind me.

"I hope he lets me do you," Tony whispered more softly. "You always thought you were so smart."

Strange how people who hardly know you are willing to tell you how much they hate you right before you die. To this day, those three sentences are the only words Tony has ever said to me.

"No weapons," Choo Choo reported.

Tony yanked me upright, grabbed me by the tricep, and led me to the back of Patsy's. The place was empty. No one playing cards. No one watching television. Just me and three sociopaths and whatever waited for me inside The Office.

Tony opened The Office door and pushed me inside. Choo Choo followed and closed the door behind us, cutting me off from the outside world. Perhaps forever.

FIFTY-TWO

TONY AND CHOO CHOO stood on either side of me. Big Lou sat at the same table where he and I had sat together and discussed my father's skills as a carpenter and the health benefits of cashews. This time I wasn't invited to sit with him. There were no offers of a drink or small talk about family. Lou just stared at me for a moment. There was a piece of paper in front of him and a pen. He wrote on the paper and held it up for me to see. It read in very neat print: *STRIP*.

"What?" I asked, completely confused by the bizarre request.

My reply annoyed Lou and he wrote quickly and angrily on the paper once more. This time his handwriting wasn't nearly as neat. The note read: *Get naked or you will be suffocated.*

Lou looked to his right. I followed his gaze to a clear plastic bag and a cord of rope on the couch. I knew Lou was serious. He wanted me to get undressed. I just didn't understand why but I was no position to argue.

I unbuttoned my shirt and dropped it on the sofa. Without untying them, I pushed off my shoes and then slid off my pants. I thought maybe they were prepping me to be tortured. Or maybe it was easier to burn a body without any clothes. Or maybe Big Lou was some sick rapist who was going to have some fun with me before putting a bullet in my head. A million different scenarios were playing out in my mind and not one of them ended with me going home safely.

I stood there in my boxers and socks. Tony gave me a sharp elbow in the side and indicated that I was still wearing too much clothing. I removed each sock and then my boxers. I was thankful the room wasn't cold because the last thing I needed was to be in a showdown with Big Louie Turro and literally look like I had no balls.

As soon as I was totally naked, Choo Choo yanked up both of my arms and looked under them. Then he grabbed my balls and lifted them to look underneath. And for the second time in five minutes, Tony bent me over a table, except this time, instead of whispering in my ear how badly he wanted to kill me, he spread my cheeks with his hand and stared up my ass. If he had any idea how bad my stomach was feeling and how nervous I was at that moment, he would have backed up quickly. In less than a minute, my mafia physical was over. Tony looked at Lou and shook his head.

I realized then that they were looking to see if I was wired. Although I was glad to know why I had to get undressed, I was terrified. Since Lou now knew I wasn't miked, he could kill me with impunity. I immediately learned I was correct to feel that way.

"Do it," Lou said.

Choo Choo crossed the room and opened the door to a large storage closet. One look inside and I knew I was about to die. In the closet was a huge industrial metal tub; a large sheet of plastic covered the floor; and a restaurant-quality kitchen knife hung from a hook behind the door. They were going to gut me and bleed me out like a pig.

Instinct took over. Completely naked, I bolted for The Office door but Tony stopped me with a punch to the face. I fell to the floor but I got right back up, trying to run through Tony—run through the wall if I had to—anything to get out of there.

Choo Choo grabbed me from behind by the arms. Tony grabbed my legs by the ankles. They carried me back toward the storage closet. I flailed, jerking my body up and down, back and forth, trying in vain to break free. *Fight or flight* became one as I was pathetically attempting the former so I could achieve the latter. My last words to Janine had been that I'd be okay. I wasn't going to let these bastards make me lie to her again.

I screamed and thrashed and pulled but could not break free. I had come into the world naked, kicking, and screaming and I was going out the same way. This was all going horribly wrong. I had gone in there with a plan. A strategy. I was going to negotiate my way out of this, like a good lawyer, like the lawyer I always knew I was. But like all my other legal endeavors in life, this one had turned out to be a disaster.

When we reached the closet, Tony punched me again to subdue me. It worked. I blacked out for a few seconds and awoke to discover Choo Choo using conductor wire to bind my ankles and tie my hands behind my back. They lifted me off the ground and placed me in the tub. I had less than a minute to live if I didn't act fast.

"Lou, think about it!" I shouted. "Why would I come here? I knew you'd want to kill me, so why would I come here?"

"Shut him up," Choo Choo said.

Tony walked from the closet into The Office. It gave me a moment to further plead my case.

"They have Jackie dead to rights!" I screamed, panicked. "I bet he didn't tell you that. He just said I was picked up, right? But he didn't tell you how they got me, did he? He didn't tell you that they've got him, too!"

Tony appeared with a roll of silver electrical tape. He pulled off a length of tape from the roll. It made the most sickening "ripping" sound I had ever heard.

"I could have run!" I pleaded. "But I came here!"

Tony leaned over me to place the tape on my mouth. I bit the tape and spit it out.

"Son of a bitch!" Tony said.

As he pulled off another piece of tape, I turned my head to the side and looked right into Lou's eyes and begged for my life.

"They have Jackie. So they have you! They've got the proof that can send you away! I have it here with me! I'm the only one who can keep you out of prison!"

I barely got the last words out before the tape silenced me. Lying in the tub, I struggled to stand but I couldn't. I watched Tony reach for the knife hanging on the back of the door. It's funny the things you think of right before you die. I suddenly remembered reading in an article somewhere that stabbing victims often claim they didn't feel the knife go into them. I hoped that was true.

Tony turned back toward me. I closed my eyes and began to pray. But I didn't pray to God. I prayed to my unborn child.

Please forgive me, sweetheart. I never meant to leave you like this. I'll watch over you always. Amen. Then I took a deep breath, held it, and waited to die.

The stabbing victims quoted in that article are full of shit. I felt the blade as soon as it entered my right arm. Strangely enough, the worst pain came when the knife was pulled out.

"Hold him still," I heard Tony bark. "I missed and hit his arm."

I felt Choo Choo's catcher's-mitt sized hands press down on my sternum and legs. I pressed my eyes even tighter and braced for the second stab.

FIFTY-THREE

THE SECOND stab never came.

"Get dressed," Lou told me as he sat down at the marble-topped table.

Getting dressed was difficult because I was still shaking, amazed that I had been pulled from the tub as per BLT's orders. I put on my clothes, except for one of my socks that I tied over my shirt, tightly around my upper arm, to help stop the bleeding. The blood soaked through the shirt and was quickly making its way through the sock. Tony and Choo Choo stood by the door, so I couldn't have run if I had wanted to, and believe me, I wanted to.

"What do you mean, you have the proof that can send me away?" Lou asked. "Feds don't have nothin' on me. If they did, I'd have been picked up already."

I sat down across from Lou, uninvited. Tony bristled. I placed my hands in front of me, trying to appear calm and unemotional. I knew that whatever I said over the next few minutes would determine if I was going back in that storage closet, if I'd ever see Janine again, if I'd ever hold my child, if I'd live or die.

In my Trial Advocacy class I was taught all about the art of *"Persuasive Argument and Negotiation."* I learned how to understand what your audience's concerns were and how to alleviate them, how to present your opinion in a clear and logical manner, and how to be prepared for any counterpoints. I kicked ass in that class—got an A+. Professor Bauer said I was a natural speaker and debater.

Problem was that instead of presenting my case to Professor Bauer in a classroom on 116th Street, I was in The Office and my adversary was a Mafia crime boss who had already tried to kill me once that day. I was about to engage in the most important negotiation of my life. A negotiation *for* my life. I knew that in order to pull it off I had to be the kind of lawyer I had always dreamed of becoming. I had to be like the lawyers I watched when I was in law school. I had to *dance.*

"You're absolutely right," I said, which is Rule Number One when presenting your position to an adversary—*Agree with the parts of their argument that are not objectionable—It helps you gain credibility.* "They don't have anything on you. But once they bring in Jackie and dangle twenty-five to life in his face, he'll tell them whatever they want to know. They don't care about Jackie, they want you."

"Bullshit," Lou said.

"You think the feds went through all this trouble to convict Jackie Masella?" I scoffed and pointed at Big Lou. "They wanna land the big fish ... Jackie's just the bait."

"Fuck you." Lou tried to sound confident but I was certain I picked up a bit of uncertainty in his voice. I pounced on the opportunity.

"How much faith do you really have in Jackie Masella?" I asked as if Lou was on the stand and I was doing a cross-examination. "Does he have any reason not to cut a deal and rat you out? If he points a finger at you, they'll toss him in Witness Protection and he'll spend his golden years working at a Wal-Mart in Topeka—a much better alternative than life in lock-up. And in case you haven't noticed, Jackie hates your guts. He thinks you treat him like shit because he doesn't earn. He'd like nothin' better than for you to die in prison."

Rule Number Two—*Find common ground through a common enemy*—in this case, Jackie Masella.

"Jackie won't roll over," Lou said. "He's dumb, but he's not stupid."

"Really? You might want to take a look at this. It might change your mind."

I reached into my pocket and pulled out the photocopy of the Salvatore Tangelino check.

Rule Number Three—*Whenever possible, counter an argument with objective, tangible evidence.*

Blood, which had now soaked through my shirt sleeve down to my cuff, curled around my fingers and smeared onto the copy of the check. It was now, literally, blood money. I slid the paper across the table to Lou. Lou glanced at the check but didn't touch it.

"That's the proof that can send you away. Because it can send Jackie away and he'll sell you out in a heartbeat. It's the check I wrote out to Tangelino when his case settled. Jackie had him sign it directly over to him because he was scared Tangelino would run away with the money. This check is enough to put Jackie inside for a long time. You still so sure he won't flip on ya?"

I was getting to him. At least I thought I was. At the time

I couldn't really tell. I don't know if it was the stress of the situation or my blood loss, but I was feeling dizzy and was having trouble concentrating.

Lou pushed the check back at me with disgust.

"Nice try, counselor. This isn't even the real check. Tangelino settled for seventy-five grand. This check is for ninety-eight thousand," he said. "You think I'm stupid?"

He turned to Tony. "Throw him back in the tub, he's fucking with us."

I didn't understand what the hell Lou was talking about. Tony grabbed me by the arms, which hurt like hell considering the gash I had sustained, and tried to lift me from the chair. I held onto the table with both hands. I don't know where my strength came from, but Tony couldn't pull me away.

"Tangelino settled for one hundred fifty thousand! Not seventy-five!" I shouted as Tony pulled my injured arm loose. I somehow yanked it back and desperately grabbed the table again. "If you don't believe me look it up in the court file! The Case Closing Statement is public record! You can see for yourself! If you don't let me help you, you're going to prison!"

Big Lou took this in. He signaled to Tony to let go of me. I stood there, dizzy as hell, trying to keep my balance, pressing my hand tightly against my wound, as Big Lou looked at me, totally confused. So was I for a moment but then everything became crystal clear. Despite the circumstances, I couldn't help but crack a small smile.

"Looks like Jackie isn't as dumb as we thought," I said. "He had Tangelino sign the check directly over to him so he could deposit it into his own account. Then he told you the case settled for seventy-five when it really settled for one fifty. You thought your share was only fifty grand so that's all Jackie gave you. But you were really supposed to get ninety-eight large. Looks like Jackie ripped you off of about forty-eight thousand dollars."

Lou grabbed the check and stared at it. His jaw locked tight. His nostrils flared and his face went flush with anger. I wouldn't have been shocked if the check had burst into flames from the intensity of his gaze.

I realized right then that Big Lou was going to kill my cousin. And I had set things in motion by showing BLT the check. I wanted to live and I wanted my family to be safe, but I never wanted Lou Turro to kill Jackie. But that's exactly what was going to happen. I knew it—I could see it on Lou's face. And there was nothing I could do about it except use it to my advantage.

Rule Number Four—*When an unforeseen opportunity arises, adapt and exploit.*

"This is what I'm offering," I said. "I'll go to the feds and sign a confession that the entire scheme was mine and Jackie's. I'll say you had nothing to do with it. The check being signed over to Jackie backs up my story that he was keeping all the money for himself. There's nothing to tie you to this but me and Jackie."

"If there's nothing to tie me to this but you two, why don't I just make you both disappear?"

And, finally, Rule Number Five—*When a question is asked for which you don't have an adequate response, bluff your fucking ass off.*

"Mr. Turro, you're a smart man. Think about it for a moment. I knew you could have killed me as soon as I walked into Patsy's. In fact, you almost did. But I walked right in anyway. Without weapons. Without the FBI. So you have to ask yourself, why would I come here without protection? The answer is obvious—I wouldn't. And because I wouldn't, you almost caused yourself an unnecessary prison stint with that whole stabbing in the tub thing."

"What the hell are you talking about?"

"I drafted a quit-claim trust. It's locked away in my safe deposit box, in a bank somewhere in this state. And you don't know where."

I don't know if I was high from the blood loss or maybe when your life is at stake you don't know the bullshit you're capable of spewing, but there's no such thing as a quit-claim trust. There is something in the law called a quit-claim deed, but that has to do with real estate transactions. I just made it up on the spot because I had to say something and *quit-claim trust* just sounded real good. Besides, I was in no position to worry about legal accuracy. I was trying to save my life. I knew my audience—all I had to do was sound like I knew what I was talking about and I had a chance. So I made up a term that had all the right legal bells and whistles and proceeded to give the performance of a lifetime, a lifetime that I was hoping wasn't about to come to an end.

"A quit-claim trust is a document that operates kind of like a will. But instead of giving away my assets to my heirs, it gives specific instructions to those who hold power of attorney as to how certain documents, in my case videos and papers, need to be distributed upon my death."

"Videos?" Lou scoffed, trying not to sound concerned, but I could tell he was.

He wasn't nearly as concerned as I was because I could have sworn I had just heard myself slur a word or two. I couldn't let Lou know I was feeling weak. Weakness equates to desperation, and desperate people lie and I couldn't have Lou know I was lying. I had to appear confident, almost cocky. So I sucked it up and, despite the pain, kept on dancing.

"Right. I made a video explaining the entire scam. How it worked. Who was involved. How we got paid. Everything. I implicated myself. Jackie. *And you*. And I made copies of all the relevant documents, pleadings, checks. Everything's in a safe deposit box with specific instructions to a lawyer from another state, you don't know who he is and never will, that in the event of my death or if I go missing for more than seventy-two hours, everything in the safe deposit box is to be sent to the FBI."

I was really lying my ass off, but it sounded good. Problem was I wasn't sure if Big Lou thought I was lying.

"I don't believe you," he said.

Now I was positive Big Lou thought I was lying.

"That's your choice," I said. "But you're taking a risk. You already know that *I* won't talk to the feds. I told them to stick it up their ass when I had the chance. But what happens when Jackie is arrested? He *has* to cut a deal because he knows if this thing goes to trial and all the facts come out, he's a dead man because you'll learn he stole fifty grand from you. The only way he can survive is to rat you out while he walks. That's what the government wants. In fact, it's what they're banking on. Why else do you think Jackie hasn't been arrested yet? They want to pressure him first. Get him to flip on you before he lawyers up."

Lou considered this for a moment. I really had him reeling. He didn't know what to think, which was good because the longer he was confused, the longer I got to live. I waited for his response. Once again, my line dangled in the water, waiting for a bite. Lou stared straight into my eyes.

"How's this gonna work?" he asked.

I didn't hesitate in answering.

"You pay two hundred grand, cash, to my wife. Leave it in

a duffel bag in the grass catcher of the lawn mower that's in my backyard shed. I also want your word that you'll let everyone know that my family and I are untouchable. In exchange, I do your time for you. I take the heat, say Jackie told me himself that you knew nothing about this thing, that he was doing it on his own to rip you off. I confess to everything and give you your walking papers."

"Two hundred grand is a lot of money."

"It's a bargain considering how many years you'd get."

Lou stared at me. Five seconds passed. Then ten. He didn't blink once. He put the check down on the table. I swear he was about to agree to everything when his goddamn cell phone rang. He answered.

"Hey, Jackie. No, Rob's down here. Yeah, down here with me. Really? Good. Bring her down here, too. Now."

My heart began to pound out of control when I heard Lou say *"Bring her down here."* Jackie had somehow gotten to Janine. And if he had gotten to her, what had happened to the rest of my family?

"Now we'll get to the bottom of this bullshit," Lou snorted. I fell back down into my chair. Nervous sweat began to pour down my forehead as I tried to comprehend the fact that I might have just caused my wife's death.

FIFTY-FOUR

MY MIND FLOODED with horrendous scenarios of what would happen to Janine when she arrived. *Would they beat her? Torture her? Rape her? Kill her in front of me?* Maybe they would do all of those things—all to teach me a lesson. More important than my lesson, they would create another urban legend that would permeate the streets of Brooklyn like the stories of Sammy "The Barber" Scala who walked into The Office but never walked out and Charlie Campo, the dead high school quarterback. I'd become just another story to solidify Lou's terror hold on Bensonhurst.

I had no idea what Big Lou had in mind. All I knew was that my wife was about to undergo unimaginable pain because of something I had done. But the pain wasn't unimaginable at all because as I sat in my chair and waited for Janine to arrive, I thought of every possible thing they could do to her to the point that I was driving myself mad.

I jumped out of my seat when The Office door opened. I had mentally prepared myself to die fighting to protect my wife. I figured they had already stabbed me once and I was still alive. Truth be told, after all I had been through in the prior twenty-four hours, I was starting to feel like I was invincible.

I quickly learned I wouldn't have to worry about Janine. I'd have to worry about Joey. The Office door opened and my terrified ex-secretary was shoved in at gunpoint by Jackie. Joey took one look at my beat-up face and my bloody arm and broke into tears.

"Jesus Christ, shut up already," Jackie said and slapped Joey across the face. She fell backward onto the couch.

"Hey!" I shouted and moved toward Jackie. I took less than a step before Choo Choo intercepted me.

"You wanna play, cuz?" Jackie threatened. He slammed his gun down on the table and rushed me. Big Lou cut him off.

"Settle down," he said.

Jackie looked at me and smiled.

"Think you're smart, you little prick?" he mocked. "Running over here? I'm gonna kill you myself ... and then I'll find where you hid your family."

"Have a seat, Jackie," Lou said calmly.

A little too calmly for Jackie's taste. He could tell right away something was wrong.

"What's up?" he asked.

"Nothing. Just have a seat."

Jackie instinctively looked back toward the table for his gun but it was gone. When Jackie charged me, I had noticed Tony picking up the gun and pocketing it.

Jackie quickly tried to turn the attention elsewhere.

"This wetback, she's been cryin' the whole time," Jackie said. "She's lucky I didn't plug her in the car."

"Where are your kids?" I asked Joey, worried that Jackie had done something to them.

"They're okay. They slept at my brother's last night," she blubbered.

"Shut the fuck up!" Jackie shouted. "Where the hell do you think you are? At the fuckin' firm? By the fuckin' water cooler? Shut up!"

Jackie looked around for some kind of approval from his paisans. He got nothing.

"Maybe you need to shut up for a while, Jack," Lou said coldly.

"What?" Jackie stammered. "What are you talkin' about?"

"Maybe I need to shut you up myself."

"What the fuck's goin' on here?" Jackie said.

He spun, panicked, and pointed to me.

"Anything this bastard said to you is bullshit!"

Lou motioned to Choo Choo.

"Take her out front."

Choo Choo pulled Joey off the couch and led her out the door into the main room of Patsy's. She looked at me the entire time, her eyes locked on mine—she wanted me to do something, anything, to help her. She was scared. So was I, but at that moment I was helpless and there was nothing I could do for her.

"I'm going to get you out of this" was all I could say as the door closed, cutting us off from each other. It was a hollow promise at best.

Lou turned back to Jackie.

"What would he have said?" Lou asked Jackie.

"What do you mean?" Jackie responded.

"You said anything Bobby said is bullshit. What would he lie about that would get you so riled up?"

"I don't know, but he's a fuckin' liar! He's tryin' to save his own ass!"

"I'm confused," Lou continued. "What would he have to lie about?"

Lou was toying with Jackie, dragging it out, trying to trip up Masella.

"I don't ... I don't know," Jackie sputtered. "He's just a liar."

Jackie had grown pale and he was nervously rubbing the tips of his fingers into his sweaty palms. I don't think he was even aware he was doing it.

"You don't know?" Lou asked.

Jackie just shut up now. He knew he was in trouble.

Lou pulled his chair around so that he faced Masella. He sat right across from him, no more than a foot away. Lou was done playing games.

"How much did Tangelino settle for?" Lou asked him pointedly.

"What?" Jackie was terrified.

"Simple question, Jackie."

Jackie, unbelievably, looked to me as if he wanted my help.

"Hey!" Lou scolded, "I'm over here. Look me in the fuckin' eye and tell me how much that case settled for."

Jackie didn't answer. He knew right then it was over. All of it. The scheme. The lies. His life.

"This help you remember?" Lou said, and he pulled the copy of the check from his pocket and held it up in front of Jackie.

Jackie still didn't say a word. Again he looked to me, his eyes filled with tears, searching for help.

"You think your cousin can do something for you? Okay, let's ask him. Hey Prince, if I go to the Adams Street

Courthouse and pull the Tangelino file, how much will it say the case settled for?"

I looked down at the ground. I didn't answer. I couldn't. Lou wasn't in the mood to play games with me either.

"You have one second to answer or I'll go tell Choo Choo to blow that little spic's head off."

"One fifty," I said softly without lifting my head.

That was it—I had just killed my cousin. I looked up to find Jackie looking straight at me.

"I'm sorry," I said, barely audible.

Lou wrapped his fingers around Jackie's face by the chin and turned his head so they were looking at each other again.

"You sorry nickel-and-dimer," Lou said.

Jackie began to sob. "I'm sorry, Lou," he cried.

"You're gonna die over forty-eight grand. You were always the dumbest guy I had workin' for me."

"I got problems. You know I do," Jackie continued.

Lou ignored Jackie. He stood and nodded to Tony. Tony approached, gun drawn, and motioned for Jackie to stand.

"Take your clothes off," Tony told him.

Jackie looked to his boss.

"I didn't think this one out!" he shouted, tears running down his face and into his mouth. That night in my office, when Jackie cried to me, he had cried out of shame and sorrow. But now he was crying out of terror.

"I'm so sorry! I'll give the money back! All of it! I can get it! Please. I'm so sorry."

"Take 'em off," Tony repeated, tapping Jackie's cheek with the muzzle of the gun.

"Tony," Jackie pleaded, "I'm your kid's godfather for Christ's sake. I'm your kid's godfather."

"Get up," Tony commanded.

Jackie slowly stood from his chair. He quietly cried as he raised his hands to his shirt collar and his fingers began unfastening each button on his shirt.

Lou turned his attention from Jackie to me.

"I'm gonna hold on to your friend out there," Lou told me as my cousin continued to disrobe in relative silence. "If you don't follow through on our deal, she'll wish I had put her in the tub to drain her out. Instead, I'll take her to East New York, introduce her to some of the big, pumped-up coons I got watching over my warehouses. They'll ride her brown ass until it bleeds and then they'll leave her in some project basement to die. You got me?"

"Before the end of the day my lawyer will deliver you a copy of my plea agreement in which I will totally clear you of any wrongdoing. Then as soon as Joey is released, I'll send my attorney to destroy the contents of the safe deposit box."

Lou thought this through a moment. It satisfied him.

"Come on."

Lou led me to the door, past Jackie who was standing completely naked just a few feet away. He was just standing there, letting Tony bind his hands behind his back. He wasn't crying any more. He wasn't struggling like I had done. He had accepted his fate. It was part of the job. I think Jackie had always known that one day his life would end like that, or something close to it. Our eyes locked but we said nothing.

As I stepped out of The Office, Jackie called out to me.

"Prince."

I turned back.

"I still love you," he said. And I knew he meant it.

I don't know if he said that to make me feel guilty or if he said it to make me feel better. But, in truth, it made me feel neither.

I didn't say anything back to Jackie. There was nothing I could say. I just did what I had to do, which was turn my back on my cousin and leave him behind to die.

FIFTY-FIVE

THE BLINDS IN THE BAR area were shut tight as usual and, since the front door was closed, Patsy's was almost pitch dark except for the small lamp on the corner table where Choo Choo was watching over Joey.

Lou stopped at the door.

"I'll be back in half an hour."

Choo Choo nodded. Lou opened the door but I didn't move. I glared at Choo Choo.

"If you or Tony lay so much as a finger on her," I said, "I'll choke the life out of both of you with my bare hands the day I get out. You can set your watch on that one you fat fuck."

I heard my own voice, and I sounded crazy. Since I had a battered face and my entire arm was covered in blood, I must have looked crazy as well. Considering all that had happened, I don't think I was playing with a full deck. And that worked in my favor because at that moment I meant every word I had just said. And Choo Choo knew I did. I looked at Joey a moment, tried to give her a look that would instill some confidence, and then walked out of Patsy's and into the sunshine.

Lou's Cadillac was a whale with white exterior and red leather seats. A real mob mobile. He made me lean forward in the car seat the entire way so that I wouldn't get blood on his interior. We rode in silence. No talking. No radio. Nothing. Twenty-seven minutes of silence. We didn't say a word to each other until he dropped me off about a quarter mile from the Federal Detention Center.

"You get out here," he said.

"Okay."

He pressed the automatic door lock.

"You think Jackie's dead by now?" I asked.

Lou didn't answer. Instead he flipped on the radio and looked straight ahead through the windshield.

"You don't have to answer, but you should know that after I confess, they'll go to arrest Jackie. They'll come to Patsy's looking for him. So, do what you have to do to make sure everything is … just do what you need to do."

"Don't worry, kid," Lou said. "This ain't my first picnic."

I pulled on the door handle and got one foot onto the street when I felt Lou's hand grab my arm.

"If I'm implicated in this thing, in any way, you'll wish you'd never met me," he said.

"I already do," I replied.

I got out of the car and closed the door. Lou made an illegal U-turn and drove away. Despite the bleeding and the dizziness, and even though I hadn't run a quarter mile since I was fifteen, I started sprinting as fast as I could. I couldn't wait to turn myself in.

FIFTY-SIX

"THAT'S ALL YOU'RE GIVING ME?" McLean asked.

He leaned back in his government-issued uncomfortable desk chair and gave Townsend a look like I was wasting their time. Up to that point, I basically had been. I'd been with McLean and Townsend for over two hours and we were just getting to the plea negotiations.

After running from Lou's car, I barged into the lobby of the federal building out of breath and looking like a Bosnian refugee. I'm lucky I didn't get shot right there. Townsend, the good cop, had to take me to a doctor who gave me some shots of antibiotics, an IV, and then he stitched me up. Forty-nine sutures. I had lost a little over one and a half pints of blood. The doc said a little more and I could have gone into shock. He wanted to admit me for observation to see if I'd eventually need a transfusion, but I refused. They made me sign out AMA (against medical advice), which I gladly did. I didn't care about saving my arm. All I wanted to do was to sit down with McLean and Townsend and try to save my ass.

"What do you mean, '*that's all*'?" I responded. "I gave you Jackie Masella on a silver platter. Not to mention hanging my own ass out to dry. Now I wanna walk."

"You wanna walk, give us Lou Turro."

"I've told you already, he had nothin' to do with this. Jackie was pissed because Louie wasn't giving him enough of the action. Masella thought this scam was a good way to put some dough in his pocket without having to share with his boss. Why do you think he had the check signed directly over to him?"

McLean considered this.

"Give us Masella and you get five."

McLean looked to Townsend again, who was standing by the door.

"We'll get Masella to tell us what we need to know about Turro," he said to his partner.

"You want me to squeal on my own cousin and still do five years," I said incredulously. "I give you Jackie and get six months, minimum security, upstate."

"Three years."

"One year," I countered. "And I want a letter from each of you jerkoffs in my file saying that I cooperated in the arrest of Jackie Masella. I gotta have something for the Parole Board."

I was just acting now, trying to sell the lie, because I knew damn well that Jackie was forever unarrestable, to say the least.

"Two years. That's the best I can do," McLean said.

I'd negotiated enough cases to know when someone couldn't bend anymore, and two years was as far as McLean could go. I thought about it for a moment. Two years of my life. Two years away from Janine and my family. Two years of seeing my kid only in photos, because I sure as hell wasn't going to have Janine drag our baby to a prison for visits. I knew I probably wouldn't serve the entire sentence, but I'd still be in for a long time. But it was better than going to trial. At trial I could have gotten a decade or worse.

"Two years," I said. "And you have to appear at my parole hearing and testify in favor of my early release. You gotta say that I'm a solid citizen who was pressured into this by the mob."

"You've got brass balls, you know that, Principe?"

"That's what my doctor tells me."

"Fine. But I can't put the last part about us testifying in the written plea agreement. I'd get canned."

"Then I'll have to take your word for it, won't I?"

"You have my word."

McLean extended his hand and I shook it.

"Write it up and I'll sign it," I said.

McLean turned to Townsend.

"Go pick up Masella."

Townsend hurried out the door to look for a man whom I knew he would never find.

I was wrong. My cousin was eventually found. Jackie was picked up about a week later by a tuna boat off the north end of Long Island. He was chained to a metal chair. The chain tangled with one of the fishing lines, and Jackie got pulled up into the net. It was a million-to-one shot. Lou must have really thought hard about what I said about the feds looking for Jackie at Patsy's and called Tony with a change of plans.

Forensic teams poured over Jackie's body. The only thing they knew for sure was that Jackie was alive when he was dumped in the ocean. He had drowned. There was bruising on his wrists. The examiners believe Jackie struggled to get free while he was stuck at the bottom. I guess at some point he had decided to not be so accepting of his fate. They searched all over him for other clues but they never found anything. The water had washed away all of the evidence. Everyone knew who killed Jackie but there was never an arrest.

It's strange but, despite all that happened, there are times when I really miss him. Like when the Yankees beat up on the Red Sox. Jackie hated the Sox as much as he worshipped the Yanks and he and I used to love reading the *New York Post* sports page together, having a good laugh at the expense of Red Sox Nation. Or like this one time, when a cherry 1965 Mustang convertible drove by. I knew Jackie would've cracked, *"Man I gotta steal me one of those one of these days"* because he always said that when he saw a Mustang. Same joke, every time—but he always managed to get me to laugh.

I know he was a bad man who did vicious, horrible things, some of them to me, but he had a good side, too. Just like all of us.

Besides, I have no right to judge anyone anymore. I'm a convicted felon.

FIFTY-SEVEN

EVERYTHING YOU'VE HEARD about white-collar prisons being country clubs is true. There are no gang rapes or guard beatings or four guys sharing a cell. I did have one cellmate, though—an accountant. It turned out that he had gone to college with one of my friends from law school. So he and I hung out a lot, played cards, talked sports, shit like that— things to help pass the time.

Most of the guys at Otisville were accountants. There were a lot of corporate executives, too. A few lawyers and even a couple of judges. One of them was Judge Batton. I had argued in front of him several times in New York. He was doing six years for taking bribes. We played basketball together every Tuesday and Thursday. I asked him once, just out of curiosity, why he never approached me about a bribe. He said that in a million years he never would have thought that I'd fix a trial— my reputation, he claimed, was better than a Boy Scout's.

The first few months were hard though. I couldn't stand being away from Janine. I didn't realize it until my first night in prison, but I hadn't slept without her by my side since the day we were married. The first couple of nights I'd spoon my pillow and pretend it was her, just to help me fall asleep. After a while I got used to sleeping alone, and that really bothered me.

Janine wasn't angry with me. She knew me. She knew how much pressure I put on myself to be a success, to achieve, to carry the Principe name to the next level. Problem is I did exactly that but it was a level down. She understood my fears and the pathetic rationalizations and logic I used to justify what I was doing while I was doing it. She understood me. What made me tick was what eventually caused me to blow up.

Just because she wasn't angry with me doesn't mean she wasn't disappointed in me. And that was a hundred times worse than anger. After I confessed, Roland picked up my family in Pennsylvania and eventually brought Janine to the Detention Center to see me before I was transferred. I told her everything. In detail. When I was done her beautiful eyes were filled with tears.

"Who do I look up to now?" she asked.

That blew me away. I always knew she loved me. But I never had any idea that she actually looked up to me. I couldn't imagine a worse way to find out. Like I said, I would have rather that she was angry with me. In fact, it would have been easier if she had just hated my guts.

But she's an amazing woman and she's forgiving. She visited every week. It was all I looked forward to.

I turned thirty-four while in prison. Janine came to see me on my birthday. She wasn't allowed to give me a present, but she gave me a card. I opened it and a picture of my son, Robert Junior, fell out.

My child has my first name but this was not my decision. I didn't want him growing up anything like me. I wanted him to be a stronger, better man than I was. I felt that breaking Principe tradition and not naming him after his father would be a good start. But Janine wouldn't have it. She insisted on the name. So now I just tell people that even though our names are the same, he was really named for his grandfather.

When Janine gave me the photo, I studied it, trying to see any differences from the other pictures I had seen of my son. He was getting big. He was born soon after I was locked up and by my birthday he was about six months old.

"He's longer," I said.

"I tell him about you every day," Janine said. "Your mom sends her love."

"Did you tell her it's more like day camp than prison?"

"I told her. She still won't come. She says she can't bear to see you in here."

"What about my dad?"

Janine shook her head.

"He won't come either. He's just kind of confused by all of this. He doesn't understand why you did it."

"He still won't come see me?" I asked, even though Janine had just told me the answer.

"He loves you, Rob. He's just confused. He'll come around."

"What about you?"

"You know I love you. But it's not about me. It's about your son. He's going to have to live the first two years of his life without a daddy …"

Janine trailed off. She began to cry. I took her hand in mine.

"It's been half a year, baby. A few more months and I've got a shot at parole. And then you'll see. Things will be back to normal."

"Not exactly."

Janine reached into her purse and took out an envelope. She handed it to me. The return address read: New York State Bar Association–Disciplinary Committee. I opened the envelope and read the letter. After the first few lines I crumpled it up and threw it on the floor. I didn't need to finish reading it.

"They took my license away."

"What did you expect?" Janine said.

"I don't know."

Janine changed the subject.

"Roland came by the house the other day. Says he's gonna come up here again next month."

"Good. Did he do what I said about Joey?"

"He tried but she won't work for him. She won't have anything to do with anyone or anything that is related to you. She's terrified."

"Have Roland go see her. She's got kids. She needs the work …"

"She got a job. Out of state. She already moved."

"Where?"

"She wouldn't tell me. Her brother passed along a message. She wants you to know that she'll miss the Rob that wanted to help Mrs. Guzman. But she never wants to see you or speak to you again."

I couldn't argue with Joey's request. After all the pain I had caused her, the least I could do was stay out of her life.

"Well, at least she got a new job" was all I could think of to say.

"Right," Janine said. "Now everyone has a job except you."

"Actually, I sorta do."

"Sorta do what?"

"Have a job," I said. "I met this guy in here, Andrew Solomon. Insurance exec. He's finishing up five years for embezzlement. When he gets out he's starting a business that trains corporations on how to catch fraud in its early stages. He's got investors and everything. He offered me a job teaching insurance companies how to not get screwed over by someone like me. You ready for this? Hundred grand a year."

"Are you serious?"

"Like a heart attack. That plus the money from Louie and we'll be in great shape."

"I still don't like taking that money from him."

"You didn't. I did."

"It's hush money."

"Bullshit. I'm earning that money right now as we speak. Did you hide it where we talked about?"

"Yes."

"Good."

I ended this visit like I did every visit with Janine. I kissed her softly and told her I was sorry for everything I'd done and I'd spend the rest of my life trying to make up for it. And she believed me. Because I had promised to never lie to her again.

FIFTY-EIGHT

I DIDN'T GET OUT early on parole. McLean and Townsend fucked me. Turned out there's no such thing as parole in federal prison, just something called GCT (good conduct time). GCT knocks off fifty-four days for every year of good time. I didn't know about this 'cause I had never done any federal criminal cases. So I wound up doing about a year and nine months! That's what I get for being my own lawyer. But it worked out okay. I got out at the same time as Andrew Solomon and he gave me a job, just like he said he would.

Janine had hid the money from Lou in a hole in the cement wall underneath our basement steps. With that money and the new job, we're better off financially now than we've ever been.

A lot of people say I got off easy. Some even say I benefited from the experience; they say I'm sort of a legend in the neighborhood—the guy who tangled with Big Lou and lived to tell about it. As a result, no one dares mess with me. What they don't know is that I haven't slept more than two hours straight since the day I was arrested because I still hear Luke Kozzowski screaming every time I close my eyes.

I hear it during the day when I'm eating or reading or whenever it's quiet. I hear it the loudest when I'm at church. I'll be on my knees praying and I'll look up at Grampa's Jesus. When I see the thin tiles Grampa used for the nails that were driven into the Son of God's hands and feet, I think of the nail that was driven into that young boy's eye in the Bronx. Father Dolan can be preaching and the organ can be blaring and the choir can be singing, but all I ever hear are the screams of Luke Kozzowski echoing off the rafters of St. Joseph's.

The folks who say I'm better off now don't know that every day when I walk to the subway to go to work, I have to pass my old office and go by the door where I first hung my shingle. The letters have been scraped from the glass, but you can still see the outline of my name and the words "Attorney at Law." And every day, when I walk by my old firm, I feel like the biggest failure in the world. The people who say I got off easy don't know about that. About how I feel. About how much, and how often, I hate myself.

Just last week I walked across the Brooklyn Bridge footpath. I stopped in the middle and looked out at the Statue of Liberty, the same statue my grandfather saw when the ship he stowed away on first pulled into New York Harbor. I slid off the class ring my father had given me at Umberto's and stared at it. I held it up so the sunlight bounced off the blue stone and made it look like a huge diamond. I reared back and threw the ring as far as I could. It hit the water over a hundred feet below and was sucked down into the blackness. I didn't deserve the ring any more. I never really deserved it in the first place.

I was a lawyer once. I was going to make my family proud.

ACKNOWLEDGMENTS

AS I TYPE THIS ACKNOWLEDGMENT, I know that it will be incredibly more difficult to write than the novel itself. So many people have contributed to these 77,000 or so words being printed and bound that I am certain someone will unintentionally be omitted, but I will do my best.

I'll begin where I began ... St. Joseph's Hospital in Far Rockaway, Queens, three plus decades ago when I was placed into the arms of the two most incredible parents any child could wish for. You've protected, nurtured, and loved me in a way all children should be. You set the example I follow for parenthood. I'm truly blessed to be your son.

Further, this book, and hence this acknowledgement, do not get published without my agent Brian Lipson who believed in *Slip & Fall* from the first time he read it, probably more so than I did. His passion for this novel never waned even as my hopes that it would ever be read by anyone other than Brian did. His great faith and efforts translated into a lifelong dream of mine becoming reality. Thank you, Brian—you're a man of your word and that's hard to find nowadays. I will be eternally grateful.

Once I declared that I was giving up law and turning in my briefcase for a trip West to become a professional writer, many people (family, friends, associates, and colleagues) assisted, encouraged, taught, and guided me through this adventure I've been on. In no particular order I give my most sincere thanks and appreciation to my trailblazing grandparents, my inspiring sister and my wonderful in-laws, The Endeavor Talent Agency (including, but not limited to, Ari Greenburg, Jason Spitz, Adam Levine, Hugh Fitzpatrick, and Tom Wellington), Rich DeMato, the McLeans, the Kolbrenners, Mel Damski, Doug and Rusty Greiff, Lindsay Sloane, Andrew Solomon, Marc Rosner, David Chase and Terry Winter, David Kramer and Brett Hansen, Bob Lee, and the entire *Prison Break* team (the most talented group of writers with whom I've ever had the pleasure to work).

Additionally, it cannot be stressed enough that without Borders Group, Inc. this story remains nothing but a file on my laptop. I offer my deepest gratitude to George Jones, Bill Nasshan, Rob Gruen, Ken Armstrong, Lynne Lyman, Ann Binkley, Beryl Needham, all of the managers I met in Denver, and everyone else at Borders for taking a chance on me and my story. You all brought an energy and enthusiasm to this project that was contagious. This book doesn't happen without you. Thank you so very much.

Most importantly, however, I want to acknowledge my wife, Janine, not for her support in all of my endeavors—that goes without saying as she is truly selfless. I want to acknowledge her for her kindness and decency and love ... Janine, you are the most beautiful person I have ever had the honor of knowing. Thanks for shacking up with me.

And thanks to you, Sophie. Every day you make me want to be a better Daddy and a better person.